THE NINE

Terry Cloutier

Terry Cloutier

This novel is entirely a work of fiction. The names, characters and incidents portrayed in it are the work of the author's imagination.

THE NINE

Is for my wife, with love, always

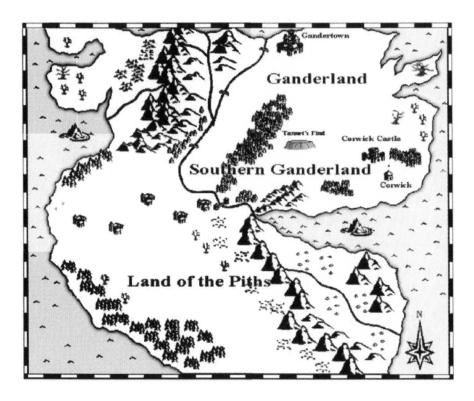

The Nine - List of Characters

- Alwin of Corwick: Hadrack's father, a peasant farmer and town elder.
- Lord Hadrack, the Wolf of Corwick Castle
- Renfry: Brother of Hadrack
- Lallo: Brother of Hadrack
- Jeanna: Sister of Hadrack
- King Jorquin: Ruler of Ganderland and Southern Ganderland
- Carwin: Peasant. Son of Garin
- Klasper: Peasant. Father to Carwin
- Hestan of Corwick: Peasant farmer and town elder
- Son Fadrian: Priest
- Daughter Elias: Priestess
- Jinian: Peasant farmer. Son of Hestan
- Garen: Peasant farmer. Son of Hestan
- Gilbin: Reeve of Corwick
- Quant Ranes: Leader of the nine
- Hape: One of the nine
- Calen: One of the nine
- Jayner of Corwick: Peasant farmer
- Widow Meade: Peasant
- Gerber the Smith: Peasant
- Meanda: Peasant
- Little Jinny: Infant daughter of Meanda
- Carspen Tuft: Slave dealer
- Hielda: Carspen Tuft's wife
- Jebido: Soldier
- Klotter: Slave
- Twent: Slave
- Quarrymaster: Commander of Tannet's Find
- Fanch Evenon: Soldier
- Listern Wes: Slave
- Baine: Pickpocket, slave, Hadrack's friend
- Hervi Desh (Heavy Beard): One of the nine
- Segar: Head in Tannet's Find
- Wigo Jedin: Slave
- Folclind: Slave
- Uhin Eby: Slave
- Einhard: Leader of the Piths. The Sword of the King
- Eriz: Pith
- Ania: Pith
- Alesia: Pith. Wife of Einhard

Terry Cloutier

- Orixe and Priam: Piths
- Megy: Quarrymaster's wife
- Urdin: Pith Pathfinder
- Tato: Pith
- Rand Lassan: Gate Commander
- Prince Tyro: Heir to the throne of Ganderland
- Dolan: Soldier
- Son Oriell: Priest
- Searl Merk (Crooked Nose): One of the nine
- Betania: Nursemaid

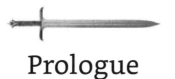

Prologue

I was eight years old the first time that I killed a man. I am old now, bent and broken, but it was not always so. I think of that simple, innocent young boy from so many years ago and I shake my head, remembering. It hardly seems possible that such a fresh-faced boy as he, and the withered husk of a man sitting here now, could possibly be one and the same. Sometimes, while lying in my bed at night unable to sleep, I'm almost fooled into thinking that what had happened had just been a dream, or perhaps had even been told to me by another. But then I picture that first bastard, his rat-ugly face as clear to me now as it had been on the day that I'd killed him, and I know that it had been no dream. I have killed many men in almost every way imaginable since that first whore-son. With long sword and battle axe, spear and knife, lance and the great halberd, men have died by my hand. I killed them with my short sword, the powerful war-hammer and mace, or sometimes, when naught else was available, I killed them with my bare hands. Once, I even killed a man with a practice wooden sword, and, truth be told, I gloried in it all. I don't care if you judge me harshly for what I am telling you. I'm not writing these words looking for absolution from anyone. Try living my life first; then you can speak to me of judgment.

I was born to a poor, peasant family, and though I didn't realize it at the time, I know now without any doubt that I was never meant to be a farmer. I was destined to become a warrior, this much has been proven, and even now, with my hands shaking from age as I put my thoughts to paper, I can feel my blood pumping faster in my veins at the memory of the smells and sounds of battle. Ah, what I wouldn't give to be young again, with the wind in my hair, a trusty shield on my arm and the solid grip of a sword in my hand. Recently, my six-year-old grandson caught me off guard when he asked me how many men I'd killed in my life. I'd never actually given it any thought before. I told him truthfully that I would guess hundreds, surprising even myself with the number. He'd seemed quite impressed and I tried to explain to him that it's no small thing to kill a man. That though their body and soul might be gone to the next world, the memory of them is always with you here on this one and that is the price you must accept for taking a man's life. Truth be told, he did not seem to understand, and I chose not to tell him that lately the dead seem to delight in taunting me when I try to sleep. My grandson does not need to hear that the dead know I'm close to joining them, and, I daresay, are clearly looking forward to it. I console myself with the thought that most of the men that I killed deserved to die, or at least I like to believe so, though I'd wager they might not agree with my take on things. I sent them into the arms of Mother Above or Father Below, and that's just as it should be, as I know they would gladly have done the same to me if their sword arm had been stronger or their feet quicker.

The past, is just that, the past. It cannot be undone, but even so, I know that some of the choices that I made over the years has caused great suffering and pain to those who least deserved it. For this, I will always feel guilty. I was young and headstrong, and not content to leave things alone, as most young men tend to be. Because of this, I became what I am. But in my youth I didn't understand that the choices I made would eventually come with a cost. Now that I'm old I realize the price I must pay for my actions is guilt and regret. One thing I know without a doubt, however, is that there is no guilt or regret in my heart for killing that first man. No shame. No remorse. No, not for that bastard. My only regret, I suppose, is I did not kill him sooner. He's the one that started it all. He's the one that changed my life forever and set me on this path. As I've grown older and frailer, a shadow of what I had been, I sometimes reflect on what would have become of me, had that bastard not done what he did.

I was the son of a peasant, Alwin of Corwick, a farmer and town elder. My mother had died giving birth to my younger brother, Renfry, who, as fate would have it, survived long enough to see his mother buried, only to be dragged off by wolves a few months later. My elder brother, Lallo, was killed in the Border War and my sister, Jeanna, whom I worshipped, was left caring for my father and me, taking on the unenviable task of running the farm while we worked the fields from first light to sundown. Other than the occasional raid from the heathen Piths to the south, things were peaceful in our village. Life was hard, true, but no harder than anywhere else I imagine. We were poor, but reasonably happy. As happy as peasants can be. That all changed when King Jorquin of Ganderland decided he would add our lands to his own. The conflict became known as the Border War, but in fairness, it was hardly a war. More like a slaughter, I would say. Our king was a stubborn old fool and despite being counselled against it, he arrogantly rode out to meet the forces of King Jorquin in the fields north of Halhaven. There his standard fell, as did he and many good men along with him. Just like that, we had been conquered. Our lands became known as Southern Ganderland, which in itself meant nothing to us at first. We were peasants after all. But soon the implications of our new king's rule became apparent. We had always paid a tax to our vassal lord, the Lord of Corwick, but he had fallen in battle, as had his heir, and now there was a new Lord Corwick, and soon to be new taxes. I remember my father shrugging his great shoulders when rumours first reached us of the new taxation coming. "A tax by this lord or a tax by the one before," he had said to me. "It hardly matters. That's just the way of things."

I confess at eight that I didn't understand any of what was happening. I had lost an older brother to war, which pained me greatly, but life is harsh for a peasant and death common, as our family knew all too well. Fiefdoms, vassals, taxes, new kings and new lords, for all of this I cared not at all. I was young and all I wanted to do was hunt and fish and wrestle with the other boys from the surrounding farms. What did I care about a new lord or some king far away to the north? It had nothing to do with me, or so I naively thought. That would change. My name is Lord Hadrack, the Wolf of Corwick Castle, and this is my story.

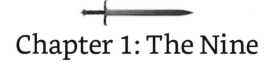

Chapter 1: The Nine

My father was a big man, well over-six feet tall, and he had arms rippled and hardened by years of heavy labor. Each arm seemed to me like a great tree trunk, hard, unrelenting and unstoppable. On many occasions I would watch as he'd strip down to his waist and grab his great axe and chop firewood behind the sty. With uncanny precision the double-bladed axe, a gift from the first Lord Corwick himself no less, would cleave the wood in half effortlessly, or so it seemed to me anyway. We burned oak or white maple mostly, and the hard wood was no match for the combined power of axe and man. Now, I know you must be asking yourself at this point, how could a mere peasant such as my father possess such a weapon? Corwick is a poor town and no one had an axe like my father's with its intricately carved handle. Most had crude stone axes or well-worn iron ones. But my father was not always a farmer. Once upon a time, before I was born, my father was a soldier and was a man to be reckoned with. He rarely spoke of it. Of what he had been and now what he had become. He was a dashing, handsome man with long brown hair tied back and deep brown eyes. To me he looked like a giant with his great arms and shoulders and he was everything a man should be. Except for the leg. I don't know how it happened, but the misshapen, crushed and almost useless leg my father dragged behind him clearly must have occurred in battle. My father never spoke of it, though. Nor would he speak of the great axe or how a lord had come to give it to him. The few things I learned of him from the before time, as my mother liked to call it, I learned from her.

My mother, ah, what a fine woman she was. It pains me, even after all these years to think of her. I remember she was beautiful, strong and stubborn, and when it came to decisions around the farm, she was never afraid to voice an opinion. My father was a hard man. A man used to getting his way in all things, except when it came to her. He loved her completely and utterly and could never say no to her. When she died, I remember seeing some of the light fade from his eyes, never to return. I see all the faces of my family in my mind as I write, and though it was all so long ago, I grieve for them still. I have avenged them as I promised The Mother and The Father that I would, but still that knowledge does little to appease the pain in my heart. The only thing that makes the pain bearable these days is that soon I know I will see them all again. I long for that day more and more, but I also know that seeing them remains in the future, and I am here to speak of the past.

The day my life changed forever began with a crisp north wind and a weak sun just rising above the Two-Heads Hills behind our house to the east. It was early March, and as such, plowing the fields had begun in earnest. The village was poor and so we only had one ox to share between the seven farms that surrounded the village of Corwick. My father and the other elders had pleaded more than once with Lord Corwick for another ox, but their words had fallen upon deaf ears. "There is no money," he would just say, waving them away. So today we were off to plow Hestan of Corwick's fields, ours having finally been finished the day before.

"You're looking bright and eager this morning," my father said to me as I entered the main room. Our house was what was called a wattle and daub house, basically a wood-framed building filled with woven twigs and straw, with the outer layer covered in mud, which when dry created a hard wall. The house was larger than most, perhaps another perk for my father from the before time. I never asked. We actually had two sleeping chambers as well as the main living quarters. Something no one else in Corwick had.

"I was hoping to meet Carwin over by the stream for a bit this morning," I mumbled, knowing even as I said it that it wasn't going to happen.

"I thought you and Carwin were enemies this week," my sister said with a grin as she placed a hot bowl of pottage before my father. Pottage was a basic stew Jeanna made from peas, beans and onions from the garden. My sister was almost fifteen and already strikingly beautiful. Like me, she'd inherited my mother's dark black hair and light blue, almost grey eyes. Her hair, though rarely seen beneath her wimple, which was a long cloth made of hemp or linen wrapped around her head, I knew was long and luxurious. She was dressed in a drab, sleeveless wool tunic over a wool shift. Her feet were bare and a pair of small brooches that were once my mother's sat perched, one to each shoulder. The brooch on her left shoulder depicted the bright and cheerful yellow Blazing Sun, the sign of Mother Above. The one on her right shoulder showed the dark black Rock of Life, the sign of Father Below. I wore a similar combined pendant called a Pair Stone around my neck that had belonged to my older brother and which had thankfully been returned to us after his death. The Pair Stone was one of my few possessions and I cherished the polished circular stone that swirled with equal parts yellow and black colors in homage to The First Pair.

I grinned at my sister. "Carwin just needed a good thumping to come to his senses. I decided I would do the thumping."

"I told you already what I thought about fighting," my father said with a frown. He was dressed in an ill-made tunic, as Jeanna was still learning the art of sewing, and well-worn trousers. On his feet he wore heavy boots which had been repaired many, many times. I suspected they came from his soldiering days, but he never said. He indicated the hard oak bench beside him. "Sit. Eat. We have a long day before us."

I sat down and nodded my thanks to Jeanna as she placed a steaming bowl on the table in front of me. "I know, father," I said before I lifted the rough wooden bowl to my lips and cautiously slurped a mouthful of stew. I thought for a moment as I chewed, trying to put into words how I felt. "I try not to fight," I finally said, "but then something happens and I can't stop myself." I realized it wasn't much. Wasn't even close to an explanation of the heat, the white-hot rage that sometimes brims out of me. How could I possibly explain something that I didn't even understand myself?

"Something happens, eh," my father grunted. He glanced at my sister briefly, then back to me. "I saw Fitch yesterday," he said as he wiped his mouth on his sleeve. He gave me a hard look. "It would appear that something happened to him too."

"But he was-"

My father held up one large, calloused hand, cutting me off. "I don't care, Hadrack." He shifted on the bench, wincing as his bad leg moved reluctantly. He put his hand on my shoulder. "You must learn to control yourself. You're big and strong. I dare say bigger and stronger than I was at your age. But just because you're bigger and stronger than someone else does not give you the right to beat them senseless. You must always think first. That's why The Mother and The Father gave you a brain. You only resort to using your fists if all else fails."

I thought about that for a moment and then said, "Did you feel that way when you fought in the army?"

My father's face tightened and he looked away. "What I did or did not do long ago has no bearing on the here and now. You are my son and I am your father. You will abide by my word and will stop fighting or I will tan your hide. Am I clear?"

I wet my lips and nodded. "Very clear," I said, looking away so that he couldn't see the doubt that I knew lay clearly across my face. At least he hadn't made me swear to Mother Above or Father Below on it. My father took oaths to The First Pair very seriously and I knew that would have been one promise I probably couldn't keep. Fighting might be wrong, at least in my father's eyes, but it certainly was fun!

"Good!" my father said. "This afternoon you will take time away from the fields and go to the Holy House and confess your sins to Son Fadrian or Daughter Elias and ask their forgiveness for what you have done." He hesitated with his bowl almost to his lips and scowled at me. "Do you understand me, Hadrack?"

"I do, father," I said, groaning silently to myself, knowing that I'd probably get stuck with Son Fadrian. The priest was incredibly old and looked like a toad to me with his wrinkled and pock-marked flesh and his breath smelled like rotten fish. Daughter Elias was young and pretty and I liked her a lot and always preferred confessing to her. But the last three times I'd gone, I'd had to confess to Son Fadrian. I'm pretty sure the old priest was starting to wonder about me.

We finished eating in silence and when we were done my father and I headed out, leaving Jeanna to do whatever girls do back at the farm. I make light of it, but truth be told, without Jeanna I don't know what father and I would have done. She was always the first awake and the last to bed and never once complained at the heap of chores that needed doing every day just to keep the farm running smoothly. We crossed our yard and headed for the western path that led to Hestan's farm and I turned back to glance over my shoulder at our house. Jeanna was standing in the yard watching us with one hand holding her wimple against the steady breeze while the other hand held a basket perched easily on her hip. Around her chickens were already congregating and I shaded my eyes from the sun just breaking over the roof of our house. I waved to her, grinning when she waved enthusiastically back.

"She'll make someone a fine wife," my father grunted.

"Really?" I said, looking at my father in surprise. As ridiculous as it may seem, I never thought of Jeanna that way. To me she was just my older sister. Bossy, protective and annoying sometimes, but surely not ready for marriage. "She's too young," I stammered, not wanting to imagine life at the farm without her.

My father chuckled. "She's almost fifteen, Hadrack," he said. "Your mother was of the same age when I met her, you know."

"I didn't know that," I said, still trying to come to grips with the idea of losing Jeanna.

We were walking along the rambling path that led to

Hestan of Corwick's house and I slowed, waiting patiently for father to catch up. It was painful to watch him half-waddle, half-drag his body along, his one good leg strong and sure footed, the other wizened and limp, leaving a furrow in the well-travelled, dusty path dotted along the sides with shoots of Hollyhock and Ladybird plants.

"Well, what did you think?" my father snorted at me. "That she'd stay unwed forever watching over an old cripple and an impatient and impertinent boy who likes to fight?" He put his hand on my shoulder, pausing as he caught his breath. Above us a feeding party of swifts swooped and looped in intricate patterns. Probably feeding on bog flies, I thought idly. I glanced to the north where a small stand of thick hemlocks sat perched high on a hill that was surrounded by a low wall of stones that we villagers had plucked from the fields. It never seemed to matter how many stones were turned up from the plow and removed each year, as we had to do it all over again the next year as more stones appeared in their place. My father liked to joke that it was Father Below's way of keeping us busy and out of trouble. I stared at the dark trees which stood out starkly from the freshly turned fields around them and I shuddered, knowing the trees encircled Patter's Bog like sentinels of warning. Tread not here, they seemed to say. An evil spirit lived in the bog. We had all heard the stories. It was said that you could see for miles up there, but even so, no one ever went near it.

"Let's get moving," my father finally said, giving my shoulder a friendly squeeze. "I don't want to be late."

I took one last glance at the trees, feeling a chill I knew was not from the morning breeze and I rubbed the Pair Stone around my neck with two fingers to ward off the bog spirit as I slowly followed my father. It wasn't long before we crested a small hill speckled with corncockle flowers and sighted the Hestan farm snuggled below in a shallow valley. Around us the bright purple flowers weaved and danced in the breeze as if delighted we had arrived. The Hestan house was almost as big as ours, but the farm had more outbuildings, as they not only had chickens and pigs like we did, but sheep and a goat as well. I glanced at the shearing shed, where I could see a small cluster of men and boys talking among themselves. As we approached, Hestan turned to greet us with an anxious look on his face. Hestan was a short man and thick bodied, with greying hair that receded noticeably at the temples. He wore a short, sleeveless tunic over a second, longer tunic which was cinched by a worn, black leather belt. Wool trousers, rough leather shoes and leggings that were only one step away from being called rags completed his attire.

"Ah, there you are," Hestan muttered to my father. He barely glanced at me.

I looked around at the faces staring at us, all of them with the same uneasy look. Beside Hestan stood his two sons, Jinian and Garen. His other son, Wildern, had died fighting in the Border War. The Lord of Corwick, as was his right, had mustered all the able-bodied peasants in defence of the king's lands and many of the older boys and men I had known all my life had lost their lives, my brother included. Now we had a new king and a new Lord Corwick, whom we had all sworn fealty to, as though we'd had any choice in the matter. Beside Garen stood Fitch, Garen's son. Fitch was big, almost as big as me and he was glaring at me with open hatred. I smiled at him and pointed to my right eye and then smirked. Fitch unconsciously started to touch his battered right eye, which was even now turning a wonderful shade of black. I made a face at him and then looked away, nodding to my friend, Carwin, who nodded back. Like Fitch, Carwin also sported a bruised eye, though his was now mostly yellow, with still some hint of black. Beside Carwin stood his father, Klasper, a tall, extremely thin man known for his quiet demeanour and seemingly limitless endurance in the fields.

"So, Hestan," my father said, looking up at the sky. "A good day for it, I'd say."

"Yes, yes," Hestan agreed brusquely, waving away my father's words. He folded his thick arms across his chest. "We have a problem, Alwin." My father raised his eyebrows and waited patiently. "Gilbin is dead," Hestan continued bluntly, "and there's a new reeve."

"Dead!" I gasped out.

My father glanced at me with disapproval, then turned back to Hestan. "What happened?" he said, unable to hide the worry in his voice.

Hestan gestured to his son, Garen. "I'll let him tell the tale."

Garen pointed to the east. "Late last night horsemen came to my house. There were ten of them."

"You said nine earlier," Jinian cut in.

Garen glanced at his brother and frowned. "Nine, ten, what does it matter? The fact is there were many of them and they were spoiling for trouble by the looks of them."

"Were they the king's men?" my father asked.

Garen shook his head. "No, they were Lord Corwick's men. They spent the night in my barn and I had to feed the lot of them. Their leader was an ugly-looking bastard and he told me he was the new reeve by order of the Lord himself. He said Gilbin was a traitor and had been executed for..." Garen hesitated, searching for the word. All of us waited, spellbound by the story. "For treasonous acts," he finally managed to say.

"This doesn't make any sense," my father muttered. "Gilbin has been reeve here since long before my time and he's always been faithful to Lord Corwick."

"Maybe so," Hestan rumbled. "But our new lord clearly does not think so."

"So what do we do?" Jinian asked.

Everyone automatically looked to my father, who stood slowly rubbing his chin with his left hand as he thought. "We do nothing," he finally said with a shrug. He looked at each face briefly. "What can we do? Our souls belong to The Mother or The Father on judgment day, as it should be, but we swore an oath to our new lord and, until judgment day arrives, our lives belong to him."

"So that's it then?" Garin demanded. He threw his hands up in the air and snorted. "We just do nothing?"

My father fixed his calm brown eyes on Garin. "What would you have us do?" he asked softly. He looked around. "Shall we arm ourselves with pitchforks and blunted hoes and march on Corwick Castle and demand to know why Gilbin was killed? Is that what you suggest?"

"Well, no..."

"Riders on the hill!" Klasper hissed, cutting Garin off.

We turned, watching as a group of riders crested the hill. They paused for a moment to study us, their mail winking faintly in the morning light before a sharp word from their leader, heard clearly across the crisp air, galvanized them forward and they trotted down the hill toward us.

"Let me do the talking," my father whispered out of the side of his mouth as they approached.

I studied them openly as only an eight-year-old boy yet without fear of the world could. There were nine of them, all similarly dressed, wearing dusty, long-sleeved hauberks that went to their knees and were slit at the sides to enable better mobility on horseback. The hauberk, or mail, was essentially a long tunic or shirt with metal loops woven into it for protection during battle. They each wore a mail coif that covered their heads and necks, leaving just their faces visible. All nine wore matching red trousers and heavy leather boots. Over their hauberks each wore a surcoat of white emblazoned with the flaming dragon banner of the new Lord of Corwick. I could see the pommel of each mans' sword moving by their sides with the motion of the horses as they slowly cantered forward. Finally, the lead man raised his mailed fist almost casually and the horses came to a stop several paces from us, where they stood stomping their feet and swishing their tails. A cloud of dust dug up by the horses' hooves hung in the air around us for a moment before being whisked away by the wind.

"A good day to you, lord," my father said to the leader.

"That remains to be seen," the man replied quietly. He

studied us with sharp, almost feral eyes. I liked him not at all. "My name is Quant Ranes," he said, drawing the name out. His cold eyes rested on me for a moment and I actually felt my heart skip a beat before his gaze drifted away to focus on my father. "You are the peasant, Alwin, are you not?"

"I am, lord," my father nodded.

"Excellent," Quant said with a smile. I noticed his teeth were crooked and yellow, those that he still possessed. "Just the man I'm looking for. The reeve has instructed me to inform you and the other elders that the tithe from this village will hence-forth be paid four times a year rather than once."

"What's a tithe?" I heard Fitch whisper to his father.

"A tax," Garen whispered back. "Now be quiet!"

My father seemed perplexed. "Four times, my lord?"

"Precisely," Quant agreed. He looked down at us, unable to hide his contempt. "Your days of slacking in the fields has come to an end. Your old reeve was a lazy fool and a drunkard and let things slide here." Quant swung his right arm in the air, gesturing to the fields still waiting the bite of the plow. "The lands of Corwick are rich and plentiful, and your lord, in his generosity, has opened his heart and allowed you to live and prosper here. All that he asks of you is that you do an honest day's work." He frowned and shook his head. "But you took his generosity and thumbed your noses at it." Quant glared at us, none of us able to meet his eyes until finally he sighed and looked to the sky. "I suppose you can't really be to blame. Perhaps too much is expected of you? Perhaps your old reeve did not fully understand your, um, limitations?" He shrugged. "After all, if you bring a cow into your house and it shits on the floor, is it the cow's fault or is it yours?"

I didn't really understand what Quant meant, I mean, what do cows have to do with working the fields? It was a puzzle and made no sense to me, but my father seemed to understand.

"We will strive to do better, lord," my father said, his voice low and even as he looked to the ground.

"Good," Quant said. "See that you do." He glanced over his

shoulder at the hill behind him and then focused on my father. "The reeve is currently delayed and might be a while." Behind him one of the men-at-arms snickered as Quant continued, "So that will give you time to gather the rest of the elders here so that he can properly explain to you his expectations." I saw my father's head come up and he stiffened as he studied Quant, then turned his gaze to the hill. A look crossed his face that I'd never seen before and it took me a moment to realize what it was. Fear! My heart lurched and I too looked to the hill and the path that lead to our farm. I knew why the reeve was delayed. Jeanna! I felt recklessness overtake me and without thinking I broke from the group and started to run, my only thought that I had to get to my sister. "Stop that boy!" I heard Quant shout. A mailed hand reached for me as I ran past the mounted men, the man's fingers just grasping my tunic and tearing it slightly before I was free. Most boy's that are as big as I am are usually slow runners, but luckily I was not and I headed as fast as I could for the hill. I heard shouts behind me and I glanced back over my shoulder to see that my father and Hestan were lying on the ground surrounded by the soldiers, who had dismounted and now stood in a ring around the two men with drawn swords. Several of the soldiers began heartily kicking the fallen men and I realized they must have tried to distract the men-at-arms so that I could escape and were now paying the price for it. I reached the base of the hill and I hesitated, torn between heading back to help father or continuing on to help Jeanna. My father saw me stop in indecision and he shook his head at me just as a booted foot caught him in the stomach. He shuddered and tried to twist away, only to be kicked by another of the men-at-arms from the other side.

"Father!" I shouted in impotent rage.

Quant glanced up at me and said something to one of the men-at-arms standing over my father, gesturing my way with his thumb. I saw the man grin through his heavy beard and he kicked my father twice more in the stomach before sauntering over to his horse. I looked again to my father just as he lifted his hand weakly off the ground and pointed behind me. I knew what he wanted and I turned and fled up the hill, while behind me I could hear the pounding of hoof beats as the heavily-bearded man-at-arms gave chase. I reached the hilltop and hesitated, searching desperately for an escape. Fast as I was, I had no illusions about trying to outrun a horse. I glanced at the silent trees surrounding Patter's Bog, but even as desperate as I was there was no way I was going in there, even supposing I could make it in time. Around me the corncockles danced merrily, unperturbed by the drama unfolding around them. I looked back. Heavy Beard had reached the base of the hill and was coming on fast, his right hand whipping the horse's flank, urging it on. I could hear the beast wheezing and see the whites of its eyes as little flecks of foam flickered at its nostrils. The horse! It was my only chance. I dove off the path to the ground and crouched down, idly noticing the heavy, sickly-sweet scent of the purple flowers around me. I heard the mounted man crest the hill, the great bulk of the horse filling my vision and I moved, leaping up and waving my arms.

"Hurrrrraggggggh!" I yelled as loud as I could.

The horse rolled its eyes in fright and let out a high-pitched squeal. It reared back on its hind legs and I narrowly managed to jump aside as one of its heavy-shod front hooves grazed my forehead. At the same time, Heavy Beard cried out in surprise and desperately pulled back on the reins, but it was too late. With a cry of dismay and a comical look on his face, the soldier somersaulted backward and fell heavily to the ground and lay still. The riderless horse spun away from me in fear and headed at break-neck speed back down the hill toward its companions. I'd bought myself some time, I knew, I just didn't know how much. I could see our farm off in the distance and I sprinted toward it. "Jeanna! Jeanna!" I cried out, over and over again as I ran. I knew I should conserve my breath, but I couldn't stop myself and I continued to call her name. Finally I reached the house and came to an exhausted halt in the dusty yard, gasping for air as I looked around. A large black horse was tied to the fencing on the right side of the house. The front door to our house was open and a sword still in its leather scabbard leaned nonchalantly against the door frame. There was no sign of the owner of the sword or Jeanna.

"Jeanna?" I called again. I raced into the house, searching frantically, but the main room and sleeping rooms were empty. "Where are you?" I shouted. I ran back outside, my eyes searching desperately for any sign of her. I paused as I heard something, a soft mewling sound followed by a grunt. It had come from behind the covered sty and it hadn't sounded like pigs. I barrelled forward, hurtling around the sty only to once again come to a crashing halt, my mouth falling open, my young mind unable to comprehend what I was seeing. My sister lay spread-eagled on the ground, her clothes torn from her slight body and thrown haphazardly around. Her wimple had come off and her long black hair lay splayed out around her head like a fan I had once seen the reeve's wife use to cool herself with. The white nakedness of my sister's flesh stood out in stark contrast to the filth of the muddy ground and a trickle of blood ran from her scalp, down to her cheek and then to her ear. Her eyes were fixed and staring upward and for a moment I feared that she was dead, but then she blinked and relief flooded over me. Above her, a man grunted and groaned, thrusting himself into her, oblivious to me standing there. The man's mail had been discarded and the tunic he wore underneath was hitched up above his waist while his red trousers lay bunched at his feet. His hairy white buttocks moved in a steady rhythm with the animal grunts coming from him. All of this I took in in a moment, a moment I shall never forget to my last day in this world. I screamed, what I cried out I have no idea, and I rushed forward with murder in my heart. I pounced on the man and began to pommel his back with my fists.

"Stop it! Stop it!" I cried. Incredibly, the man seemed not to notice me and he continued, not losing a beat. I sobbed in frustration and glanced around for a weapon. Then I froze. Jeanna was looking at me with the light of recognition in her eyes.

Slowly a tear welled in her left eye and trickled down through the blood on her cheek.

"Hadrack," she mouthed softly.

I crouched beside her, unable to move as I was held by the look of both love and shame in my sister's eyes. Finally she turned her head, releasing me as she once again stared up at the sky. The moment gone, I again searched the yard frantically for a weapon. Not far away I spied a rock the size of my fist lying nearly submerged in the muck. I half-ran, half-crawled over to it and I grasped it in my hand. The reeve, for that's who I knew this foul creature to be, cried out just then and slammed himself one last time into Jeanna, lifting his head and upper body off of her and contorting his spine as he planted his seed within her. Never before or since have I felt hatred for another man more than I did that day. I raised the rock over my head and screamed as I raced toward him, intent on bashing in his skull. Just as I reached him, the rock already descending, he seemed to come out of whatever trance he had been in. The reeve looked up in surprise, automatically raising his arm to ward off the blow. Instead of his head, the rock cracked against the bone of his wrist, snapping it. The man screamed and fell sideways, clutching his wrist to his chest. This is when I should have finished him. It still pains me even after so long to think of it. I should have pounced while he was down and crushed in his face with the rock, beating into it over and over again till naught was left but a bloody wet mess. But I was eight years old, I was scared, and I didn't think. Instead, I ignored the reeve, tossed the rock aside and knelt down beside my sister.

"Jeanna! Jeanna!" I sobbed. I gently shook her arm, trying to get her to look at me, but her eyes stayed fixated on the sky. Beside us I heard the reeve moaning in pain as he dragged himself away, but I ignored him. "Jeanna!" I whispered, wiping away a tear. "Tell me what to do! I don't know what to do!" I looked at my sister, lying there naked and violated and I felt sick, wondering at the kind of evil that could do something like this. The sun, which had been hidden by clouds earlier, came out, gleaming off her white flesh and I wished I had a blanket to cover her nakedness. Just then a shadow fell over us and I looked up. I only had a moment to register that the reeve stood above us with a look of rage dominating his truly ugly face. His right arm hung limply by his side, the wrist already red and swelling, but his left hand was free and that's what he struck me with. I was a healthy eight-year-old boy who'd been in a lot of fights and been hit many times, but never like that. The reeve was a big man and very strong and he hit me backhanded, across the face. With a cry of pain and shock I flew backward, falling into the muck as the reeve stalked toward me. In his good hand he now held a knife and I scuttled backwards through the mire, trying to get away from him.

"You broke my wrist you little bastard!" the reeve hissed at me. His tunic was splattered with mud and stained with dark blood, my sister's I presumed, and he'd somehow managed to pull up his trousers. How with only one good hand, I couldn't imagine. "I'm going to make you suffer for that!"

I tried to get to my feet, but I slipped in the mud and fell heavily on my rear as the reeve laughed unpleasantly. I scurried backwards awkwardly as he moved toward me, but stopped as my back came into contact with something hard and unyielding behind me. I looked over my shoulder and felt my heart sink. The woodshed. I was trapped! I was against the outer wall, several feet away from the door that led into the woodshed and I felt defeat overcoming me. The door was open slightly and something gleamed at me from where it leaned against the inside wall and suddenly I felt my spirits soar. My father's axe!

"Hadrack?" my sister called out at that moment in a tiny voice. "Are you there?" I glanced past the reeve and stared dumbly at my sister. She was sitting up, looking dazed and confused, one hand propped in the mud, holding her up, the other clutched to her small breasts.

"Stupid whore!" the reeve growled. He whirled and in several quick strides was by her side. Before I could even comprehend what he was about to do, the knife flashed and blood spurted in a wide arc from my sister's neck.

I sat there for a moment in stunned, incredulous silence, not daring to believe what I'd just seen. Then anger descended over me like a veil, stronger than anything I'd ever felt before. I moved without even knowing it, screaming incoherently as I reached into the woodshed and grabbed my father's axe. The axe was made for battle, a weapon to cut and to maim and to bludgeon, with two heads, both razor sharp. Carvings of battle scenes ran along both sides of the shaft and I'd spent many hours staring at them, daydreaming of war. Normally I found the axe to be heavy, but at that moment it weighed nothing at all and I turned, raising it over my head as I charged toward my sister's murderer. For his part, the reeve seemed strangely calm as I bore down on him. I didn't realize until much later that he'd had a right to be. I was just a boy and untrained in the art of warfare. An easy mark for one such as him, even if I did have an axe and he only a knife. If it hadn't been for the rock, things would have turned out much different and I wouldn't be here. The very rock I'd meant to bash his head in with, in the end, did the job it was meant to after all. For, as I ran, my right foot stepped on it where it had fallen after I had tossed it aside. I lost my balance and pitched forward, crying out in dismay as I lost my grip on the axe. I hit the mud face first, and, as I fell, I heard a strange sucking sound coupled with a low grunt. I desperately got to my knees, panicking as I wiped away the mud that covered my face and had blinded me. When I could finally see again I stared in disbelief. The reeve lay on his back, his arms flung out to either side of him. His face, or what was left of it, was nearly cut in two by my father's axe. The reeve was dead.

Chapter 2: Patter's Bog

I don't how long I grieved, lying there in the muck while I held my sister to my chest with only the occasional grunting and huffing of the pigs in the sty to keep me company. My memory of that day tells me hours, but in reality it could only have been minutes. After I'd realized that the reeve was dead, I had rushed to Jeanna's side even though I knew it was too late and that she was dead as well. I fell to my knees beside her body, unable to accept that she was gone and I tried to shake her awake, crying out her name over and over again before finally giving up and pulling her to my chest. Tears streamed down my cheeks seemingly without end and the feeling of loss and guilt was overwhelming beyond description. If only I had been faster, I cursed to myself. If only I had finished the reeve when I'd had the chance, Jeanna would still be alive. I had failed her and I had failed father and I didn't know how I could possibly face him and tell him what I had done. I sniffed in misery and wiped tears from my eyes as I looked down at my dead sister. I thought of the reeve and what he'd done to her and I glanced over at his corpse, feeling the hatred still pulsing wetly in my veins. I stared at the carved handle of my father's axe, the head embedded deep into the man's face and suddenly I knew what I had to do. I gently lowered Jeanna to the ground and I stood up, pausing to look down at her. She seemed so small and frail, I thought. So vulnerable lying there naked in the filth and mud. I glanced around, then stooped to pick up the reeve's mail that he had tossed aside. Gently I knelt and covered my sister's nakedness with it, pausing to wipe mud from her face and kiss her one last time while trying to ignore the hideous slash in her neck as I did so.

"Goodbye, sister," I whispered. I stood up and stared down at her small form as I clutched the Pair Stone hanging around my neck in both my hands. "I swear to both The Mother and The Father that I will avenge you," I promised her. I felt hardness take over my heart and I turned away from her and approached the reeve. The axe had caught the man square in the middle of his face, slicing through his nose and mouth and it was angled deep into his forehead. He had to be one of the ugliest men I'd ever seen when alive and having his face cut in two did nothing for his appearance. I noticed his eyes were blue and had a strange look, as though surprised that he was actually dead. Blood and gore and bits of bone lay about his head, staining the mud even blacker, yet I ignored it. All I cared about, all I could think about were the others. The other men-at-arms and their leader, Quant. There were nine of them, and they were just as responsible as the reeve was for my sister's death, so they would share his fate. I pictured the battle to come. How I'd crush and maim and kill each of them with my father's axe. It all seemed so easy. So effortless. In my eight-year-old mind nothing could go wrong. Then I went for the axe. I grabbed the handle and pulled, but it wouldn't budge. I tried again, pushing forward and up on it, trying to dislodge it. But all I accomplished was slipping and falling in the mud. "Please, Mother," I whispered, glancing to the skies. "I need that axe! Help me!" But Mother Above either didn't care or wasn't listening that day and, try as I might, I could not pull the axe free from the reeve's face. Finally I gave up and flopped down in the muck beside the corpse, my chest heaving from exertion. That's when I heard the horses. I scurried on all fours to the corner of the sty and I looked around its wall. There were three men-at-arms on horseback in the yard and they were all facing the farmhouse and seemed nervous.

The largest of the three, a man with heavy rounded shoulders and a crooked nose, spoke to the other two, "Keep your eyes open for the boy."

"What for?" The man who had spoken grinned black teeth and glanced around. "That little bastard is probably long gone by now." He turned to the house and licked his lips. "I'm thinking maybe when the reeve is finished we can all have a go, eh?"

"You shouldn't try thinking, Hape," Crooked Nose said. "You don't have the talent for it." Crooked Nose and the other man, a youth of maybe seventeen, both laughed as Hape scowled at them. Crooked Nose turned back to the house and he cleared his throat. "Er, my lord?" he said tentatively. He waited a moment, then cleared his throat again and spoke louder, "Uh, my Lord Reeve? Sorry to disturb you, but might we have a word?"

"He's too busy cunny-catching to hear you," Hape muttered. "Don't seem fair is all I have to say."

"Enough out of you!" Crooked Nose hissed at him. He glanced to the youth. "Calen, you go in there and tell the reeve that Quant needs to speak with him."

"What!" Calen said, his voice tweaking slightly. "Why do I have to do it?"

"Because I said so," Crooked Nose said.

Calen glanced at the house, then reluctantly dismounted and handed the reins of his horse to Hape. I was surprised at how short Calen was as he stood there shifting his weight nervously from one foot to the other. On horseback it's hard to tell a man's height. The youth glanced at the house, straightened the sword at his side and squared his shoulders, and then stepped forward.

"Oh, and, Calen," Crooked Nose called out.

Calen hesitated, pausing in midstep. "Sir?"

"Whatever you do, don't look."

The youth's face reddened and he nodded. "Right. Got it. Don't look." He stepped carefully around the sword at the door and crossed the threshold into my home. I could hear him calling out to the reeve several times and then he was back in the doorway. "He's not in here."

"What do you mean he's not in there?" Crooked Nose said with a frown as he looked around the yard.

I knew they'd check the outbuildings next and so I carefully eased backward around the sty. Once I was sure they couldn't see me, I stood up in a half-crouch and turned away from them and started to run. I paused as I glimpsed something winking at me in the muck, having to force myself not to cry out with joy when I realized it was the reeve's knife. I scooped it up and kept running, wiping the blade clean as I ran. It wasn't my father's axe and I certainly couldn't kill nine men-at-arms with it, but it was better than nothing. Directly before me lay the field my father and I had recently harvested the winter wheat from. Like all the farms in Corwick, ours was separated into four fields, all of which had been plowed by now, but it was this field's turn to lie fallow this year and not be replanted so the ground could recover strength and nutrients while we planted rye, oats and barley in the other three. I headed for the freshly-turned earth of the open field just as I heard a shout of discovery ring out from behind me. They had found the reeve and my sister, I guessed. I glanced over my shoulder to see that Crooked Nose, Hape and Calen had come around the sty and were standing beside the reeve and staring down at his body. Hape turned away from the man's corpse and walked over to stare at my sister. He bent over and dragged the mail from her body and even from here I could see the gleam of lust on his face. Rage and disgust boiled up in me and I almost turned back. Then better sense prevailed and I kept running. Glancing back again, I realized they were so intent on the bodies that they hadn't actually seen me yet.

To the east lay open land that ran on for several miles before finally meeting up with the Two-Heads Hills in the distance. To the north lay more open fields and beyond that, almost a mile away, stood a small forest with a fast running stream where the other boy's from the village and I liked to hunt and fish. Hestan's farm sat to the west of me and I knew more men-at-arms were waiting there, so I chose to run north, heading for the safety of the forest. I figured if I was lucky maybe they wouldn't see me, but unfortunately there was no luck for me that morning and a startled shout sounded almost immediately. I looked back to see the youth, Calen, pointing at me and motioning to the others.

Crooked Nose cupped his hands to his mouth and he shouted, "You there! Boy! Get back here!"

I looked to the forest still so far away and knew I had no chance to make it now as the three men-at-arms were already turning and running for their horses. There had to be somewhere to hide from them, I thought frantically.

I glanced to the northwest and felt my skin go cold as I stared at the stone wall and mass of trees up on the hill that hid Patter's Bog. The trees swayed back and forth in the breeze and it seemed to me as though their dark branches were moving in unison as though controlled by someone or something else. "No, you can't!" my mind screamed at me even as my body ignored it and turned toward the bog. I started to run, faster and faster as the trees waved me closer, encouraging me. Behind me the men-at-arms were now mounted and had given chase and I looked back and grinned painfully as I sucked in air. The freshly-turned ground was slowing the horses down, the soft soil and ruts causing the horses to lose their balance as they tried to cut across the field to catch me. I kept running, ignoring the stitch in my side as I forced my feet to fight their way through the loose dirt. The slope up to the bog was steep and, as I drew nearer, I almost lost my footing several times on smaller pieces of rock that had rolled away from the stone wall. I finally reached that wall and scurried over it, tearing my trousers on a sharp stone before I made it to the treeline. I paused to catch my breath, turning to check on the soldiers. Crooked Nose was in the lead almost fifty yards away with his companions not far behind him. The horses were laboring up the incline, fighting to gain proper footing, but even so they were making progress. I didn't have much time, I knew, so I turned and plunged into the trees.

Patter's Bog was named after a peasant who, it was said, drowned himself in its dark waters many years ago after being rejected by a woman he'd loved. He'd asked for her hand in marriage, so the story goes, only to be spurned for another man. Depressed and angry, he'd found the two lovers rutting and had killed them both in a fit of rage before dragging their bodies into the bog and then jumping in after them. Legend has it that anyone who dares enter will feel Patter's wrath and be pulled into the bog as well to spend all of eternity with him and the two lovers. I shuddered, trying to forget about the story of Patter as I pushed my way through the trees. I was hoping there would be somewhere to hide in the bog, but I was about to be disappointed.

Once past the trees and in the open, I found myself staring down at a heart-shaped basin of murky black water that was maybe fifteen feet wide and surrounded by weathered, moss-encrusted stones. That's it? I thought. This is the bog? On one of the stones a large brown and green frog stared up at me, looking unimpressed by my sudden appearance as its chin expanded and contracted grotesquely. At the back of the water hole two thick holly bushes grew, though neither of them were much higher than my shoulder. Beyond that the trees rose again. That was it. I looked at the bright red berries on the bushes and willed my mind to think. There had to be a way. I could run through the trees at the back and keep going, I thought. Instantly I rejected the idea as just plain stupid. They would catch me if I tried that. The frog abruptly moved, jumping from one stone to another before, with a soft plop, it leapt into the water and disappeared. I stared at the expanding ripple it had left behind as an idea began to form in my mind. I ran to the edge of the bog, searching the ground until I found what I was looking for, then I walked backward a few paces. Behind me I heard someone curse and the sounds of horses and I knew they had reached the wall. I purposefully stepped forward, jabbing my foot deeply into the soft, damp ground, then another step. I looked back and down, satisfied, then continued like this right to the water's edge. I grabbed my pendant with my left hand and closed my eyes. "Please Mother, please Father, do not let Patter take me down there," I whispered.

I opened my eyes and, hopeful that The First Pair had been listening, I tucked the reeve's knife into the back of my trousers and took a tentative step into the water. My foot instantly sank into the mire and I froze and waited with my heart thudding in my ears. Finally, after my foot had sunk down several inches, I felt resistance to my weight. Reasonably confident that I had solid footing beneath me now, I took another step, then another and another. I could feel the bog pulling at my feet and I fought rising panic, trying not to picture a hand reaching for my legs from beneath the water. Behind me I heard the unmistakable sound of metal against metal as someone drew their sword from its scabbard, then a thud as a branch was cut. I knew I had to hurry. When I judged I was in deep enough, I started moving sideways, shuffling my feet as I moved so that they wouldn't sink. I headed for some flat-looking rocks to my left and when I reached them I lifted first one foot out of the water onto a rock, then with a grunt and a heavy sucking sound, pulled my other foot out and up. I breathed a huge sigh of relief. Patter had not taken me!

I was standing about ten feet from where I'd entered the bog and I hurried along the slippery rocks toward the bushes as fast as I safely could. I took off my tunic, careful not to lose my pendant as I pulled the garment over my head, and as I took each step, I crouched down and reached behind me with the tunic, wiping my wet, muddy footprints off the rocks as best I could. It wasn't perfect, I knew, but it would have to do. Finally I reached the bushes and I threw my tunic into the middle of the water and climbed off the rocks, pushing my way through the branches and ignoring the pain as they scratched and tore at my naked flesh. I crouched down and touched the Pair Stone lying against my chest just as the men-at-arms burst through the trees. The men hesitated, clearly not having expected the bog to be there and they looked around in surprise.

"Where'd he go?" Calen finally asked.

I watched them through the branches and prayed again to The Mother and The Father that none of them knew how to track well. Not even the smallest boy in our village would have fallen for what I'd done. Hopefully these men would.

"He must have run out the back," Crooked Nose said.

"Maybe not," Hape said as he dropped to one knee to peer intently at the obvious tracks I'd left. He followed my trail with his eyes and then snickered and stood up. "It looks like he went into the water right about there," he said, pointing to where I'd entered the bog.

"Now why would he do that?" Crooked Nose asked suspiciously.

"Because he's a peasant," Hape said, "and they're stupid." He drew his sword and reached into the murky water, hooking my tunic with it and holding the dripping cloth up for the others to see. "Silly bastard didn't know about the quicksand," Hape said with a grin. "Some of the bogs around here are like this. I once saw a horse step into one and it was gone faster than a whore after you've paid her."

Crooked Nose shrugged his rounded shoulders and motioned behind him with a thumb. "Let's get back, then. I'm not looking forward to telling Quant about the reeve."

"That bastard will probably blame us somehow," I heard Hape grumble faintly as the men turned and left.

I watched them go, hardly able to believe that it had worked and I pressed the Pair Stone to my lips in thanks. My body was shaking uncontrollably by now, both from fear and relief. I wrapped my arms around myself and concentrated on stopping my teeth from chattering, afraid the men might hear the clacking. Hape had been right about the bogs around here, but he'd been wrong about me. I might be a peasant, but I wasn't stupid. I'd known there might be quicksand, but I'd taken the chance rather than risk getting caught. I heard the men-at-arms mount up and ride away, their voices too far away to make out clearly now. I realized I'd been holding my breath the whole time and finally I let it out in a whoosh as I stood up. I saw my tunic lying wetly on the ground where Hape had tossed it aside and I ran around the bog to fetch it. The sun was breaking through the tops of the trees by now and a small section of the bog was bathed in sunlight, so I wrung the tunic out the best that I could and draped it over a rock, waiting for it to dry.

I sat down on another rock and felt the sun warm my flesh, enjoying the thought that for the moment I was safe where I was. I had a sudden image of Patter sneaking up behind me and I glanced quickly over my shoulder, relieved to see that there was nothing there. I grinned self-consciously at myself and pulled the knife from my trousers. If Patter came for me I'd deal with him just like I would deal with the nine. I stared at the small knife in my hand, thinking that I now had two names, Hape and Calen. No, wait! Three names! I couldn't forget, Quant. Three names plus Crooked Nose and Heavy Beard out of nine. It was a start. Once the soldiers had left the village I'd find my father and tell him what had happened. I'd give him the names I knew and my father and I would go to Corwick Castle and tell Lord Corwick what his men had done. I pictured the wrath on the lord's face when he learned of the crime they had committed. He would judge them harshly, I knew, as well he should. There would be no trial, for there would be no need. Everyone would know of their guilt. I saw the nine dancing from the gallows in the castle courtyard, their feet kicking helplessly as the ropes around their necks slowly strangled them. In my mind the entire village was there that day, cheering as the men swung slowly back and forth. They would pay for Jeanna! They would all pay!

I sat there, smiling as I envisioned different, horrible ways for the nine to die while enjoying the warm sunlight on my bare skin. My smile slowly faded after a while as a deep feeling of guilt slowly returned, pushing the warmth of the sun away. I wrapped my arms around myself and shuddered as I realized I still had to tell my father about Jeanna. Father! I shot to my feet as I remembered the last I'd seen of him he'd been on the ground being kicked by the men-at-arms. How could I have forgotten? I cursed myself for being a terrible son and I snatched my tunic off the rock. It was still damp, but dry enough to wear and I pulled the cloth over my head even as I hurried into the trees. I reached the edge and stopped along the treeline, knowing no one could see me in the dark shadows here. Above me several chickadees chirped at me playfully. From where I stood high on the hill I had a good view of our farm. The yard was empty save for several of our chickens pecking at the ground. One of them lay still near the house, clearly dead. Probably trampled by the horses when the men-at-arms came chasing after me, I thought. Thankfully I could not see Jeanna or the reeve from this angle and I looked past the stone wall to the west, pausing to glance up at the sun. It had to be well past noon by now and I wondered where the time had gone.

In the distance I could see people sitting on the dusty ground in Hestan's front yard. It looked like some women were there as well. Probably Hestan's wife and two daughters, I figured. The villagers were huddled together in a tight circle but, even with my sharp young eyes, I was having trouble making out their faces clearly from this far away. I looked for my father and thought I saw him off to one side, but I wasn't certain. I saw two men-at-arms sitting astride their horses and conversing a little distance away from the villagers. I instantly recognized the rounded shoulders of the man talking and waving his arms. Crooked Nose! I was pretty sure the other one was Quant just by the arrogant way that he sat his horse. I saw a flash of white surcoats reflecting the sun near where the shearing shed stood and I realized that there were two more men-at-arms there. They were both on foot and leading their horses by the reins to where I knew a water trough lay. Both horses ducked their heads and drank for a long time. One of the men-at-arms was very short and I guessed that it had to be the youth, Calen. The other one was probably Hape. That's four, I thought. Where were the others? I scanned the area, then widened my search into the fields. There! Another rider was waiting in the middle of Hestan's field, almost invisible from here if not for the white surcoat. What was he doing there? His back was to me and he was facing the narrow western path that led from Hestan's farm to that of Jayner of Corwick's farm. The land at that point dipped dramatically, so I couldn't see what he was looking at.

I pictured Jayner's farm in my mind and knew that further west from there sat the tiny village of Corwick, though calling it a village might be a bit of a stretch. There were only five or six houses in the village, as well as an ancient smithy and, of course, the Holy House, where we all congregated to pray twice a week. The man on horseback suddenly waved his arm in the air, then turned toward Hestan's farm and cupped his hands over his mouth. I heard a faint, "Ho!" echo across the field from him. Down in the yard, Quant said something to Crooked Nose, who nodded and waved back to the man in the field. I watched as Hape and Calen mounted their horses and joined the other two. What was going on? Quant, Crooked Nose and Hape kicked their horses into a gallop, leaving Calen behind. The three men-at-arms rode along the western path and the soldier in the field fell in behind them. When they reached the hilltop they spread out on each side of the path, two per side, and stopped. It wasn't long before I saw movement as a pair of mounted soldiers crested the hill, their white surcoats matching those of the waiting men. Two more of them, I thought grimly. That made seven. One of the new riders said something to Quant, who motioned toward Hestan's farm with this hand. The man nodded and headed that way, while behind him a large knot of people marched along on foot. As the walkers drew closer I recognized several of the ones in the lead. There was the Widow Meade, unmistakable bent over almost double like that. She'd broken her back years ago and it was a miracle that she could walk at all. Beside her, clearly helping her, walked the great bulk of Gerber the Smith, who was almost as big as my father. A tall woman carrying a small child walked just behind the Widow Meade and the smith. Meanda and her daughter, Little Jinny, I knew. I identified more people as they drew ever closer to the farm and I chewed on my lower lip with worry as I realized that except for Son Fadrian and Daughter Elias, the entire village was on the march. Another of the men-at-arms, the eighth one, appeared at the rear of the marchers, urging them on as if he were herding sheep. I wondered idly what had become of the last soldier. The procession moved forward raggedly, with Quant, Crooked Nose,

Hape and the other man following along at the sides. I heard Calen shout something and I shifted my gaze to Hestan's farm, where I watched as the people sitting there rose stiffly to their feet. With a sigh of relief escaping my lips, I saw that my father was standing among them, towering over them all. It looked as though he had a bandage wrapped around his head, but other than that he seemed fine. The marchers had reached the farm by this time and they joined my father and the others. Many of the villagers began crying and hugging each other and everyone seemed to be talking at once, a gabble of noise that slowly drifted up to me on the hill. Quant kicked his heels angrily against his horse's flanks and the animal sprinted forward before coming to a halt in a cloud of dust in the yard as Quant yanked up viciously on the reins.

"Be quiet!" I heard him shout. The words echoed across the fields and silence fell as all eyes turned to him. Even the birds above me stopped chirping at the sound of Quant's wrath. The leader of the men-at-arms pointed his finger at the villagers and said something, but his words were lost to me. Little Jinny immediately started to cry, which seemed to anger Quant even more and he began shouting and swinging one arm wildly through the air. The only words I could make out clearly, however, were, "cut," and, "tongue." When Quant was finally done ranting, a large figure stepped away from the villagers and I watched my father slowly drag himself forward before he stopped only paces from Quant's fidgeting horse. My father looked up at the man and started speaking, his arms spread out to each side as he talked. I strained my ears, but I couldn't make out more than a few garbled words and I cursed softly in frustration. Maybe I should sneak down there, I thought. I glanced at the rock wall and plowed field below me, then over to the corncockles covering the small hill above Hestan's farm. All the men-at-arms were watching my father and I thought if I hurried maybe I could make it to the flowers and hide there so I could hear. And then what? I asked myself. Then what will you do? I realized I didn't know and that I'd just have to wait where I was and see what happened, much as it galled me.

Below me, Quant leaned down toward my father, his face just inches above his horse's twitching ears. "You want to know, peasant!" I heard him shout. The word "peasant" echoed over and over and I clutched my Pair Stone fearfully as my father straightened his shoulders. He stared up at Quant and nodded to him firmly and I felt a jolt of pride flow through me at his bravery. Quant pointed past me to the east and said something to my father, then kicked his horse into motion, heading up the hill to our farm. Behind him the other men-at-arms herded the villagers into a tight formation before urging them onward. I saw my father say something to the Widow Meade and then fall into step beside her, the two making an odd pair as they both forced their broken bodies up the short hill and along the path. Once the procession finally reached our farm, the villagers all bunched together in the middle of the yard like a flock of sheep surrounded by hungry wolves. Everything was silent save for the odd squeak and grunt from the pigs in the sty and the occasional cluck of a chicken. "Peasant," Quant finally said, addressing my father. I could hear much clearer now that they were closer and for that I was thankful, though the pounding of my heart threatened to drown out whatever words might be spoken. "You wished to know what became of your children," Quant said. He pointed with a mailed hand to the sty. "The answer to your question lies behind there."

"Mother Above!" I whispered in horror, knowing what he was about to see and helpless to prevent it. My father simply nodded at Quant's words, his face set in a white mask. What must he be thinking, I thought, knowing that whatever it was it couldn't be worse than what he was about to see. The Widow Meade grabbed my father's hand in hers and brought it to her lips. I think she said something to him as well, but it was so low that I couldn't hear the words. My father nodded to her and patted her hand gently before he slowly turned away and shuffled toward the sty. I watched his broad back disappear behind the building and I closed my eyes, feeling the tears start to roll down my cheeks when I heard his horrified screams. I didn't realize it, but I was stabbing the tree beside me over and over again with the reeve's knife as the sounds of my grieving father echoed over the farmland. After a time, the cries ended with nothing left but the sounds of soft sobbing. At some point I'd fallen to my knees, but I don't remember doing it. Above me the reeve's knife was stuck in the trunk of the tree, gleaming down at me as though mocking my helplessness.

"Enough!" Quant barked gruffly. He motioned to Crooked Nose and Hape. "Bring him back here."

The two men-at-arms nodded in unison and dismounted, then strode purposefully around the sty. Within moments they were back, dragging my weeping father between them. They dropped him roughly in the yard and then stepped back as Hestan and his son, Jinian, moved to go help him. Crooked Nose drew his sword and lifted it toward the two villagers in warning and they reluctantly fell back.

"So, peasant," Quant said. "Are you satisfied now?"

"My son," my father finally gasped out as he pushed himself up on his elbows. "What have you bastards done to my son?"

Quant smirked. "We have done nothing to your son." He nodded to Patter's Bog. "That, however, cannot be said for that bog over there."

I saw my father's puzzlement as he glanced toward where I knelt hidden under the trees. For just a moment it seemed as though he was staring right at me, but then he slowly looked away and turned back to Quant. "I don't understand," he said weakly.

"The quicksand took him," Hape said as he leaned down to look at my father with a lopsided grin on his face. "Ate him up it did and burped back nothing but his rags."

"No!" my father shouted. "No!" His great shoulders bunched and his face twisted in pain as he fought to push himself to his knees. "No, you bastards!" my father cried again as he used his good leg to support his bad leg and trembling, rose shakily to his feet. Rage and grief had twisted his features into an ugly mask and as he rose to his full height he tore the bandage from his head and glared up at Quant with a murderous look. I stared across the plowed field at my enraged father, terrified for him and feeling small and helpless as I clutched the Pair Stone in my hands. I closed my eyes and prayed to The First Pair for a miracle, because I knew that without one my father was about to die.

"Ho!" a shout rose, echoing across the fields from the west. I opened my eyes and turned, shocked to see that horsemen were coming over the hill from Hestan's farm. There were perhaps twenty of them riding two by two in tight formation and they were wearing the white surcoat and dragon emblem of the Lord of Corwick. The two lead riders held long spears in their right hands at the end of which fluttered the lord's gold and white standard with the dragon emblem. I caught my breath as I saw the rider directly behind the standard bearers. He was lean and fit looking, dressed in gold-plated armour and a golden helm which gleamed in the sunlight. A red cape lined with fox fur was thrown over his shoulders and was clasped by a shiny black pendant that shimmered as he moved. His face under the helm was hard to make out from my vantage point, but having seen him once before I knew that he was young, with short blond hair and a beard that was closely trimmed on the sides and left long in the front and then braided so that it hung below his chin. "The Lord of Corwick!" I whispered as I felt my body sag with relief. A sudden curt command from Lord Corwick halted the column some distance from our farm house and the standard bearers in the lead guided their horses aside as Lord Corwick and another rider continued on. The man with Lord Corwick looked familiar and, as they drew closer and entered the yard, I realized that it was Heavy Beard, the man who'd chased me this morning and fallen off his horse. It seemed like that had happened so long ago that it might have actually been a dream. "The ninth one," I muttered as Heavy Beard nodded to Quant before guiding his horse near where Hestan stood with his two sons. Heavy Beard glowered down at the three men and

I could clearly see the fear on their faces as they quickly looked to the ground.

"My lord," Quant said, bowing his head slightly as Lord Corwick halted in front of him. Quant picked at his teeth and then turned away and spit on the ground. "A messy business, this."

"Show me," Lord Corwick said in a clipped tone. I could clearly see the rage smouldering across the lord's young face and I chortled to myself. Just you wait! I thought. Just you wait until he sees what you did!

"My Lord Corwick!" my father implored as the two men rode past him. "I need-"

Lord Corwick cut him off with a raised hand, barely giving him a glance as he and Quant rode around the sty and disappeared from view.

I can still see that day clearly in mind, though it happened over sixty years ago now. Nothing moved while they were gone, not even the lazy swish of a horse's tail. I remember the fetid stench of the decaying bog back through the trees behind me and the smell of my own sweat mixed with the mud on my skin as though it were yesterday. I close my eyes and I see again the silent men-at-arms on horseback surrounding the terrified villagers huddled together and holding each other for comfort. I can see the motionless column of men sitting and waiting for their lord halfway between Hestan's farm and ours, their faces mere white blurs in the distance. I picture my father standing between Crooked Nose and Hape, his body hunched over with pain and his face etched with grief. He'd always seemed like a giant to me before, but now it seemed as though he'd shrunk, as though what life he'd had left in him had been sucked away, leaving nothing left but a husk. I spoke before of regrets, and this is one that I carry with me always. I should have run to him at that moment. If I could do it all over again, that's what I would do. It would be foolish, I know, but at least if I had he would have known I was alive and even if that knowledge had given him just a moment of freedom from his grief, it would have been worth it. I was so young and so unprepared for what was about to happen, and as I write this I weep for that boy, and for them all.

Quant and Lord Corwick finally reappeared around the sty and they rode silently into the yard and stopped their horses facing the villagers. Lord Corwick's face was red and angry looking and Quant seemed amused for some reason. "My lord," my father said hoarsely as he stood swaying on his feet. He lifted his arms and took a weak step toward the two mounted men.

"Be quiet!" Crooked Nose hissed, putting his hand on my father's chest and stopping him. He gestured with the sword he held in his other hand. "Go back and join the others and keep your ugly mouth shut!" My father looked at Crooked Nose with lifeless eyes and he shook his massive head and raised his right hand. What he was going to do I'll never know because Crooked Nose saw the upraised hand and he stepped back and swung his sword. My eyes were blinded by a sudden flash of sunlight on metal and just like that my father's head fell sideways from his neck and rolled slowly several paces through the dust as a torrent of blood spurted from his neck. The headless body sagged like an empty sack and fell limply to the ground. I looked at the grotesque figure lying in the dirt in numb disbelief as my father's wizened leg jerked several times and then was still. The rest of the villagers started moaning in fear and clutching at each other as they screamed at Lord Corwick for mercy. I saw the look of anger on the lord's face turn to hatred as he stared at his people begging for their lives and I felt sickened. There would be no mercy this day, I knew. For I now realized that Lord Corwick hadn't come to mete out justice for my sister's murder. He was here to avenge the death of the reeve!

"Nobody lives," I heard Lord Corwick say harshly. He glanced at Quant. "Kill them all and destroy everything just as we discussed."

Quant grinned wolfish teeth. "Yes, my lord."

Lord Corwick nodded to him and then galloped back down the path in an angry cloud of dust. When he reached his men they moved aside to allow him through before falling in behind him as the standard bearers raced their horses to each side of the column to take the lead once again in front of their lord. Quant waited for them to leave, his unfeeling eyes studying the villagers with disdain as several of the younger men tried to run. They didn't get far, however, as the men-at-arms herded them back with their horses and the flats of their swords. Most of the villagers gave up after that and they fell to their knees, either begging for their lives or calling out to The Mother or The Father to save them. When Lord Corwick and his men finally disappeared from sight, Quant grinned his yellow smile and drew his sword. "You heard his lordship!" Quant cried. He lifted his sword into the air. "Kill them all!"

I couldn't bear what I knew was about to happen, so I turned and fled back into the bog. The last words I heard before the screaming began were from Hape encouraging the others to save the women until the end. I shuddered at the fate that awaited those women and I ran to the stone I'd sat on earlier, then plugged my ears and rocked myself back and forth. My father had told me this morning that The Mother and The Father had given me a brain to think with and I focused on that. I was eight and armed with only a knife against nine men-at-arms. There was nothing that I could do, but I also knew that that wouldn't always be the case. I would live, I promised myself. I would live, and when I was ready, I would find the nine. I would find them and I would kill them all. I wouldn't be a boy forever!

Chapter 3: Carspen Tuft

That night in Patter's Bog was one of the longest nights of my life. At some point darkness had set in while I sat shivering on the cold stone and a red glow began to fill the sky above the trees. I smelled smoke and I realized numbly that they had fired the buildings. I briefly considered going to look, but I felt drained of the will to move and I just sat there and stared into the dark, murky waters of the bog. Earlier I'd headed back to the treeline once the screams had mercifully stopped; hoping that the nine had left, but it had been a mistake. They were still there and the sight that had greeted me had turned my stomach and I'd heaved up what little food was still in me before I'd stumbled back to the bog. I wasn't going back out there to look again. Not for any reason. I don't know how many hours I sat in the darkness afraid to close my eyes and sleep, but eventually the sky began to brighten above the trees. I had no plan and I was at a loss as to what I should do next. I had the reeve's knife, a torn tunic, thin trousers and worn leather shoes that had belonged to my older brother and were still a bit too big for my feet. I had to stuff rags in them so that they stayed on. That was it. I felt hopelessness and despair wash over me, my earlier bravado gone now, and I fought back tears just as a sudden vision of my father appeared standing over me.

"You know what you have to do," my father said, looking down at me kindly.

"I'm so tired," I said to him listlessly, knowing that what I was seeing wasn't real. My father was with Mother Above now, or possibly, Father Below, and he was long gone from this world.

"You can't stay here," my father insisted. "You must leave this place."

"What does it matter where I am?" I asked, fighting to keep the tremor from my voice as I felt a crushing loneliness come over me. "Everyone is dead anyway."

My father sighed and squeezed my shoulder like he had done so many times in the past. It felt like his fingers were actually on me and I sagged with fatigue in his firm grip. "You must stay strong, Hadrack. I need you to survive and grow powerful so that when the time comes you can avenge us."

"But what if I can't?" I asked him. "What if I'm never strong enough to do that?"

"You will find a way," my father said. He smiled at me sadly as he began to fade. "It is your destiny."

I felt overwhelmed with exhaustion and loss and I rubbed my tired eyes with my fists and then blinked as I looked up at the silent trees circling me. Had he really just been there or had I imagined it? I wondered as doubt began to wiggle its way into my tired thoughts. I realized that either way, what my father had said was right. If I didn't move I'd die here of starvation sooner or later, and then no one would be left to avenge the deaths of the villagers and my family. I stood up, pausing to stretch my aching limbs before I turned and headed for the treeline. The reeve's knife was still where I had left it and I pulled it from the tree trunk as I passed by. The sun was rising in the east now and the soothing morning rays lit up the land where our farm had once stood. Nothing much remained of our house save for blackened, smouldering ruins, and even though I had been expecting to see it like that, expecting something and actually seeing it are two very different things. I watched with a heavy heart as thick columns of black smoke rose upward from the charred ashes of the house and partially blocked the sun before being whisked away by the early morning breeze. Heavy smoke and flames danced and swirled where the sty and woodshed had stood and I saw that the chicken coop and toolshed were completely gone as well. Bodies lay everywhere in the front yard and across the plowed fields, lying twisted and torn in every way imaginable. I stuck the knife in the back of my trousers and squared my shoulders just like I'd seen my father do when he had set his mind to something. I stepped out from the trees and paused, my nose wrinkling in distaste. There was something underlying the smell of smoke, an almost sweet, sickly smell and I grimaced when I realized it was the stench of burnt flesh. Great plumes of black smoke rose from the west and I knew that Hestan's farm had suffered the same fate as my own. I could see similar dark smoke coming from where Jayner's farm lay below the horizon and more smoke rose to the east where the other farms lay. "Destroy everything," I remembered Lord Corwick saying.

I started forward, heading south through the soft soil of the field until I reached the western path, choosing the longer route to delay what I knew I was going to see for as long as possible. I reached the path and turned toward the ruins of my home and slowly walked the worn trail, until finally I entered our yard. Not much was left of the house at all, as the walls and roof had long since collapsed, but the sty and woodshed continued to burn briskly. I coughed repeatedly as the stench of charred flesh filled my nostrils while thick black smoke billowed around me. The wind was blowing from the north that morning and sending the smoke right at me and it was so thick at times that I was having trouble seeing. I covered my nose and mouth with my tunic, coughing and blinking my stinging eyes as I crouched down to examine the closest bodies, looking for my father. The first body I came to was that of Hestan's son, Garen. He was lying on his back with his throat slashed open and his son, Fitch, lay face down across his chest. The back of Fitch's head had been crushed in. Not far away from them lay Garen's brother, Jinian, and close to him lay his father and the twisted body of the Widow Meade. I moved on, keeping low as I examined body after body. I suppressed a moan as I came upon Little Jinny where she was lying almost peacefully on the ground with her knees drawn up to her chest. She looked as though she could have been sleeping if not for the patch of blood staining her small dress. I searched through the smoke, but there was no sign of Little Jinny's mother and I grit my teeth, pretty sure I knew what had happened to her.

I turned away from Little Jinny and glanced toward the sty just as there was a break in the smoke. I gasped in shock as my gaze fell upon my father's head staring at me with sightless eyes. Someone had taken a fence board and impaled the head on it before driving the board into the ground. I saw that my father's body lay not far from the board and I stood up and walked through the smoke toward it. As I drew closer, the sweet sickly smell grew stronger and I realized it was coming from the dead pigs in the sty. I reached the fence board and with shaking hands I gingerly pulled father's head from it, trying not to look at the slack face as I crouched down and carefully placed it by his corpse. Then I stood up and forced my way through the smoke and past the remnants of the sty. The woodshed was still burning quite briskly on the other side, but the smoke was being blown away from me now so that I could breathe and see much better. I looked down at the ground and I can only imagine what the expression on my face must have been as I stared at the row of naked bodies that lay there. I'd been expecting it, but even so I was unprepared for the sight of women that I'd known all of my life lying there with their throats slashed. Each of the women had been staked out with their legs spread and their ankles cruelly tied to the stakes with ropes. Their arms had been drawn over their heads and their wrists had been tied to stakes as well. Many of their faces were frozen in terror and anguish, with their eyes bulging out of their sockets grotesquely.

I heard a rattling coming from deep in my throat and I turned away, leaning over with my hands on my knees as I retched up a small amount of white bile. I heaved painfully several more times and then finally stood up and wiped my mouth as I turned back to the women and burned the scene of their murders into my memory. This too the nine would pay for, I vowed. I glanced around for the reeve, not surprised to see that his body was gone from where it had lain, as was my father's axe. Then I focused my gaze on my sister lying among the dead. I moved purposely to her side and picked her up in my arms, trying not to stare at the gaping wound in her neck as her head flopped back and forth. She was slight and though I was tired, it seemed to me her body had no weight at all, as though the essence of her flesh had fled along with her soul when she'd died. I started to walk, heading north toward the forest, my eyes focused on nothing but the trees in the distance. I don't know how long it took me to get there, but I remember I fell many times as my feet kept catching in the soil, tripping me as I stumbled along. But each time I pushed myself to my feet and picked my sister's body back up and continued on. Finally, when I reached the trees, I made my way to the stream that I knew well, and there, near a spot where Jeanna and I had fished and laughed, I buried her.

When I was done, I turned and headed back to the farm to get my. I had no illusions that I could even drag, let alone carry his great bulk, so I picked up his head and tucked it under my arm and walked back to the trees with it. It would have to do. I dug a small hole with the knife beside where Jeanna lay and I placed my father's head gently inside, then I covered it up. I knelt by the graves and placed a hand on each one. "I repeat my vow," I said formally. "The nine will die. I will not rest until it has been fulfilled or I am dead and have joined you in the world after. This I swear to you both." I stood up and stared at the graves for a time while I toyed with the Pair Stone around my neck and prayed. Finally I realized it was time to go and I crossed the stream and struck out through the trees to the north. In hindsight I probably should have gone back and salvaged whatever I could from the ravaged farms, but with father and Jeanna properly buried, I was anxious to put as much space between me and what had happened in Corwick as I could.

It's funny the things that you remember as old age sets in. I can tell you what color the sky was, the smells, even what each individual tree looked like when I set out on that first day. After that it becomes a blur of walking, sleeping and scrounging for food and just trying to stay alive. My best guess is I was on my own for a month, if not more. I remember something about a bear and having to spend a day or two stuck in a tree before it finally gave up and left me alone. I also remember being sick with a fever and the never-ending ache of hunger pounding away at me. Other than that, not much of that time remains with me. One thing I have not forgotten, though, is Carspen Tuft and his wife. How could I possibly forget them? I'd been sick with fever for almost a week, and though I was coming out of it by then, I still wasn't myself yet when I saw them sitting around a weak campfire one morning in a hollow surrounded by elm and maple trees. They were roasting a rabbit over the flames and I stood and watched them for a time, hidden by the trees as my stomach rumbled at the smells drifting over to me. A matching set of mules stood tethered nearby, the animals grazing on sparse grass that grew near an ancient elm that was wider than I could spread my arms. The gnarled, dark-grey roots beneath the tree wound their way in all directions along the ground and a battered wagon that looked like it had seen many years of hard use stood almost hidden in the shadows of the great elm. I noticed that an opening no bigger than my head was cut into the back door of the wagon and that it was protected by three stout iron bars. That should have been a warning to me, I suppose, but my mind was not as sharp as it should have been and I dismissed it. Had I been thinking clearer, I have no doubt I would have continued on around them, despite the maddening smells that filled my nostrils. I only wish that I had. Instead, having checked the man and woman out, I decided that they were harmless and I stepped from the trees into view.

Carspen Tuft was a small man, not much taller than me at the time, and he was easily into his fortieth year. I actually thought at first that he was one of the little people he was so short. Tuft was almost completely bald, with just a tired ring of wispy grey-black hair encircling his head. A thatch of greying beard hung from his chin and this was heavily stained yellow with juices. He was dressed in a dark brown cloak over an equally brown tunic and a small knife in a worn leather scabbard hung at his hip. The cloak was clasped around his shoulders with a heavy Pair Stone pendant, and what may have once been white trousers were stuffed into scuffed leather boots. "What have we here?" Tuft exclaimed in surprise when he saw me. He stood up, one hand automatically going to the hilt of his knife. His eyes looked like a rat's, cunning and mean, though his features were set in a pleasant look of welcome.

"I smelled your fire," I mumbled, my voice sounding odd to me after going so long without speaking to anyone. I took two steps forward into the hollow, barley able to keep my gaze from the flames. I gestured weakly to the cooking meat. "I haven't eaten anything in a long time."

"I understand, lad," Tuft said kindly. He glanced into the trees almost casually. "Are you alone?" I nodded and the little man visibly relaxed and he let his hand drop away from his knife as the hardness left his eyes. "My name is Carspen Tuft," he told me as he motioned to the fire. "Come. Sit and join us. There's plenty to go around." I was moving closer even as the words were coming out of his mouth. I'd lost my knife weeks ago and had been living on grubs and whatever edible plants I could find, so the thought of cooked meat was beyond intoxicating. "Sit here, by the fire," Tuft said, motioning to where the woman sat on a flat rock. She still hadn't said anything and she just stared at me in silence. "Hielda, move your fat ass so the boy can sit!" Tuft commanded gruffly. The woman snorted and stood up and I realized that Tuft was right. She was fat. Very fat. She was dressed in a dark cloak with the hood up, hiding half of her face. All I could see was her rounded chin, the tip of her squat nose and a bulbous mouth, with just a hint of her eyes gleaming at me when she lifted her head. Long grey hair spilled out from the hood and fell to her shoulders and her hands were bare and enormous, looking puffy and unhealthy as though from disease.

"We don't have any room, Husband," Hielda said in an annoyed voice.

"Tut tut, my dear," Tuft said, waving her words away casually. "There's always room for one more." I had no idea what they were talking about, nor did I much care. All I could think about was food and so I sat down on the stone that Tuft had offered as my stomach grumbled loudly with desire. Tuft smiled at me in a friendly fashion and he squatted beside me and turned the meat on its spit while I stared, mesmerized. The fire crackled pleasantly and I felt my eyes start to droop with exhaustion as an ember jumped out from the flames and landed near my foot, sizzling in the grass before going out.

"The Quarrymaster told us last time that he wouldn't pay for any that were sick," Hielda said in a low voice.

"Bah," Tuft said with a shrug. "He's said that before. He'll pay. He always pays." He glanced sideways at me, studying me critically. "Besides, I don't think he's that sick. Just tired and hungry is all."

"He's not worth the trouble," Hielda grumbled.

"I'll say what's worth the trouble or not!" Tuft said sharply, glaring up at Hielda. I was having trouble keeping up with their conversation, as by now I was completely lost to the smells and the warmth coming from the fire and I closed my eyes. I don't know how long I sat like that, but eventually I felt a hand on my arm, gently shaking me and I opened my eyes to see that Tuft was looking at me pityingly. "Poor boy," he said sadly. "You're all done in." Tuft shifted his gaze to his wife who still stood near the fire and was watching us closely. "Get the boy some ale," he ordered. "The brown bottle in my sack will do nicely. You know the one." Hielda opened her mouth as if to protest, then she snorted again and stalked off. While she was gone, Tuft poked at the rabbit with his finger, wincing as he yanked his finger back almost immediately and sucked on it. "It's ready, but Mother Above that stings!" he said around his burnt finger as he winked at me not unkindly. He took the spit off of the fire and slid the cooked rabbit onto a large piece of bark and then cut the meat into sections using his knife. "Eat up, lad," he said, smiling as he stabbed a steaming wedge and offered it to me. I nodded eagerly and took it, switching it from palm to palm and waiting impatiently for it to cool. My mouth was almost dripping with desire and finally I couldn't wait any longer and I crammed it into my mouth. Nothing I have ever eaten since has tasted as good as that rabbit did that day and I chewed hungrily as Hielda reappeared with a bottle in her hand. "Ah, just in time my love," Tuft said to her. She silently handed him the small brown bottle and then crossed around the fire to sit on the other side of it and glare at us. Tuft ignored her and he turned and offered the bottle to me. "Try it," Tuft said. "It will restore your strength and I promise you'll feel as good as new in no time. You'll see."

"What is it?" I asked as I took it from him and pulled out the stopper and sniffed it cautiously. It smelled a bit like the ale my father and Hestan drank sometimes, but it had a sweeter tint to it.

"My own recipe," Tuft announced as he stabbed a piece of meat with his knife and put it in his mouth. He chewed noisily and added around the food, "Take just a little to start."

I nodded and took a tentative sip. It tasted sweet at first, but then it began to burn my throat as it went down. I choked and coughed and Tuft laughed heartily while Hielda just sat there and never said a word. "Burns!" I managed to gasp out.

"Only at first," Tuft nodded. He motioned with his hand. "Take another. It gets easier."

I did as he suggested, then took a third, longer sip, starting to enjoy it. He was right. It did get easier. I wiped my mouth with the back of my hand and smiled contentedly at Tuft as I felt a pleasant numbness start to travel down my limbs. I took another hunk of the meat that Tuft offered me and I popped it into my mouth and chewed, then washed it down with a gulp of ale. I glanced at the bottle in my hand and frowned, blinking as I tried unsuccessfully to focus on it. I rubbed my eyes with the back of my hand and glanced at Tuft, only to gasp out in surprise. A moment ago there had been only one Tuft, but now there were three of them and they were all grinning and talking to me at once. I looked away in confusion and shook my head, then turned and looked again. Still three Tufts. I barely felt the bottle drop from my hand as I tried to say something, anything, but I couldn't get my mouth to work properly. The three Tufts just kept staring at me, their faces now expressionless except for their identical, unfeeling rat eyes watching me before blackness took over and I knew nothing else.

When I awoke, it was to the sensation of motion, and I cautiously opened my eyes. Darkness surrounded me save for a faint glow above me and to my left. I realized I was sitting propped up with my back against something hard and unyielding and I couldn't move my arms. A sharp smell of sweat, piss and shit filled my nostrils and I gagged and tried to breathe through my mouth as I felt a rising panic. Where in the name of The Mother was I? My shoes had fallen apart weeks ago and I'd been barefoot ever since and I wiggled my toes cautiously, trying to restore feeling in them. I instantly felt contact with someone and heard an annoyed grunt and I quickly pulled my knees up to my chest. I groaned as pain flared in my temple.

"Your head hurts something awful right about now, I expect," a man's voice whispered beside me.

"Where am-?" I began.

"Not so loud!" the voice hissed, cutting me off. I blinked, just able to discern a vague form sitting beside me. "We'll be stopping for the night any time now," the man continued softly, "and that bitch gets mad if she hears us talking, so keep your voice low."

My eyes were becoming accustomed to the darkness by now and I realized the faint light was moonlight coming in through a small barred window. I was in Tuft's wagon! I leaned toward my companion. "The bitch? Do you mean, Hielda?"

"Who else?" the man said bitterly. I shifted my rear end on the hard floor and looked down at my hands. A band of iron with a ring at the base was clamped around each wrist and another iron ring encircled the one on my wrist and was then attached to a similar ring embedded in the floor. I closed my eyes and let my head fall back against the hard plank behind me. I was a prisoner! How could I have been so stupid? My head swam and I felt my stomach heave as a wave of nausea came over me and I moaned faintly. "The dizziness will pass," my companion said kindly. "Just give it time." I opened my eyes, wincing at the stabbing pain in my head and studied him. His features seemed strange in the dim light, with his eyes showing up only as deep bottomless black sockets and his nose looked huge and hooked. Probably a trick of the shadows, I thought. "The name's Jebido," he added.

"I'm Hadrack," I mumbled in reply. "How long have I been asleep?"

"Since this morning," Jebido replied. "That brown bottle of theirs hits hard."

My head felt like it was starting to clear a bit and I nodded to him in agreement and took a better look around the wagon, surprised to see that Jebido and I weren't the only prisoners. In front of me sat a fat man with a bushy blond beard, dirty blond hair and large ears that stuck out oddly from his head. He was wearing a long soiled tunic that reached almost to his knees, which I could see were bare and covered in filth as he wore no trousers. Beside this man sat a thin, ragged looking fellow with his chin lolling on his chest, clearly sleeping. The thin man was wearing what must have once been a fine tunic and jacket, but was now heavily stained and torn in many places. On the other side of Jebido near the door sat a boy of about my age, though he was much smaller than me, with a thin, intelligent looking face.

"That there is Klotter," Jebido said, motioning with his chin to the fat man. Klotter nodded slightly, but said nothing. "The skinny fellow sleeping is Twent," Jebido continued. "Claims to be a teacher or something," he added doubtfully. He motioned with his head to the boy by the door. "Don't know this one's name. He doesn't talk much."

The wagon came to a shuddering halt just then and Tuft called out in a muffled, but cheerful voice, "That's enough for tonight, my love. We'll get an early start in the morning and be at the quarry before noon."

"As you wish, Husband," Hielda responded flatly. A small square suddenly creaked open in the planking at the front of the wagon and Hielda's pale white face peered in at us suspiciously. "I'll be listening, so there better not be a sound coming from in here!" she hissed, "or you'll feel the burn!" The opening snapped shut with an angry clack and the wagon rocked back and forth as Tuft and Hielda dismounted. I could hear Tuft chattering away happily as he unhooked the mules and led them away until finally their voices receded.

I leaned as close to Jebido as I could. "What did she mean by we'll feel the burn?" I asked in a whisper.

Jebido glanced at Klotter. "Show him so he understands."

Klotter pursed his lips and with his manacled right hand he pulled at his tunic, raising it until he revealed the red, angry burnt flesh of his manhood. I swallowed loudly and shared a long look with Jebido and then turned away and closed my eyes. There was no more talking after that from any of us. I slept fitfully that night, unable to find any comfort from the hard, unforgiving wood of the wagon floor and the unrelenting smell inside the wagon. By the time morning came around I was sore, hungry and thirsty, but worst of all, I had to piss. I tried not to think about it, but the more I tried, the more I had to piss. I noticed Jebido was awake, his face looking less odd now in the light of day, though his nose was still incredibly large and hooked like a great bird of prey. Despite our surroundings he looked lean and fit, with thick brown hair and an unkempt dark beard shot through with grey on the sides of his chin. I guessed him to be about thirty years of age. I leaned as close to him as I could. "I have to piss," I whispered.

Jebido just shrugged. "Then go ahead and piss. They used to have two guards who let us out twice a day, but that lying little bastard out there disagreed with them about something two nights ago and they left. We haven't had anything to eat or drink or been let out since, so there's not much point in trying to hold it."

I grimaced and nodded to him, knowing that I couldn't ignore the pressing need any longer. I closed my eyes and leaned my head against the wall, ignoring the wetness pooling under me as I pictured the nine in my mind. Crooked Nose, Hape, Calen, Heavy Beard and Quant. I pursed my lips, concentrating, trying to remember the other four who I didn't have names for. There had been two men with reddish beards, I recalled, and another one with blond hair that had curled outside his coif like a girl's. The ninth one I couldn't picture at all no matter how hard I tried and finally I just shrugged and gave up. I would track them down one way or another, I knew. I had made a vow, and, as far as I was concerned, it was only a matter of time before I found them all. Beneath me the wagon abruptly lurched, snapping me back to reality and I heard Tuft calling out to the mules as he snapped his whip.

We were under way again and for the rest of the morning we rumbled along steadily, rarely if ever saying anything to each other. The heat and stench inside the wagon became oppressive, but we endured it simply because we had no choice. Every once in a while Hielda would snap open the tiny door and peer in at us eagerly, only to look disappointed when she saw us sitting in dejected silence.

We finally arrived at our destination just around noon, just as Tuft had predicted, and the wagon came to a lumbering halt. Jebido and I shared a glance as the wagon rocked beneath us as Tuft and Hielda jumped down and I clearly heard Tuft greet someone cheerfully. The reply back was gruff and abrupt, with little warmth to it, and then heavy-booted feet sounded outside the wagon before the back door swung open, flooding us with warm sunlight. I blinked at the sudden brightness and studied the big man who stood in the doorway staring in at us. He was dressed in mail and stood with one mailed hand braced on the hilt of his sword and his helmet tucked beneath his other arm. His beard was long and grey, the color matching his closely-cropped hair and bushy eyebrows that were arched in disgust as he looked in at us and wrinkled his nose. "Mother's tit!" the man snapped. He turned to glare down at Tuft, who stood beside him holding a large iron key ring in his hand. "You didn't even let the bastards out to shit?"

"We wanted to, Quarrymaster," Tuft whined as he tucked the keys away in his trousers. "Truly we did, but I normally bring you boys, as you well know, and they are easily handled compared to full grown men."

"Your point being?" the Quarrymaster growled.

Tuft spread his arms. "My point, my lord, is that because you contracted us to bring as many men as I could find this time, I hired what I thought were trustworthy guards to protect us. How could I possibly have known that those murderous rogues would rob us and then flee, barely leaving us with our lives intact? It was a harrowing experience, I must say." I glanced at Jebido and he rolled his eyes at me as Tuft sniffed and actually dabbed at his eyes and then continued, "But, my wife and I were determined not to let you down and, despite the great personal risk to us both, we brought them to you anyway."

"And you didn't let them out to shit because?" the Quarrymaster prompted.

"Well," Tuft said, looking up at the bigger man as he swept his arm toward us. "I'm old and frail now, a far cry from the strapping man of my youth, and these men are dangerous. I was afraid they would murder me if I set them free to do their business and then do only The Mother knows what to my beautiful wife. I couldn't let something ghastly like that happen to my precious flower, now could I? Surely you, in your great wisdom, can understand that I had no choice?"

"Uh huh," the Quarrymaster grunted, looking unimpressed by Tuft's story. "Even hogs get slopped out once in a while you know."

"Yes, of course you're right," Tuft said apologetically. "It won't happen again. You have the word of Carspen Tuft on that!"

"See that it doesn't," the Quarrymaster grumbled. He glanced into the wagon and his eyes fell on me and he pointed. "What's wrong with that one?" he demanded as he turned on Tuft. "Is he sick? I thought I told you not to bring me any sick ones!"

"He's not sick, I assure you," Tuft said, raising his hands

in the air in protest. He grabbed the Pair Stone pendant around his neck in both of his hands. "I swear by both The Mother and The Father that he is well. He's just a little under nourished is all and, to that end, I've been feeding him twice a day with my own hands to help him regain his strength." Tuft looked in at me and winked and I glowered back at him in anger. "Look at those mighty shoulders, my lord. He just needs a little fattening up and I'll wager he'll be one of your best boys."

"Well," the Quarrymaster muttered doubtfully as he peered in at me again. "I guess he'll do, but those grey eyes of his are strange."

"The sign of the wolf," Tuft assured him, patting his arm. "A well-known symbol of strength and endurance." He motioned with his right hand. "Now, shall we retire to your tent and finalize payment?"

"Very well," the Quarrymaster grunted. He slammed his helmet back on his head and barked, "Fanch, bring them down and get them settled in!"

A man appeared beside Tuft and the Quarrymaster dressed in polished leather armour and over this he wore a yellow surcoat with a black stag emblazoned across his chest. He was shorter, but wider than the Quarrymaster, and he had a stern looking, expressionless face. He held out his hand without saying a word and Tuft smiled at him and dropped the ring of keys into his palm.

"That one there," Tuft said, pointing to the keys.

Fanch nodded to Tuft and then reached into the wagon, careful not to soil his surcoat in the filth as he unlocked the boy with no name's bonds. "Free the others and be quick about it," Fanch instructed him in an impatient voice. The boy nodded, pausing to rub his wrists before taking the keys and, though he was small and slight looking, he was very nimble and precise, so that in just a few moments we were all free. I stood up stiffly and my head almost brushed the roof of the wagon as I followed the others through the filth on the floor, trying not to slip. Jebido, Klotter and the teacher, Twent, all had to bend almost double to get out. One by one we jumped down to the ground, all of us unsteady on our feet after being locked up so long.

I breathed in deeply, enjoying the sun on my face and relief at being free from the stench in the wagon and I looked around curiously. We stood near a round pavilion tent of stark white canvas with a thick blue border running around its base. Another similar border circled the tent halfway to the top, right before the peak began and a third, smaller one circled the peak. A yellow banner depicting a black stag flew from the top of the spire. The tent flap lay open and I could see Tuft and the Quarrymaster talking animatedly inside, while the great bulk of Hielda stood beside her husband, dwarfing him as she waited in silence. Around this tent were more just like it and I guessed there had to be at least twenty of them, maybe more. To the right of the tents stood a neat row of ten high-peaked buildings made of timber and covered in sun-burnt turf. A dusty, well-travelled road cut through the buildings and led to a timber bridge spanning a small river. The road then continued on the other side of the bridge and wound its way upward through a forest of tall oak trees. The noise and commotion of a bustling encampment rose all around us as both men and women worked at hauling firewood and water, tending gardens, smoking fish on tall wooden racks or cooking in huge iron pots that sat over open flames. I saw several spry boys of roughly my own age repairing the sod roof on one of the buildings and I watched curiously as at least twenty men worked with picks and shovels at building a wall of dirt higher than a man's head around the perimeter of the encampment. More men came behind them and began placing sharpened stakes at least ten feet long on the outward slopes of the dirt wall.

"This way," Fanch said gruffly as he brushed past me and headed for the road. Four men-at-arms joined him and they fell in behind us as we meekly followed Fanch. We approached the roughly-hewn timber bridge and I studied the water flowing beneath it, guessing that the river was perhaps forty feet across at its widest. Four women knelt on the near bank of the river washing clothing and they paused in their labor to wave as a team of four horses crossed slowly above them pulling an open wagon. Two men sat on the bench in front of the wagon and one of them said something down to the women and then laughed. The wagon was loaded with several stone blocks longer than I could spread my arms and half again as wide. The bridge creaked and groaned in protest as the wagon crossed over it and one of the blocks shifted with a screech as the wagon wheels rumbled over the joints in the timber. The wagon made it safely to the other side and the driver cracked his whip, urging the horses into a canter and we had to step aside quickly to let them pass before returning to the road.

"Excuse me, lord," Twent said to Fanch's broad back. "May I have a word?"

Fanch stopped just before the bridge and lifted his head to the sky. "There's always one," he said with a sigh. He turned to face Twent and put his hands on his hips as he spread his booted feet on the ground. "What is it?" The rest of us unconsciously moved several feet away from Twent.

"Well, you see," Twent said weakly, clearly unnerved by the look on Fanch's face. I hadn't noticed before, but Twent had a huge lower lip that jutted out from his mouth and it was quivering uncontrollably. "I think there's been a mistake," Twent managed to say. "I really shouldn't be here."

Fanch leaned sideways on one foot, looking past Twent and the rest of us to the soldiers who stood in the rear. "Did you hear that?" Fanch demanded. "The dandy says there's been a mistake and that he doesn't belong here." The soldiers all laughed and Fanch grinned and then, moving faster than I would have thought possible, he punched Twent in the stomach. The skinny man doubled up, grasping his stomach in shock as the air flew from his lungs with a whoosh. Fanch cursed him and then brought his right knee up, flattening Twent's nose and sending blood spraying. Twent fell heavily onto his back and he cried desperately for mercy as Fanch grabbed him by his long, greasy brown hair, and dragged him to his knees. "Don't you ever talk to me again you worthless whore-son!" Fanch growled. He shook Twent's head from side to side. "Do you understand me?" Blood streamed freely from Twent's ravaged nose and his eyes were tearing uncontrollably as he nodded weakly. "Good," Fanch said. He glared at Jebido. "You, help him up!"

Jebido knelt and helped the skinny teacher to his feet and we proceeded over the bridge and up the hill through the trees while Twent sobbed softly to himself. Once past the trees we entered a huge clearing where several wagons and thirty or so men waited near what had to be the largest hole in the ground I'd ever seen. A wooden platform had been built overlooking the western side of the hole and as we watched, one of the wagons was carefully manoeuvred onto it. A confusing array of beams and ropes and pulleys were built above the platform, with the largest pulley set where the beams met in the middle. A long rope ran over that pulley and then dropped down through an open section of the platform into the pit and the other end was attached to a powerful looking horse that was standing patiently waiting. A small man with a club foot was holding the horse's bridle and whispering to it. I noticed there were two more platforms, one to the east, and one to the north of the pit, and that they were in use as well. Fanch led us to the eastern side of the huge quarry as the man with the club foot abruptly shouted and urged the horse forward. The rope attached to the horse and pulley began to move reluctantly and as Fanch halted us at the edge of the pit, a large stone block appeared from the hole and rose into the air. Men who'd been standing waiting for it leapt forward and, with a lot of cursing, they managed to push the stone onto the wagon using long staves. I turned my attention away from the workers as four men dressed in leather armour stepped out from a wooden guard post and greeted Fanch. The men all carried long spears in their right hand and rectangular shields painted yellow with the black stag emblem on them on their left arm. Fanch spoke with them briefly, then returned to us. He pointed at me and then to the pit. "You, down you go."

I glanced at the pit and saw that the top rung of a ladder

was sticking out over the rock rim by about a foot or so and I nodded my head in understanding. I moved cautiously to the edge of the hole and my breath caught in my throat as I looked down. The ladder sat on a narrow ledge at least twenty feet below me and was tied into the rock with rope and metal pins at the base and at the top. The ledge was perhaps two feet wide at the most and covered with moss. Below that another ladder lay propped against the ledge, leading down another twenty feet. I leaned forward to get a better view, resting my hand on the ladder to steady myself. Beneath the second ladder were more, perhaps as many as ten before finally I could see a wide basin down at the bottom. Tiny figures were moving around the basin and I drew back, suddenly feeling dizzy.

"Get your ass down that ladder, boy!" Fanch snapped at me impatiently.

I shared a look with Jebido and then grabbed the top of the ladder and swung my leg out and over onto the first rung and started to descend. I'll get out of here, I told myself as I made my way down. Somehow I'd find a way. I had no idea at the time that it would be nine long years before I finally climbed back out of that cursed pit.

Chapter 4: Tannet's Find

The quarry was called Tannet's Find, named after the Ganderman surveyor who had discovered it where it had lain overgrown and forgotten for many years deep in the forests of Southern Ganderland. We prisoners never called it that, though. We called it Father's Arse, or sometimes just the Hole, and we referred to each other as Father's Turds. The stone of Father's Arse was instantly prized by the Gandermen builders and they declared everything else inferior to it and, within a year of its discovery, almost all of the quarried stone in the kingdom came from there. The quarry had been dug a long time ago, so we were told, possibly centuries, maybe more, no one knew for certain. Whoever those original miners had been, they had just started digging straight down, slowly widening the perimeter as they mined the creamy-grey, finely-textured limestone from the surface. The original miners had expanded and deepened the quarry over the many years it had been worked, until eventually reaching a point where the limestone began to lose its fine texture and durability. Rather than abandon the site, those first miners began to dig sideways, cutting out a dizzying maze of tunnels in all directions. They'd also somehow drilled an opening on the southern side about thirty feet down from the rim and about the width of a tall man. I can't even begin to understand what it must have taken to accomplish that, but water poured continuously from this opening the entire time I was held there, rolling down the wall into a deep basin cut into the floor that formed a natural reservoir. A narrow channel led from this reservoir to another tunnel, where the water flowed back out. Sometimes when it rained the floor of Father's Arse would flood, occasionally up to our ankles, but it would always eventually drain away through that tunnel. No one but

The Mother and The Father knows why the Hole had been abandoned or where the water came from or went to, nor did we much care. We were just grateful that we had continuous fresh water to drink and to bathe in. It was the only luxury that we would ever know deep down inside that quarry.

Life in Father's Arse was harsh, as we Turds were forced to work in near darkness in teams of four in exhausting twelve-hour shifts, with two men and two boys per team. When the shift was over, we'd go to the eating hall where we were fed weak stew, crusty bread, and once in a while, a hunk of moldy cheese. A mug of acrid ale that looked, smelled, and tasted like piss, was given to us to wash it all down with and then we were free to do what we wished until our next shift. For me, at least in the beginning, that meant stumbling to the sleeping hall and collapsing in bed like one of the dead.

The boy's sleeping halls were built along the western curve of Father's Arse and the men's along the eastern curve, while the eating hall and guards' quarters were built along the middle, dividing the two. We called the guards Heads for some reason. I never thought to actually find out why. The Heads were prisoners as well, though they'd gained some trust from our captors above and had been promoted. Each Head was responsible for five teams of workers. If a team missed a quota, it was the Heads fault and he would be demoted back to being a Turd. The Heads were armed with whips and a small club and, believe me, they used them, as none of them wanted to miss their quota. It was also the Heads responsibility to keep the peace among the Turds and to guard the ladder. There were always two Heads at its base at all times, though it probably wouldn't have mattered if they were there or not, as we all knew there were still those guards at the top to contend with.

I won't lie and try to tell you that those first few weeks weren't tough, because they were, but I was young and resilient, which helped immensely. I was still recovering from the fever I'd had, but once I started getting regular food, foul as it was, I started to recoup my strength fairly quickly. Luckily for me Jebido and the boy with no name were both assigned to my team and they watched out for me as much as they could. Jebido was partnered with a huge bald man named Listern Wes, who spoke rarely, but worked tirelessly. The two men made a formidable team with picks and chisels and not once during the entire time we were teamed did we miss a quota. Jebido and Wes would use picks to expose a rough block of stone, while we boys cleared the debris away around it. It was hard, difficult work in the cramped space of the tunnels, which were weakly lit by faint candlelight. Once the stone was suitable in size, we'd use hammers, chisels and wedges to cut along its base, separating it from the rest of the rock. From there, the four of us would wrap ropes around it and we'd drag it along a specially designed trench to one of the three cutting rooms, whichever was closest. The cutting rooms were massive chambers, each one dug out of the limestone precisely the same distance from the center of Father's Arse, one to the north, one east, and one to the west. Within these great chambers teams of stonemasons labored, cutting and shaping the stones to their desired sizes with chisels and saws. The stonemasons were actually free men and they worked for wages and, I was told, would come from all across the kingdom to work in Father's Arse. Once the finished stones were shaped to the desired size, Turds would drag them away so that they could be drawn up to the surface above.

"Why don't they just shape the stones at the building site?" I remember asking Jebido after we'd delivered a particularly fine block to the cutting room.

"They're harder to carve up there," Jebido had grunted, motioning with his head to the world above. "Different air, so I've been told."

The work was hard, but so was working the fields in Corwick and, as time went by, I found myself becoming stronger and my endurance increasing. We four grew to become dependent on each other and rarely did we even need to speak while we worked, as each of us knew what to do in any given situation. As the weeks passed, the boy with no name began to talk more and we finally learned that his name was Baine. Though he was small for his age, Baine was quick and stronger than he looked and he quickly gained the admiration and respect of the rest of the team. He was a year younger than I was and we developed a deep friendship, necessitated in part, I suppose, by us working so close together every day. Not long after we arrived, Jebido began sitting on the moss-covered rocks by the reservoir and staring into the water after we ate. So now that I wasn't as tired as I had been after shift, it became a habit for me and Baine to go and sit with him and we'd talk. The sound of the water cascading into the reservoir was loud, but not enough that we had to shout to be heard and, in fact, we all found it strangely soothing. Listern Wes would join us as well sometimes, though the huge bald man never spoke more than three words at a time.

Almost a year after our captivity, Baine, Jebido and I were sitting by the reservoir in our customary place when I saw a familiar figure working with the men drawing the stones from the cutting rooms. I'd seen Klotter around from time to time, but not often as we usually worked different shifts. He was thinner and fitter looking than I remembered, but it was undoubtedly him. Klotter had originally been partnered with Twent, the skinny teacher from the wagon, but Twent had developed a wet, bloody cough and had died less than a month after we'd arrived. Over the many years that I would spend down in Father's Arse, I would see a lot of good men die that way. Seeing Klotter got me to thinking about Carspen Tuft and his fat wife Hielda, and that horrible trip in the wagon. "Baine," I said to my friend. "You never did tell us how you got caught by Carspen Tuft?"

Baine blinked his large eyes at me and I could tell he was thinking. He had a habit of doing that and rarely, if ever, did I see him speak without choosing his words carefully. He always thought about things first, chewing on the words in his head before finally spitting them out. "I don't remember you telling us how you did either," Baine eventually said. He turned to Jebido. "Or you for that matter."

I realized he was right. I don't think any of us had ever

said anything about that trip or that horrible little man since the day we climbed down into Father's Arse. I guess we'd all just wanted to wipe it from our minds. "Forget it," I said, regretting I'd brought it up.

Baine shook his head, pausing to flick his long black hair from his eyes. "Actually, I'd like to tell you," he said. He squared his thin shoulders and composed his thoughts, then said, "I met Tuft in Gandertown."

"Gandertown? You mean where the king lives?" I interrupted.

"Of course where the king lives," Baine said as he rolled his eyes. "What do you think?" I grinned and motioned for him to continue while Jebido sat listening with his arms crossed, his face expressionless. "I was heading to bed after doing my rounds on The Waste when..."

"The what?" I interrupted him again.

Baine frowned at me. "Don't you know anything? The Waste is the main street in Gandertown. That's where I lived and worked most of the time."

"By yourself?" I asked. Baine just nodded.

"Your family are dead, I take it," Jebido said, his face unchanged.

Baine just shrugged. "Maybe," he said. "I don't know for sure. I never knew them."

"Who raised you then?" I asked.

"Nobody."

"Nobody," I repeated. I thought of my mother and father and sister and two brothers. True, I hadn't had them long, but at least I'd had them. I couldn't imagine being as alone as Baine had been all his life.

"The Waste is pretty much all I've ever known," Baine said. He glanced around Father's Arse. "Until this place, that is."

"So how did you meet Carspen Tuft?" Jebido prompted.

Baine grinned sheepishly. "I tried to rob him."

"What?" I gasped. "You're a thief?"

Baine gave me a cold look. "Don't look so surprised, Hadrack," he said. "You would have been too in my place. There aren't a lot of choices on The Waste." He glanced at Jebido. "I was a pickpocket and I was good at it. Tuft was sitting up on the wagon with that woman sitting beside him. It was really early in the morning and they were just sitting there in the middle of the street talking. I couldn't believe anyone would be dumb enough to be on The Waste at that time and I figured it'd be easy. I remember wondering what was in the wagon." Baine shook his head. "I guess I know now, huh? Anyway, Tuft got down when he saw me and he waved me over, all cheery and happy like he is. You know what I mean." Both of us nodded and Baine continued, "He said that he'd taken a wrong turn and had gotten lost and he needed my help. I told him what he wanted to know and that's when he offered me the bottle. I took a few sips and we chatted while I tried to figure out where he was hiding his gold. Then I started to feel strange. The next thing I knew I was a prisoner." Baine glanced at Jebido. "I remember you tried to talk to me when I woke up."

"Yes," Jebido agreed. "You weren't much of a talker back then."

Baine grinned sheepishly at Jebido and then gestured to him. "Now you go."

Jebido shook his head and looked at me instead. "Let's hear your story first."

I hadn't spoken to anyone about what had happened over a year ago in Corwick and I looked down and swallowed, composing my thoughts. "I lived in a little village called Corwick," I began. Beside me Jebido stiffened and his eyes widened. "What?" I asked him, surprised by the expression on his face.

"Corwick?" Jebido repeated. "Would that be part of the fiefdom of the Lord of Corwick?"

"Yes," I nodded in agreement. I felt my jaw tighten at the lord's name. "We were vassals to the Lord of Corwick," I said. "The first and the second one," I added.

"Mother Above!" Jebido whispered as he ran his fingers through his hair.

"Are you all right, Jebido?" Baine asked.

"I'm fine," Jebido said. He took in a deep breath and turned to me. "Please, continue, Hadrack," he said, though his voice had an odd shake to it.

I gave him a look, perplexed by his behaviour, but by now I was starting to see that day vividly in my mind and my thoughts drifted inward and I forgot about him. I don't know how long I talked, but I told them everything. About how my father and I had gone to Hestan's farm and about the nine showing up and how I'd run back to our farm only to find the reeve and my sister that way. They sat in stunned silence as I told them of how I'd tried to stop the reeve and how he'd hit me and how, by chance I'd manage to kill him.

"Mother's tit!" Baine exploded at that point. "You killed a reeve?"

I nodded gravely to him and then told them of Crooked Nose and Hape, and of the youth Calen, and how they'd chased me into the bog. How I'd fooled them by making them think I'd been sucked down by quicksand and how I'd watched as my family and friends had been herded together at our farm. I told them of Lord Corwick's arrival and how relieved I'd been, only to see my father cut down before my eyes. I explained how the Lord of Corwick had ordered the nine to destroy everything before, like a coward, he'd slunk back to his castle with his men. I told them of burying Jeanna and my father and my vow to them that I would find the nine and kill them all. I told them of the leader of the nine, Quant, and of Heavy Beard as well, and that I didn't know the others' names, but someday I would find them. And I told them of being on my own after that, starving and ill until finally I'd stumbled across Tuft and Hielda. When I was done, I looked up at my friends and I fought back the tears that threatened to overwhelm me, determined not to cry in front of them. We sat there in silence for a time, alone with our thoughts with just the sounds of the water and the pulleys above us screeching and the men working keeping us company before finally, Jebido cleared his throat. What he said next has stayed with me my entire life. Never before or since have I been as shocked by anything as I was at that moment.

"Hadrack," Jebido said. His face looked strained and his hands were trembling. I'd never seen Jebido like that in the entire year that I'd known him. "Hadrack," he repeated. "I was there that day in Corwick and I know their names." I rocked backwards from his words as if I'd been struck. Nothing had prepared me for it and I shook my head, staring at Jebido in disbelief. He opened his mouth to say something more and white-hot rage descended on me. I was on my feet in a moment and I flung myself at him, screaming like someone possessed. Jebido was caught by surprise and he fell backward. I landed on top of him, pounding away at anything that I could with my fists. I heard Baine yelling something beside me and I could feel him trying to pull me away, but I ignored him. Jebido just lay silent beneath me, not trying to protect himself from my fists as they rained down on him. He looked up at me and I thought I could see tears in his eyes before he shifted his gaze past my shoulder and his expression changed to alarm. He shouted, "No!" just as I felt something hard crash against my skull. I sagged into Jebido's arms and he wrapped them around me protectively as I felt weakness flood my body and then everything went black. When I awoke, it was to find myself lying in my bed, which was really just some straw piled on the floor that I shared with another boy from the other shift. Jebido and Baine were sitting on the floor beside me and looking at me with obvious concern. I learned later that one of the Heads had hit me with his club and that I was lucky he hadn't crushed in my skull.

"How do you feel?" Jebido asked gently when he saw that I was awake.

"Don't you talk to me!" I screamed at him, wincing as sharp pain instantly stabbed along my temples.

"Hadrack," Jebido said softly. He went to put his hand on my shoulder and then thought better of it and he put his hands in his lap instead. "We need to talk."

"I said I don't want to talk to you!" I hissed at him. "Go

away!"

Jebido bowed his head. "I will. But can you at least let me try to explain what happened first?"

"Explain what?" I asked as I glared at him. "That you're a murdering bastard?"

"I didn't kill anybody," Jebido said softly.

"Sure!" I snorted. Jebido sighed and looked at the ceiling, not saying anything.

"You need to listen to him," Baine said.

"Why?" I demanded.

"Because he's telling the truth and he's our friend. He didn't kill anyone just as he says."

I felt doubt rise in me at the earnest look on Baine's face and my anger cooled a bit as I turned and studied Jebido. He looked terrible, worse even than when I'd first seen him in Tuft's wagon. Whatever this was about it seemed to be eating him alive. Finally, I crossed my arms and stared at Jebido coldly. "Fine. Say what you have to say and then leave me alone."

Jebido nodded and paused to compose his thoughts. "I was a soldier, Hadrack," he finally said. "One of Lord Corwick's sworn men."

"Yes, I gathered that," I said bitterly.

Jebido sighed and looked at his hands. "I'd been employed at Corwick Castle for almost three years before any of this happened." He looked at me with serious eyes. "I wasn't one of the nine, Hadrack. I swear by The First Pair that I wasn't." I pursed my lips and took a deep breath and waited as Jebido continued, "Late in the afternoon on that day, one of the nine men you spoke of, Hervi Desh, arrived at the castle with news of a murder in Corwick."

"Heavy Beard," I whispered, realizing who the man had been.

"Yes," Jebido said. "Desh told Lord Corwick that the reeve had bravely tried to stop one of the peasant's from raping a woman and that he'd been killed for it."

"That's a lie!" I shouted. "That bastard raped and murdered my sister!"

"I know that now," Jebido said, holding up his hand. "At the time all we knew is what Desh told us. Lord Corwick mustered the garrison and we rode out right away. I'd never seen him as furious as he was that day. To be honest, we all were."

"So you were one of the soldiers that came with Lord Corwick," I said as I tried to control my anger and understand what he was telling me. "The ones who stayed back and waited for him on the path."

"I was," Jebido confirmed. He let out a long sigh. "I saw your father executed, Hadrack. Lord Corwick told us that your father was the one who had tried to rape a young girl and that he had murdered the reeve when he tried to intervene."

"What!" I cried in disbelief.

Jebido shrugged. "It made sense to us at the time and we rode back to the castle believing justice had been served with your father's death. It wasn't until a few days later that we learned that the entire village had been destroyed and everyone had been killed. The official story we were told was that the Piths had raided from the south and had killed everyone."

"And you believed it?" I demanded incredulously.

"Why not?" Jebido asked. "The savageness of what happened in Corwick could only have been the Piths, or so it seemed to us. No Ganderman would do that." He looked at me gravely. "They killed the Son and Daughter, Hadrack, and burned the Holy House as well."

"No!" I gasped in shock.

"Mother Above!" Baine whispered in horror.

Jebido nodded. "So you see, why would anyone even remotely suspect it hadn't been the Piths? I only learned the truth by accident when I overheard a very drunk Hape talking with Calen about what had really happened."

"What did you do?" I asked, still shocked by what I'd heard. I thought of old Son Fadrian and pretty Daughter Elias and shook my head in disbelief. How could they have done it? I wondered. What kind of men would dare do such an evil thing?

Jebido sighed. "I foolishly went to Lord Corwick and told him what I had overheard."

"But he's the one who told them to do it!" I protested.

"Yes, but I didn't know that," Jebido said. "Hape hadn't said a word about that part. You have to remember that we rode away with Lord Corwick before any of the killings started." Jebido ran his fingers through his hair again and snorted softly. "Lord Corwick told me in very clear words that if I breathed a word of what I knew, then my head would be quickly freed from my body."

"Murdering, lying bastards," I whispered. I could feel my anger toward Jebido softening as I listened to his story. I wanted to believe him, I realized. He had befriended me. We had become close and I knew instinctively that what he was saying was the truth.

"They are all of that and more," Jebido agreed. "A nest of vipers the lot of them. I should have realized after what I'd overheard that Lord Corwick had to have ordered the village destroyed. I felt like a complete fool. I guess a part of me didn't want to believe it, I suppose."

"What happened after that?" Baine asked.

"I demanded that Lord Corwick release me from his service," Jebido said. He shrugged. "What else could I do? I couldn't be sworn to that man after what I'd learned."

"He told Quant to destroy everything," I said, feeling tired and drained of emotion. "I heard him order it. They burned all the buildings and even killed the animals too." I looked at Jebido in confusion. "And now you're telling me he ordered them to kill the Son and the Daughter as well and blame it on the Piths. It doesn't make any sense."

Jebido sighed. "I have a theory about the Piths and the Son and Daughter's murder," he said. "But it's complicated and I'll leave that for another day. I think the main reason he killed everyone else is pretty simple. Lord Corwick is a very vindictive man, Hadrack, and I'm very sorry to have to tell you this, but the reeve was his brother." I sagged back on the straw, feeling sick to my stomach as I realized that all of those lives had been lost because of me. If only I had found another way, none of it would have happened at all.

"So, did he release you?" Baine asked breathlessly.

"Yes," Jebido nodded to him. "He said he respected my feelings on the matter and asked when I'd be leaving. I told him I'd stay until the morning." Jebido chuckled dryly. "As soon as I walked away from that snake, I gathered what few belongings I had, grabbed a horse and hightailed it out of there." He grinned. "They sent men after me, of course, but I kept to the hills and stayed out of sight for weeks until I was sure they'd given up and then I headed for Gandertown."

"And that's where you met Tuft," Baine said.

"Yes," Jebido agreed. "I was drowning my sorrows in a tavern when he walked in and started a conversation. I don't really remember much of that night, but I must have told him some of what had happened and he knew no one would be looking for me. I remember he told me of the ale he brewed for himself out in his wagon and we went to sample it. That's all I remember and the rest you know."

"I want their names," I said, glaring at Jebido. "The names of the nine that I don't know. I want them all."

"And you will have them," Jebido promised. He put his hand on my arm. "I'll give you that, my young friend, and I'll give you much more. I'll give you the means to kill them."

I looked at him and shook my head. "No," I said. "I appreciate it, Jebido, I really do. But I don't want anybody's help. This is something that I have to do by myself when I'm ready."

"I didn't mean that I'd help kill them," Jebido said with a slight smile. "At least not in the way you're thinking. Believe me, I fully understand that the vow you swore to your father and sister is sacred." He stood up and put his hands on his hips, staring down at me. "The lives of those nine men belong to you, Hadrack, and no one else. I have no doubt that when you're ready, you will kill them. But it won't be easy and, if you're going to succeed, you're going to have to learn to fight."

"Here?" I said with a frown as I looked around. Nearly half the straw beds were being used by sleeping boys and I turned and looked up at Jebido. "How can I learn to fight down here?"

Jebido grinned. "I'll teach you," he said as he glanced at Baine. "I'll teach you both."

About a week after that conversation, Baine and I went to join Jebido by the reservoir and we found him sitting in his usual spot waiting for us and grinning like a fool. Two long wooden swords sat on the stones by his side and, as we approached, Jebido jumped to his feet like a child with a new toy and eagerly displayed them to us.

"Where did you get them?" I asked in amazement as Jebido handed one of the swords to me. It was made of oak, with a rough blade angled at the end and a smoothly sanded grip for the hand. The hilt and cross-guard were thick and crudely cut, but seemed more than serviceable. I took a few practice swings, surprised at the weight.

"Segar got the wood for me and I made them," Jebido said proudly. Segar was the Head in charge of our team and was a giant of a man with a badly broken nose and one eye that always seemed to focus on something to his left. He had a temper that you had to watch out for, but, as far as Head's go, Segar wasn't the worst down in Father's Arse. Jebido told us how he'd approached Segar and had requested material for the swords, and though Segar had resisted at first, he'd finally relented after extracting a promise from Jebido that we'd increase our quota by a third. Neither Baine nor I were that enthusiastic about the quota increase at the time, but in the end things worked out just fine. So began our training.

Every day after our shift and we'd eaten, Baine and I would spend at least two hours working with the wooden swords while Jebido instructed us. After we were done for the day, Jebido would return the swords to Segar, who kept them locked up in his quarters. As the months went by, more and more of the Turds would come and sit and watch us practice, yelling encouragement occasionally, but more often than not cheering when either Baine or I got whacked by Jebido's sword, which, truth be told, was more times than I care to admit.

"There are eight basic things you need to know to fight with a sword," I remember Jebido told us on that first day as he held one of the practice swords in the air. "First, you must be strong," he said. "Strength and endurance in battle are a necessity. If you are stronger and fitter than your opponent, you will win. Second, you must at all times stay focused and calm. If you let fear overcome you, you will make mistakes and you will die. Third, there is no such thing as fair play." He paused and lowered the sword and leaned on it as we listened intently. "When you face a man in combat, know that he will stop at nothing to bring you down. The moment your swords cross, it's kill or be killed. And have no illusions, my young friends. He will stop at nothing to kill you. You must do the same. Fourth, confidence. You must not just think that you can win; you must know that you can win. When the enemy sees this he will be disheartened, and this will weaken him. Fifth, patterns can kill you. A good swordsman knows how to read you. If you are predictable in your fighting patterns, he will see it and he will kill you. Sixth, don't be intimidated by your opponent. Many fighters use words or bluster to try to plant fear in you. Once the seeds of fear sprout, you are lost. Seventh, timing and distance." Jebido snapped the blade of the sword up suddenly and swung it. I instinctively drew back as the tip grazed my face. "You must know at all times how far your opponent is from your blade. A miss throws you off balance and could prove costly, as it opens you up to counter attack." Jebido lowered the sword again. "And finally, eight. The most important of all. Caution. The surest way to get yourself killed is to rush into it. Think, assess, and then act. Never underestimate your opponent."

As the years went by, I grew bigger and stronger and faster. Jebido had told me early on that I was a natural with the sword, and he was right. I took to it easily, though it would be several long years of bumps and bruises before I managed to actually hit Jebido. Baine, on the other hand, struggled. He was fast, faster than I was in fact, but he was predictable in his attacks and could be easily disarmed, even by me.

"You need to change things up," Jebido scolded him during one such practice as Baine's sword went twirling from his hand for the third time in as many minutes. "You're making it too easy."

Baine walked over to the sword and picked it up and shrugged. "I'll never be a swordsman, Jebido, and we both know it. I'm too small."

It was hard to argue with that, as I was thirteen and already as tall as Jebido, while Baine, on the other hand, though a year younger than me, still barely came up to my shoulder. Baine was stronger than he looked, but he was slightly built and we all knew he would be easily overcome in combat where strength and raw power could overwhelm speed.

"When we get out of here I'll teach you the bow," Jebido promised him. This seemed to perk Baine up and he showed more enthusiasm in the lessons, at least for a little while.

By the time I was fourteen I was taller than Jebido and I was managing to catch him with my blade every once in a while. I still had ten bruises for every one I gave him, but it was still satisfying nonetheless.

One day while we were sparring, Baine, who'd been watching intently with some of the others, mentioned he needed to piss and that he'd be right back. I remember noticing someone get up and follow Baine, but I didn't have time to dwell on it as Jebido rushed at me with his sword held above his head. I raised my sword to counter his, realizing even as I did it that it was a feint and I spun aside at the last moment as Jebido's foot narrowly missed my midriff and glanced off my hip. I managed to keep my balance and I swung back and down with my sword as I turned, gratified to hear a sold thwack as the edge of my blade caught Jebido's lower leg. The Turds sitting around watching cheered mightily at that.

"Mother's tit!" Jebido grimaced. He paused, bending his knee back and forth gingerly before grinning at me. "Well met,

Hadrack! I thought I had you with that move."

"It was a near thing," I said, grinning back at him.

I looked for Baine, intending to give him a turn with the sword, and then I remembered he'd gone to piss. I frowned as I recalled someone getting up quickly and following him, and I felt a jolt of fear as I realized it had been Wigo Jedin!

One of the first things we boys learned when we were brought to Father's Arse was to watch out for ourselves. There were no women in the Hole and many of the men had no qualms about buggering a boy if they could. Some boys went with them willingly, and if that was their choice, then so be it, as we turned a blind eye to such things down in the Hole. There were a few, though, that liked it rough and preferred to take what they wanted. Wigo Jedin was one of these. The other boys liked to joke that he'd bugger a hole in a rock if it were big enough and knew how to fight back. I thought about sharing my concerns with Jebido, but then changed my mind. It was probably nothing and Jedin had just gotten up to go get some sleep. "I'm going to take a piss," I said to Jebido. "I'll be right back." Jebido nodded, still flexing his leg and wincing as I pushed my way through the Turds. Several of them congratulated me on my swordsmanship and I grinned and nodded to them sheepishly. I reached the dimly-lit tunnel that led to the latrine, which we called the shit pit, and entered as the sounds of the Turds behind me were abruptly cut off. A candle burned weakly on a ledge halfway along the right-hand wall, the flame flickering in protest as I passed by. There was a boy, Folclind, his name was, who was not quite right in the head and whose only job down in Father's Arse was to ensure the candles never went out. Without their light, it would be very easy to get lost forever in the network of tunnels down in the Hole.

I turned left into another shadowy tunnel and then left again, instinctively wrinkling my nose as the foul stench of the shit pit began to assault my nostrils. We used tapped out tunnels for the shit pits and they were all dug the same way, roughly twenty-feet long by five-feet across and usually about six-feet deep. There was nowhere for the piss and shit to go down in Father's Arse, so over time the hole would fill up. When that happened, we'd just seal the tunnel off and dig another one.

A candle sat burning faintly near the entrance to the pit and I approached the opening cautiously, certain that I had just heard a muffled thud. I lowered my head and passed through the low entrance. The smells coming from inside were so strong that it made my head swim and I guessed the pit had to be almost full by now and would need to be sealed off soon. A wooden railing about four-inches wide and roughly waist height ran along the edge of the hole and a fat candle flickered on the bench at each end. To shit you'd have to prop yourself up with both hands and then wiggle your ass backwards. I was always terrified of falling in. I couldn't think of anything worse than that. All of this, though, meant nothing to me at that moment, for I realized my fears about Jedin had been justified. Baine lay face down on the rock floor near the back of the tunnel and I saw dark blood seeping from a wound on his temple. He wasn't moving, whether dead or unconscious, I couldn't tell. Jedin stood over him with his dirty, stained tunic in his hand as faint candlelight flickered across his broad chest. I felt rage overcome me and I gripped the wooden sword tighter in my right hand as I headed toward them. Jedin heard me approaching and he glanced up in surprise, then smiled when he saw me. "Well, well," he said as he slowly turned to face me. "The other one."

"Get away from him, you bastard, or I swear by The Mother and The Father I'll crack your head open with this!" I yelled as I showed him the practice sword I held.

Jedin glanced at the sword and laughed. "With that toy? You'll crack my head open with that?"

"Last warning, you whore-son!" I growled at him.

Jedin laughed again. "I have a sword, too," he said. He glanced down at Baine, who, I was relieved to see, was moving his head now and groaning softly. "And when I'm done poking your friend with it, maybe I'll move on to you." I was fourteen years old and big and strong for my age, but Jedin, though not as tall as I, was much wider, with massive shoulders and hugely muscled arms. I had no illusions about what would happen if he got his hands on me and we just stood there, eyes locked, at an impasse. "I guess I can wait," Jedin finally said with a sneer. "You won't always be around to protect him." Jedin started to put on his tunic and I tensed, as I knew that though his words had said one thing, his eyes had promised something else. He paused with the tunic almost over his head, then twisted it in his hand and threw the garment at my face as he rushed forward with his great arms spread to envelope me. I swept the tunic aside with my left hand even as I lifted my right arm, stabbing outward wildly with the point of my sword. The hard wood caught him between the legs, which seemed fitting considering what he'd planned to do to Baine. Jedin squealed like a hog at slaughter and then fell writhing and moaning to the floor. I looked down at him squirming at my feet and I had a sudden vision of another day and another man lying helpless on the ground. I'd had an opportunity then and I'd let it pass me by, and it had cost me dearly. I knew that if I let Jedin live today, Baine and I would forever be watching our backs and, sooner or later, the bastard would get one of us. I saw my sister in my mind and I grit my teeth. Using all of my strength, I swung downward with the sword. I hit Jedin hard, crashing the blade into his skull over and over again, not stopping or caring as the man's wet, sticky blood splattered all over me and the tunnel walls. Finally, panting and exhausted, I dropped the sword from my numb hand and I turned and gazed at Baine, who was sitting up now and staring at me with wide eyes.

"Mother's tit, Hadrack!" he whispered as he looked from me to the crumpled mess on the floor.

Baine told me many years later that that moment in the shit pit was when he'd known he'd be my sworn man some day. No one had ever stood up for him before and he told me what I'd done that day was a debt that he felt he owed me for the rest of his life. I knew nothing of that at the time, of course, and I was still trying to come to grips with what had happened, when heavy footsteps sounded along the tunnel. Baine and I tensed, expecting the worst, and then we relaxed as we recognized Jebido's hook-nosed face as he stooped down and entered the latrine. He glanced around at the blood-splattered walls and his bushy eyebrows rose slightly when he saw what was left of Jedin lying on the floor. He whistled through his teeth. "Well, boys, I guess we better get this mess cleaned up before someone needs to piss and sees it," he said. And that's exactly what we did.

Jebido and I striped Jedin's corpse, and while Baine used the dead man's clothes to wipe down the walls and floor as best he could, we dragged the body over to the shit pit and pushed it in. Jedin sank and then popped back up to the surface and I remember thinking we were going to get caught because he was going to float on top just like all the other turds. But luckily Baine had other ideas. He gathered some rocks and piled them onto the dead man's chest, until finally it sank from sight for good. Surprisingly, no one seemed to notice, or if they did, care about the smudged stains on the walls and floor of the shit pit, and the next day it was sealed up and a new one was dug. The Heads looked for him, of course, but not with much enthusiasm, as Jedin was not a popular man. Everyone in Father's Arse just assumed he'd gotten lost in the tunnels and had died, which did happen from time to time. Most of us Turds considered it good riddance and, for quite a while after he disappeared, we'd joke that you'd better look over your shoulder first before bending down because Jedin's ghost might be sneaking up behind you to bugger you. I've always thought it fitting that Jedin would be spending all of eternity buried in a tomb of shit.

The year that I turned seventeen was the year that everything changed for us Turds down in Father's Arse. Two things happened, one right after another. The first mainly just affecting myself and my team. The second, everyone in the Hole. We were working the western tunnels and having a terrible time of it, I remember, as we'd had an unusually bad stretch of persistent rain. Many of the tunnels were knee deep in water. It was the worst we'd ever seen, but the Heads insisted we continue regardless. I didn't learn until much later that the reason we continued was because King Jorquin had been strengthening his defences in Southern Ganderland for years by building a line of defensive garrisons and bridges along the border to defend against the Piths to the south. The building of these ambitious defences had begun right after the discovery of Father's Arse, about a year before Jebido, Baine and I had arrived at the quarry, and that's why we worked night and day all those years. It seemed that no matter how many stones we pulled from the earth, the builders still wanted more. The bridges and most of the garrisons were complete, but several of the key garrisons were not finished yet and war with the Piths had become a certainty.

For us Turds though, toiling in the depths of Father's Arse, the problems of the world above hardly mattered. What did matter to the team, however, was that Listern Wes had begun to cough. At first, the rest of us pretended not to notice when he would hack and cough into his hand for several minutes before finally wiping bright red blood onto his trousers. As each day went by, Wes grew weaker and weaker, refusing to let us do anything to help, probably because he knew, like we did, that there was nothing any of us could do about it. Every Turd in the Hole knew that coming down with the wet cough was a death sentence. Then, almost three weeks after that first cough, Listern Wes, now barely a hundred pounds of skin and bone, died. The Heads replaced Wes with Uhin Eby, who had a tendency to chatter on about anything or nothing for hours at a time. Eby was an inattentive worker and hugely annoying and none of us cared for him much, as we had to work even harder now to make our quota each day.

Nearly a week after Wes' death, Baine, Jebido and I were sitting by the reservoir and resting after a particularly gruelling workout. Not many of the Turds watched us practice anymore, having grown bored of our battered wooden swords I suppose. By this time, I was the tallest person down in Father's Arse, even taller than Segar. Baine and I were listening as Jebido told us an amusing tale about a watch commander and a whore with one leg, when he was interrupted by a screech coming from above us along the western rim of the Hole. The ear-splitting noise was quickly followed by shouts of alarm from the Turds on the ground as a large stone that was being lifted over the rim came hurtling back down. The men beneath the falling stone managed to dive out of the way to safety just as the block disintegrated into thousands of pieces as it hit the stone floor. In the nine years I'd been in the Hole I'd seen ropes break a handful of times, so a falling block was far from unusual. What was unusual was that the stone was quickly followed by a horse and then a man, both of them shrieking in terror before the unforgiving floor of Father's Arse silenced them forever.

"Mother Above!" Baine gasped as the three of us leapt to our feet. Heads appeared from all directions with drawn clubs, converging on the dead horse and man just as we heard a pitiful wail echo out from above us. Somehow another man had fallen from the rim, and then another man fell, followed immediately by a third man, all of them screaming and flailing their arms wildly as though somehow that might help save them. One of the falling men landed heavily near me in a cloud of dust and he lay still in a crumpled heap. He was dressed in leather armour and his shield, which was painted yellow with the king's black stag emblem embossed on it, clattered loudly to the ground beside him, followed closely by his spear, which landed point first. The spear bounced against the rock with a crack, narrowly missing impaling the already dead soldier before it then somersaulted end over end crazily to land at my feet. I instinctively crouched down and picked it up.

"Thank you Mother, thank you Father!" I whispered as I looked up at the deep blue sky far above me, feeling sudden hope. I turned to Jebido, but he was already racing across the floor to the other fallen soldiers who lay close together like sacks of broken bones. Jebido snatched up both the soldiers' spears, having to toss one aside when he realized it was broken down the shaft. Our eyes met across the distance and I pointed to the ladder, which was for the first time in my memory, free of Heads. "Baine, let's go!" I shouted as I sprinted forward. I saw a huge figure running to cut Baine and me off and I groaned as Segar beat us to the ladder.

"I can't let you do it," Segar growled as we ran up to him.

"But this is our chance to finally escape this place!" I protested. I levelled the spear at his chest. "Come with us or step aside."

"I will not," Segar stated. He crouched and whirled his club in his hand as he regarded Baine and me calmly.

I looked over my shoulder and groaned as I saw Jebido racing toward us with five or six Heads close behind him. "Either come with us or die right here!" I screamed at Segar. I'm still not sure what the big Head would have done, but in the end, it didn't matter. Jebido reached us and, without pausing, he thrust forward with his spear, impaling Segar in the chest. The big man's eyes rolled in surprise and he fell without a sound.

"Hurry!" Jebido panted, motioning to the ladder with his chin.

I nodded, held the spear against my chest and, using my thumb as a basket to grip it, pulled myself up the first rung with my fingers. When I finally reached the first ledge, I jumped to the next ladder and then looked down. Jebido was right behind me and Baine was right on his heels with a look of overjoyed excitement plastered across his thin face. I looked past Baine at the Heads that had gathered at the base of the ladder just as one of them began to climb. I looked away and clambered up the ladder, moving as fast as I could, then jumped to the next ladder and then the next, and the next, until finally, unbelievably, I climbed the last rung and dragged myself up and over the lip of Father's Arse. I stood up, panting and out of breath as I looked around at the trees and deep blue of the sky and felt the wind on my face. After being a prisoner in the Hole for nine long years, I was finally free!

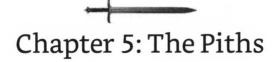

Chapter 5: The Piths

I don't know how long I stood there breathing in free air above the rim of Father's Arse, but eventually I felt a hand pushing at me urgently and I heard Jebido demanding that I move my huge ass. I turned guiltily and helped to pull him up. Then he and I helped Baine over the lip. A lot had changed since the last time we three had stood in this spot. On the far side of the quarry the trees had been cut further back and a tall wooden palisade had been constructed in their place. I noticed that a good section of the heavy oak timber had been hacked through and that there were bodies strewn in piles all around the breach. Most of the dead men wore the yellow and black stag emblem of the king, while a few wore no surcoat at all and were big and wild looking, with long, shaggy blond hair and beards.

"Those are Piths," Jebido told us, pointing to the blond men.

The guard station near the ladder seemed unchanged, but the ground around it was littered with twisted bodies, all of them the king's soldiers. The trees along the hill that had separated Father's Arse from the main encampment were all gone and the small wooden bridge crossing the river below us had been replaced by a bigger, wider one made of stone. Thirty or so soldiers of the king stood bunched together in the middle of the bridge with their backs to us, facing toward the encampment. The soldiers were armed with swords, heavy rectangular shields and many, I noted, held long spears like the ones Jebido and I carried. Thick black smoke filled the air and occasionally some of it would drift downward to dance and skip around the soldiers as the wind toyed with it. We could hear men screaming in the distance, some bellowing in fury or triumph, some crying out in mortal anguish amid the clash and thunder of metal weapons colliding. A square fortress of stone rose in the middle of the encampment where once the tents had stood and at least thirty mounted Piths were pressing a small, desperate knot of Gandermen who fought on foot back toward the closed gate. I guessed these men and the ones bunched on the bridge had been caught outside the fortress when the Piths had attacked. A tall flanking tower with a cone-shaped roof stood to each side of the gate while thick buttresses rose along the outer walls of the fortress every twenty feet or so. Yellow-clad archers appeared in the arrow slots of the flanking towers and along the ramparts, shooting down at the confused mass of men and horses. A small group of mounted Pith archers began shooting back at the archers on the walls and I grunted in surprise when I realized that they appeared to be women.

I nudged Jebido and pointed. "Is that really women down there?"

"Indeed," Jebido said. "The Pith women fight with their men and are said to be deadly with a bow."

I nodded just as a great cheer erupted from the Piths as the last of the Gandermen fighting outside the fortress fell. The Piths quickly turned their attention to the thick oak gate, attacking it enthusiastically with their great war axes while the women archers continued to give them cover. In all of the excitement we'd forgotten about the Head's pursuing us from below and with a grunt, one of them appeared on the ladder behind us. Jebido whirled and whipped his spear up, cracking the butt end across the man's temple. The Head cried out and fell backward, windmilling his arms before disappearing from view.

"Go back or you'll share his fate!" Jebido shouted as he held onto the ladder and peered into the quarry.

"Look!" Baine said, pointing down to the bridge.

A mass of wild-looking Piths appeared through the smoke, running toward the bridge and the king's soldiers that waited there. I guessed there were at least twenty of them and they held a long sword, war-hammer or battle axe in their right hands, while on their left arms they carried round metal shields painted blue and white with a circular raised boss in the center. The Piths reached the head of the bridge and they slowed, calling out insults to the soldiers who stood watching them. I noticed some of the Piths near the back had their shields slung over their shoulders and instead of swords or axes in their hands, they held long, wicked-looking poles. The tips of the poles were thin and pointed like a spear. On one side, about a foot down from the tip, was a great axe head, while on the opposite side, a nasty hook jutted out.

"Halberds," Jebido explained. "Not a weapon the Piths normally use, so I imagine they must have found them here." He grimaced and nodded to the Gandermen waiting on the bridge. "That's bad news for them. When the front lines meet in the shield wall, the Piths will use the halberds to strike from above. Hit a man's helmet just right and it'll crack like a walnut."

I could feel my heart pounding with excitement and I gripped my spear tighter, resisting the almost overwhelming urge to run down to the bridge as the Piths stopped about ten paces from the Gandermen. Most of the warriors were dressed in worn metal-plated armour lined with wolf or bear fur, while a few of them here and there wore simple leather armour. All of the Piths had long, matted blond beards and hair and wore either a leather skullcap or a conical metal helm with a nose guard that reached to the chin. A tall man in the center of the Piths caught my eye and I studied him with interest. He wore an engraved black helmet accented by gold strips around the base and crisscrossing the helm. A thick gold nose-guard covered most of his face, save for his cheeks and eyes, and above those eyes, two great golden wings flared out, giving the man a predatory look that was frightening to behold. Long black tassels fluttered in the wind at the top of his helm and his silver breastplate gleamed in the sun. A black cape with red embroidery along the edges billowed behind him and he carried a shield and held a long sword with a golden hilt in his right hand. He stepped forward a pace toward the Gandermen and slowly removed his helmet. I saw that his blond hair fell well past his shoulders, the color matching his thick beard. He grinned white teeth at the silent line of Gandermen watching him and I judged him to be in his early twenties at most. One of the king's men stepped forward a pace as well and he too removed his helmet, revealing dark grey hair cropped close to his scalp.

"Greetings," the blond man said cheerfully. He propped the point of his sword against the stone by his feet and leaned on the hilt, then gestured to the Piths to either side of him with his helmet. "Some of my men here claim that your fat king likes to rut with donkeys and pigs." He raised his eyebrows. "Is that true?"

Several of the king's men shook their swords and shouted in anger at the insult, but the blond man just smiled back at them and waited. The leader of the king's men held up a mailed hand, silencing them. "Who are you?" he demanded.

"Does it matter?" the blond man asked with a shrug.

"Yes, it does," the Ganderman said. "I like to know a man's name before I spill his guts on the ground."

The blond man laughed at that and he nonchalantly twirled his sword on the stone. "They call me, Einhard," he said, bowing his head slightly. "Sometimes I am known as Einhard the Unforgiving."

"The Sword of the King," the grey-haired man said grudgingly. "I've heard of you."

"The very same," Einhard acknowledged with a grin. "And you are?"

"Fanch Evenon," he replied. "I command the garrison here." Baine, Jebido and I all shared a glance. We remembered Fanch. He was older and greyer now, but it was unquestionably him.

"Well," Einhard said thoughtfully. "That's a mighty fine name, my friend. I'm glad you told me, since, as you pointed out, it's good to know a man's name before you spill his guts on the ground." Einhard smiled at Fanch and then he glanced over his shoulder at the besieged fortress behind him. "Shouldn't you be in there, Commander, rallying your troops or something like that?"

"I like it here just fine," Fanch growled back.

Einhard tipped his head back and laughed. "We'll see about that." His smiling face turned hard. "My terms are simple, so even you should be able to understand them. You and your men will surrender now. If you do this, one out of every three of you will live, at least until tomorrow anyway. You have my word on that."

"The word of a heathen means nothing to me," Fanch snorted. "Do your worst you piss-drinking savage!"

Einhard grinned. "I rather hoped you'd say that." He raised an eyebrow. "No quarter then?" he asked.

"No quarter," Fanch agreed grimly as he replaced his helmet and returned to his men. The Piths began to bang their weapons against their shields, hurling insults at the king's soldiers as Einhard put his winged helm on and then waited. I could see him grinning widely beneath his helmet and he looked as though he was thoroughly enjoying himself. If anyone saw us standing above the bridge on the hilltop, they gave no sign of it

"Any moment now," Jebido whispered knowingly.

"Kill them all!" Einhard abruptly screamed, raising his sword and sweeping it toward the Gandermen. The Piths cheered and surged forward as Fanch gave a single, sharp command, forming his men into two tight lines. The soldiers armed with spears took up positions in the front rank and locked their shields together, forming an imposing wall with the weapons balanced on top and bristling toward the Piths like quills on a porcupine's back. The soldiers standing in the second line then lifted their shields in a practised motion over the front ranks' heads, protecting them.

"It will help," I heard Jebido mutter.

"Will it be enough?" I asked. Jebido just shrugged as the Piths fell on this wall of steel in a wave of fury, screaming and cursing as they stabbed and hacked with sword, axe and warhammer. The halberds were rising and falling from behind them now, the steady rhythmic clang vibrating up from the bridge as the heavy axe heads crashed against the upraised wall of shields protecting the front line. I could see the legs of the soldiers in the second rank buckling under the onslaught but, despite the constant barrage raining down on them, they pushed back and steadied, holding firm. A Ganderman in front suddenly stumbled and his shield lowered just a fraction, enough for the hook of a halberd to latch on to it. The soldier was drawn forward helplessly and he fell, still struggling to protect himself as he was trampled underfoot by the seething mass of battling men above. I saw Einhard encouraging his warriors into the gap left by the fallen man even as he stepped over him and jabbed the top of his shield into an opponent's face. The Ganderman cried out as his nose shattered and then, moving faster than I would have thought possible, Einhard whipped his sword up and out and slashed the man's throat. In the same motion, he hacked downward, cutting a spearhead off at the haft before lunging forward. I don't know what became of the spearman after that as he was lost in the swirling press of bodies.

"Mother Above!" I whispered, awed by Einhard's speed and strength. I could feel my blood humming along my veins, all my senses tuned to the battle below. Without realizing it, I started to move forward as though in a trance.

Jebido saw me moving and he grabbed my arm roughly. "Don't be a fool!" he hissed at me. My cheeks felt flushed and my eyes seemed as though they were burning up within my skull. I looked at Jebido, unable to control my excitement and his face fell. "Mother's tit, boy! You only have a spear and wear no armour. They'll kill you!" I was about to tell him that I didn't care, that I needed to go down there and fight when a great cheer suddenly arose from below. Incredibly, having resisted the Pith's original onslaught, the disciplined Gandermen were now pushing the blond warriors back step by bloody step along the bridge. "A cornered rat always has the sharpest teeth," Jebido said to me grimly as we watched the fierce battle. He continued to hold firmly onto my arm, taking no chances.

I looked for Einhard in the confusing swirl of battling,

cursing men. Finally, I saw him down on one knee with his shield raised above his head as a massive Ganderman pounded his sword repeatedly against it. Another soldier swung low at the fallen Pith leader, intent on taking out his vulnerable leg, but Einhard just managed to deflect his blade and he stabbed outward, narrowly missing the man's unprotected torso. I couldn't contain myself any longer and I shrugged off Jebido's hand and pointed to the forest on the other side of Father's Arse. "You and Baine run for the trees and get out of here!" I shouted, and before either of them could say anything to stop me, I sprinted down the hill. I was seventeen and finally free, and for the first time in my young life, I felt fully, gloriously alive! I lowered my spear, screaming like a man crazed as I reached the bridge and kept running. As I drew closer to the battle, I focused on the broad back of a Ganderman in the center of the back line and I headed straight for him. The soldier had long brown hair spilling out from the back of his dented helmet and he must have heard or sensed me somehow, because he turned and glanced back and his mouth dropped open comically as I bore down on him.

"To the rear!" the soldier screamed in panic as he spun to face me. Behind him I saw a halberd come crashing down onto the helmet of the Ganderman the long-haired soldier had been protecting with his shield. The man's helmet split in two and he sagged as blood spurted and bits of bone and brains exploded outward. I snarled as I closed the distance with my target and I jabbed the spear point directly at the center of his chest. The soldier swung his shield up, deflecting the point of the spear to the side. I felt my arms and shoulders go numb at the jarring impact and my spear lowered enough for the soldier to stomp his booted foot on it, pinning it to the ground before he snapped it in half with his sword. He grinned mockingly at me and then raised his blade to strike me down just as a spear hissed past my ear. The point caught the Ganderman in the neck, sending out a spray of blood that drenched me before the man's eyes fluttered and he collapsed.

"We couldn't let you get killed all by yourself, you young fool!" Jebido grunted as he ran past me. He grabbed the end of his spear and wrenched it from the dead man. I barely had a moment to grin my thanks to him and Baine before we were suddenly surrounded by soldiers. I flinched, expecting a sword thrust at any moment, but the men bearing down on us seemed completely oblivious that we were even there. Somehow the Gander shield wall had been broken and the soldiers, who'd shown such composure moments earlier, were now in a frenzied panic as they ran for their lives. I had no idea what had changed to snatch apparent victory from the Ganders, but I was to learn over time that a battle could be won or lost simply on the morale of your men. Once fear sets in, even the most hardened men become prey to it and they will run. The fleeing Gandermen continued past us and ran up the hill, clearly heading for the safety of the trees on the other side of Father's Arse, while behind them gleeful Piths gave chase. Most of the Gandermen didn't even make it all the way up, as they were caught and brought down by Piths swinging axes and war-hammers. I noticed that one very fast soldier had not only made it to the top of the hill, but was now almost halfway around Father's Arse. He was being heartily pursued by three Piths and, as I watched, one of them drew back his arm and threw his war-hammer, which caught the fleeing Ganderman on the back of his knee. The man cried out and fell heavily to the ground, and then thrust his hands up in the air defensively as the Piths surrounded him. I heard him pleading desperately for his life, but the warriors just laughed and fell upon him, stabbing and smashing until he lay still. Afterwards, one of the Piths lifted his war-hammer in the air and whooped as he shook it at the sky.

"Hadrack," Baine whispered. He grabbed my arm and motioned to the bridge behind us. "It's Fanch."

I turned to see that the garrison commander had chosen not to run like the others and instead he stood with his back facing us, glaring at the Piths. His helmet was gone and dark red blood ran down the right side of his face. I saw that he'd lost his shield and that he held his left arm bent awkwardly against his chest. Einhard smiled at him and took off his helmet and handed it to one of the other Piths before he focused his amused eyes on me. I noticed they were a startling bright green. "Well done, Ganderman!" he called to me. "I am indebted to you."

"For what?" I managed to mumble. Beside me I heard Jebido whisper to be careful.

Einhard spread his arms and I saw blood seeping from a long gash on his bicep, but he seemed unaware of it. "For attacking their rear and distracting them. We would have won anyway, of course, but it certainly made things easier."

"We had you beaten, piss-drinker!" Fanch snarled as he pointed the tip of his red-smeared sword at the Pith. He turned and waved the sword at me and I could see rage simmering in his eyes. "The only thing that saved your asses was this overgrown puppy sneaking up behind us like a coward!" I bristled and felt my face flush and I took a step toward him. Fanch just laughed. "Don't waste my time, boy!" He deliberately turned his back on me and faced Einhard. "We have unfinished business, you and me."

Einhard bowed his head. "Ah, yes, the spilled guts I do believe." He threw his shield to one of his men and smiled at Fanch. "Shall we get on with it then?"

I could feel my entire body shaking with anger as the two men glared at each other, both having clearly forgotten about me. Fanch had called me a puppy and a coward and it had instantly enraged me. Perhaps it wasn't just the words, but also the way he'd so casually dismissed me, turning his back to me in contempt that had set my blood boiling. I don't know. All I could think about was that I had to kill that man. I glanced down, gliding several steps sideways to stoop and pick up a fallen sword and I swished it in my hand, testing its balance. I'd never actually held a real sword before and it felt marvellous.

"Don't turn your back on me, shit-eater!" I shouted at Fanch's back.

Einhard's eyebrows rose in surprise when he saw I held a

sword and then he grinned at Fanch. "Well, it would seem that the overgrown puppy has other ideas."

Fanch snorted. "This won't take long, heathen, then it's just you and me." He took three long strides toward me and as he walked, he snapped his sword back and forth like an angry cat's tail. I waited for him with my blade held awkwardly in my hand and as he drew closer, I clumsily brought my guard up. Fanch snickered in contempt and behind him I could see Einhard frowning. "You're just a big, stupid peasant!" Fanch sneered. "I bet you've never even touched a sword before today." Fanch took another step toward me and I took one back, and he laughed. "I'm going to enjoy making you squeal!"

I could hear both Jebido and Baine offering encouragement from behind me and I nodded, never taking my eyes away from my adversary. Fanch grinned and then he lunged forward with his sword without any warning. He was quick, quicker than I'd expected he would be for a wounded man and I leapt back desperately just as Fanch broke off the attack. The older man smirked at me and I realized it had just been a feint. I glowered back at him. I could hear Jebido's words in my head that he'd drilled into me repeatedly over all those years down in Father's Arse. Be smart, be quick, and be strong, but most of all, he would say, be cautious. I decided to be all of those things except the last one and I leapt forward and took a wild swing at Fanch's head. The Ganderman easily ducked the blow and then he swung his blade sideways at my legs, his face already breaking out in a triumphant grin. He'd done exactly what I'd expected him to do and I brought my sword down hard and fast, just as Jebido had taught me and I blocked his blade. Then, in the same motion, I thrust forward with the hilt, smashing it and my fist into the older man's face. Fanch grunted and his head snapped back and he staggered to one knee. I felt raw power bursting along my arms from all those years of hard labor in the quarry and I struck down at his unprotected head with all of my strength. Fanch somehow managed to bring his sword up just in time and the two blades met with a thunderous clash. I grinned at the look of utter shock on his face at the force of my blow and I swung downward a second time, and then a third as Fanch desperately tried to block me. Jebido had told me repeatedly over the years to never underestimate an opponent, and now I understood why. Fanch had badly underestimated me and it was about to cost him his life. It was a lesson I would not soon forget. I swung down a fourth time, putting everything I had into it and Fanch's blade shattered beneath me. My sword kept going, cleaving off a sizable portion of his skull as blood sprayed outward in a gush. Fanch's eyes widened and his body twitched, and then he slumped to the ground.

"That's for Twent, you shit-eater!" I snarled as I spat on the dead man.

"Well fought, Hadrack!" Jebido cried. He and Baine ran to me and began to slap my back repeatedly in congratulations before Baine gave me a warning nudge as Einhard and the rest of the Piths strode up to us.

"That was very entertaining, Ganderman," Einhard said. He stopped and stood with his hands on his hips and grinned at me. "I thought you were a dead man at first."

"I got lucky," I said. I could feel my legs and arms trembling as I fought to catch my breath and I gestured to Fanch's body, hoping Einhard wouldn't notice my shaking arm. "He was wounded and overconfident."

"True enough," Einhard said. "He was both of those things." He glanced down at the dead man and looked thoughtful. "But lucky? Maybe, maybe not. Sometimes men make their own luck." A great cheer rose up from the encampment behind us as the Piths finally breached the fortress gate and Einhard turned to look over his shoulder. "It's about time." He pointed a finger at me and glanced at a huge Pith with long blond hair tied in a braid down his back. "Eriz, I want to talk with this one later." He waved a hand at Jebido and Baine. "You can kill these two."

"What!" I gasped as the Piths began to converge on us. Beside me Jebido lowered his spear threateningly and Baine crouched to pick up a sword that lay nearby. "Wait!" I shouted, lifting a hand. "You can't do this!"

Einhard frowned and made a gesture, halting his men. "I can't?" he said in mock surprise. He swept his arm behind him at the burning encampment. "Do you see that, Ganderman? I'm in charge here now and I can do whatever I please."

"They're my friends," I pleaded.

Einhard shrugged. "So what's that to me?"

"You said that you were indebted to me," I countered, thinking desperately.

"True enough," Einhard nodded. "And I'm paying that debt back by letting you live. I owe them nothing."

I could feel my body starting to shake again, this time with anger as I glared at the Pith leader. "If it wasn't for the three of us you would have been beaten!" I shouted at him. "You know it and I know it." Einhard looked at me blankly and he crossed his arms, listening. "We've been prisoners for nine years in that stinking hole back there," I said, pointing toward Father's Arse. "We could have run the moment we were free, but we didn't." I gestured to Jebido and Baine with my sword. "They had as much to do with helping you to defeat those soldiers as I did and now you're going to reward them by killing them? Don't you have any honor or are you just an unfeeling stinking savage?"

"Careful, boy!" Einhard growled, his green eyes turning hard and dangerous.

My anger was consuming me by this time and heedless of the consequences I pointed the tip of my sword at Einhard's chest. "You don't scare me. If you want to kill them you'll have to kill me first!" I could feel the veins in my temples throbbing as I glared at Einhard. "Our blood won't be the only blood spilled here today, mark my words," I promised him.

Einhard stared at me, his eyes glittering with deadly promise as we locked gazes before finally his mouth twitched in a reluctant smile. "The puppy has teeth, I see," he said. He glanced at Jebido and Baine briefly, then shrugged and turned back to me. "Your point is well made, Ganderman. You and your friends deserve consideration for what you did. Drop your weapons and I'll let you live, at least for now while I think on it."

"How do I know that I can trust you?" I demanded.

Einhard frowned. "Because I am Einhard, Sword of the King, and you have my word as a warrior on it. If that's not good enough for you then hold onto that sword and suffer the consequences." I glanced over my shoulder at Jebido and he nodded slightly, and I felt myself start to relax. I twirled the sword in my hand and handed it hilt first to the Pith leader. Jebido and Baine both dropped their weapons to the ground and Einhard turned to the big Pith. "Eriz, see that the Gandermen are given food and drink and keep them out of the way until I call for them."

"It will be done, brother," Eriz said in a deep voice.

Einhard grinned a dazzling smile at me. "We'll talk later." He turned to go, then glanced back at me. "Remember, Ganderman, even puppies with teeth need to be careful when surrounded by wolves." He winked at me and then headed for the fortress with the rest of his men.

"This way," Eriz rumbled, motioning for us to follow him. We crossed over the bridge and made our way along the road into the encampment, where I could see many bodies strewn all across the ground. As we walked, I saw several women and children also lying among the fallen. One of the dead women was almost completely naked and had clearly been raped. I grit my teeth, averting my eyes. The innocents always paid the price when men made war, I realized. The heavy wooden gate to the fortress lay shattered in pieces on the ground and the sounds of screams and cheers could clearly be heard coming from inside the building. Eriz turned us away from the fortress toward an open area where a row of large black iron pots hung suspended from long poles held up by a tripod at each end. The fires beneath the pots had burnt themselves out and now only smoking coals remained. To our left stood a large stump with an axe leaning against it, and beyond that several haphazard rows of firewood were stacked. Twisted bodies lay on the ground near the cooking pots and we had to step over them as we walked.

A line of squat white tents rose beyond the cooking fires, and in front of them, ten or so of the king's men knelt unarmed in the grass with their heads lowered. Piths stood around the Gandermen in a half-circle and they were jeering and spitting on the kneeling men. A tall Pith with massive, heavily tattooed arms moved to stand above the first soldier in line. He drew his sword, raised it over his head and then brought it down hard across the back of the soldier's exposed neck. The man's head flew off and his body sagged, spurting blood in a stream as it collapsed. The Piths cheered mightily and one man started measuring the distance the blood had flown with his feet. I couldn't help but think of my father with sadness as I watched.

"What are they doing?" Baine whispered.

Eriz chuckled softly. "They're playing bloodline." He gestured with his chin. "Watch." The tattooed Pith moved to the next man in line and swung down again, severing the man's head. Blood spurted out in a stream onto the ground and the Piths converged on it, gesturing and arguing while the distance was measured. A moment later cries of glee and shouted curses arose, and I saw what looked like small strips of silver reluctantly changing hands. I learned later that the Piths valued silver above all else and they used small shards of it, called fingers, like we would use gold coins. "Stay here and don't move," Eriz growled at us. "I'll be right back." The big Pith glared at us and then hurried over to the tents, where we could clearly hear him placing bets. He, along with the other Piths, cheered as the next man in line lost his head.

"Savages!" Baine muttered as we stood watching helplessly.

"Yes," Jebido agreed with a sigh. "But these savages hold our lives in their hands."

"We could make a run for it," I suggested as I realized the Piths had seemingly forgotten about us in their enthusiasm for their game.

"And get how far on foot?" Jebido grunted. "They'd catch

us for certain."

"We could steal some of those horses," Baine suggested, nodding to where a bunch of the animals stood tethered and grazing near the eastern palisade wall.

Jebido snorted at him. "Can you ride?" Baine's thin face fell and he shook his head. Jebido looked at me. "What about you, Hadrack?" I shook my head as well. I was a peasant and had never been on a horse. "I didn't think so," Jebido muttered. "The Piths are magnificent horsemen. How long do you think it'd be before they caught us with a couple of inexperienced riders like you two?"

"Then what do we do?" I asked.

Jebido shrugged. "We see how this plays out, I suppose. Their leader seems to have taken a shine to you, Hadrack." He frowned at me. "So I suggest if you want us to keep our heads on our shoulders you'd better make sure he keeps on liking you."

"How am I supposed to do that?" I asked.

"For starters you can watch that temper of yours," Jebido said. "It got away from you earlier and it almost got us all killed." I started to protest that if it hadn't been for me, he and Baine would have been dead anyway, but then I thought better of it. Jebido was right. Losing my temper with Einhard had worked out for us this time. The next time we might not be so lucky and I resolved to try and think more before letting my emotions take over.

"They're finished!" Baine hissed to us in warning, gesturing with his chin to the Piths. The king's men had all lost their heads and the Piths began walking back to the fortress, laughing and joking among themselves. Eriz returned to us with a grin on his face and I saw a flash of silver as he dropped something into a small leather bag he held.

"Come along," Eriz said as he tucked the bag into his tunic. We followed him around the sprawled bodies of the headless Gandermen and made our way toward one of the white tents. Eriz swept aside the flap and ushered us inside. The interior of the tent was damp and smelled strongly of mould, sweat, and piss. Filthy looking furs lined the floor and a small wooden bench with a chunk missing from the top sat near the back of the tent. "Stay here until I return for you," Eriz ordered as he stood in the entrance. He wrapped his big fingers around the hilt of his sword and glared at us. "If you try to leave, I will kill you." He motioned to the furs. "Sleep if you like. Food and drink will be brought shortly." The big Pith left and the three of us sat on the furs and talked for a while before a frightened looking old woman came in carrying a wooden tray with mugs of ale and food on it. She was dressed in a drab tunic and skirt and refused to meet our eyes as she gave us the ale and a hunk each of barley bread. I tried talking to her but she just shook her head slightly and glanced at the entrance with haunted eyes. She left as quickly as she could. The bread was mouldy and dry, but having spent nine years down in Father's Arse, we barely even noticed.

"What do you know about these Piths?" I asked Jebido around a mouthful of bread.

Jebido drained his mug, then lifted one cheek and farted mightily before he answered. "Nasty in a fight," he said. "Deadly with a sword or bow on foot or on horseback. They like to strike hard and fast, take whatever plunder and women they can and then disappear back to their lands." He slapped at his arm and fished through the dark hairs before crushing and tossing a flea that had bitten him aside. "Rutting, gambling and fighting is what those bastards live for, so I've heard."

"So you mean they're like most soldiers, then?" I said with a grin.

"I guess that's fair enough," Jebido laughed. His face turned serious. "One thing I find curious is Fanch referred to Einhard as the Sword of the King."

I shrugged. "What's so curious about that?"

"The last I knew the Piths had no king," Jebido said.

"So who's in charge then?" Baine asked.

"That's just it," Jebido said. "The Piths have always been separated into tribes, with each tribe commanded by a warlord. They never had a king before and from what I heard, spent more time fighting each other than anyone else."

"I guess that's changed," I said.

"I'd say so," Jebido agreed.

"Is it true they don't believe in The Mother and The Father?" Baine asked.

"What?" I gasped in surprise. I couldn't even fathom such an idea. What kind of savages were these Piths? I wondered.

"True," Jebido nodded with a look of distaste on his face. "They believe that only one god created the earth and the skies and they call him the Master."

"That's just stupid," I snorted. "The First Pair made this world for us, Their children. Only a fool would think otherwise."

Jebido lifted a hand. "I agree wholeheartedly, Hadrack, but I wouldn't go calling these Piths fools to their faces and pissing on their beliefs if I were you. Fools they may well be. But these fools can kill us whenever they choose."

"Do you think the Piths and Ganderland are at war now, Jebido?" Baine asked. "Or is this just some kind of random raid?"

Jebido looked thoughtful. "This seems too targeted to be that," he said. "When the Piths raided in the past, they usually just hit easy prey like unprotected towns and villages. As far as I know they've never attacked a fortified position like this one before." He grimaced. "Then again, since they seem to have united under a single king, this might be a common thing now."

I thought of Corwick and how the Piths had been blamed for its destruction and I frowned as I remembered something Jebido had told me about it years ago. "Jebido," I said. "You once told me you had a theory about why the Lord of Corwick blamed what happened in Corwick on the Piths. What was it?"

Jebido made a face "I did?"

"Yes," Baine said. "I remember you saying it. It was right after that time the Head tried to bash in Hadrack's skull with his club. Remember?"

"That's right," Jebido said. He grinned. "I must be getting old or something. I forgot all about that."

"You told me you thought the nine killed the Son and Daughter for a reason," I prompted him.

"Well, it's just a theory I had at the time," Jebido said. He turned to Baine. "Did you ever go to The First Holy House in Gandertown?"

"A few times," Baine nodded. He looked at me. "That's where The First Son and First Daughter live."

"I know that," I said. "I'm not stupid, you know."

"Could have fooled me," Baine said with a grin.

I ignored Baine and looked at Jebido. "Son Fadrian and Daughter Elias taught us all about it. They even had a painting of The First Holy House on one wall of the nave."

"I saw them once," Baine said. "The First Son and Daughter." He made a face. "Both of them were old and shrivelled."

"That may be so," Jebido grunted, "but old or not, they live close to the king and wield enormous power and influence over him."

"Power over the king?" Baine said, looking shocked by the idea. "Really?"

Jebido nodded. "King Jorquin is very devout. Some say overly so, and he always listens to what they say."

"What does any of this have to do with Corwick?" I asked.

"Well, I'm just guessing," Jebido said. "But I think blaming the murders of The Son and Daughter on the Piths was done so the king had a reason to attack them."

"I don't understand," Baine said. "He's the king. He can attack anyone he wants, can't he?"

Jebido shook his head. "Not in this case. I know for a fact that King Jorquin wants the Piths' lands. The problem is The First Son and Daughter expressly forbade him from attacking them."

"But why?" Baine asked. "The Piths are savages. Why would they care?"

"The First Son and Daughter were convinced they could save the Piths souls by bringing them back to The Mother and The Father," Jebido explained. "So the king's hands were tied and he could do nothing."

"Until word got out about what had happened in Corwick," I said in sudden understanding.

"Exactly," Jebido agreed. "That's my theory, anyway."

Baine shook his head, looking thoughtful. "But it doesn't make any sense," he protested. "Are you saying what happened at Corwick was planned all along by the king just so he could attack the Piths?"

Jebido snorted. "Of course not! Corwick was seen as an opportunity is what I'm suggesting."

"An opportunity by who?" I asked, pretty sure I already knew the answer.

"Lord Corwick," Jebido said. He glanced at me. "Lord Corwick is King Jorquin's nephew. I think the killing of Lord Corwick's brother, the reeve, was a perfect opportunity to not only exact revenge for his brother's death, but also help his uncle get what he wanted." Jebido stretched out his legs on the furs and yawned. "Obviously I don't know what's happened in the last nine years, but there you have it. That's my take on the whole thing."

"But you said the Piths had attacked villages before," I pointed out.

"Yes," Jebido agreed. "But they always left the Holy Houses strictly alone. I think that's what made this time so unforgivable for The First Son and Daughter."

I nodded to him in understanding and lay down on the foul smelling furs, suddenly feeling exhausted. I closed my eyes and pictured that day in Corwick, seeing again the young lord riding up to my farm with Hervi Desh by his side. Had the bastard been planning it even then? I wondered. I thought about my father and Son Fadrian and Daughter Elias and all the others murdered that day. They'd just been pawns in a game they neither knew, nor cared about. I felt my stomach churn with hatred for Lord Corwick and the nine and I tried to sleep, but as tired as I was, I couldn't stop thinking about it and sleep eluded me. I don't know how long I lay that way, but eventually the great bulk of Eriz appeared in the entrance.

"Gandermen, the Sword requests your presence," the big Pith rumbled as he peered in at us. I sat up immediately and noticed that Baine was awake as well. He turned and shook Jebido out of his slumber and together we stood and joined Eriz outside. Darkness had fallen at some point while we lay in the tent and a weak half-moon shone down on us. Two silent Piths fell into step behind us as Eriz led us toward the stone fortress in the distance. Four Piths appeared out of the gloom and one of them said something in a slurred voice to Eriz, who just shook his head and kept moving. The four Piths laughed and stumbled away, clearly drunk. We made our way across the compound and as we drew closer to the fortress, I saw that long poles with torches on the ends had been shoved into the ground every ten feet or so, lighting our path. A man and woman stood by one of the poles holding hands and talking and they smiled and nodded to Eriz. The man wasn't overly tall, but he was built like an ox, with massive arms and legs. The woman was wearing a long white tunic under leather armour and had a bow slung over her shoulder. I realized she must have been one of the archers I'd seen protecting the Piths attacking the fortress gate. She was slim and pretty and had long blonde hair on one side of her head and on the other side it was completely shaven. I was to learn that this was a common style for the Pith women.

"Eriz, there you are!" the woman said as we approached. I noticed she held a bottle in her right hand and was slurring her words slightly. "I looked everywhere for you." She glanced at her companion and grinned. "Tato beat you to me, so you'll have to wait."

Eriz laughed. "I don't have time right now, anyway, Ania," he said. He gestured to us with his thumb. "I've got to deliver these Gandermen to Einhard. I'll find you when I'm finished." Ania glanced at the three of us, pausing to study me with interest before finally she shrugged and took a swig from the bottle. Eriz slapped the shoulder of the Pith holding her hand. "Don't wear her out, you bastard!"

"Not possible!" Ania called out cheerfully to our backs as we moved on.

Many of the buildings outside the fortress had burnt themselves out, I noted, though the air still smelled heavily of charred wood. I glanced around as more Piths stumbled past us. Other than Eriz and our two silent guards, everyone else appeared to be drunk. I didn't see any sentries posted anywhere. Einhard hadn't struck me as such a reckless leader and I thought that perhaps an opportunity to escape might show itself. I shared a look with Jebido, pretty sure he was thinking the same thing. Eriz guided us through the shattered gates of the fortress and into the outer courtyard. To the left of the gate stood a modest stable, and to the right a row of long, low buildings. The biggest building sat in the middle of these and the sign of the Blazing Sun and the Rock of Life hung side by side over the door. A man wearing the flowing black robes of a priest was hung by his wrists in front of the door from a rope that had been nailed to the top of the Holy House. The priest's bare feet dangled several inches off the ground and I could see the immense agony he was in on his face. Several Piths stood around him pricking him with their knives and laughing each time the priest tried to wiggle away from the points. There was no sign of the priestess anywhere, but I spied her yellow robes lying on the ground and I grimaced, not wanting to imagine what had become of her. Eriz led us across the outer courtyard and then through the inner gateway, which was protected by an archery tower on each side and a long gatehouse. The inner gate lay open and undamaged and we passed through it into the inner courtyard, where we saw a Pith man and woman rutting openly. Dead Ganderland soldiers lay everywhere in the courtyard, but the Piths seemed completely oblivious to the dead as they coupled.

"Motherless heathens," Baine whispered. He opened his mouth as if to say more, but Jebido gave him a hard look and he fell silent. Luckily, the guards behind us and Eriz were all focused on the rutting couple and they appeared not to have heard. Finally, having grown bored of watching, Eriz gruffly ushered us up a set of stone steps and into the great hall.

"Watch your tongues in here," Eriz warned as we stepped inside. "Your lives hang on the Sword's word and nothing else." He pointed to the back of the hall, where I could see Einhard splayed out on furs on a raised wooden platform. A woman lay beside him with a goblet in her hand and my breath caught in my throat as I stared at her. She was dressed in a long-sleeved, fur-trimmed white dress cut low at the neckline. Red and yellow swirling patterns ran along the arms and down each side from her armpits to the hemline. The dress was cinched at her thin waist by a black belt and two gold broaches shaped like shields and about the size of my hand covered her large, full breasts, which threatened to spill out from the top of the dress. A single blue pendant hung around her neck on a gold chain and her hair was long and blonde and done in the traditional Pith fashion. Her face was pale white and fine, with a long straight nose and thick lips that seemed too red to be real. I saw her smile in amusement at something Einhard said to her and she tilted her head back, laughing. Our eyes met across the room and I felt trapped like a fly in a web and couldn't look away as she studied me curiously. Finally she said something to Einhard and gestured toward us with her chin.

"Ah!" Einhard shouted when he saw us. He jumped up unsteadily to his feet and beckoned to us. "Come here, men from Gander! I have something I want you to see!"

Eriz folded his arms across his chest and stood in the doorway as our guards moved to stand on each side of the entrance. Four dead Gandermen with ropes around their necks hung from the rafters and Baine, Jebido and I were forced to make our way through their dangling feet. Piths lay everywhere on the wooden floor, many of the warriors obviously drunk and passed out in each other's arms. Beer, piss and vomit covered the planks in pools and at first I tried to avoid the worst of it, but finally just gave it up as impossible and walked through it. A naked female Pith lay unconscious and draped across the legs of two male Piths who sat with their backs propped up against the raised platform. I made my way around them, glancing back to share a look with Baine behind me just as one of the Piths began slapping the woman's bare ass with his hand as he sang happily to himself.

"Come! Come!" Einhard gestured to us impatiently. He fell back on his rump with a grunt and then banged his open hand on the furs beside him. "You sit here, puppy!" he roared at me with a lopsided grin. His green eyes seemed glazed and out of focus and I realized that he was quite drunk. "Your friends can sit back there," Einhard added, waving vaguely behind him. Jebido put his hand on my arm and squeezed gently, giving me a look before he and Baine made their way to the furs that lined the wall at the back of the room. Torches flickered along the walls, creating a smoky haze that enveloped us all like a cloak. I coughed and wiped at my eyes as they started to sting. Several large planks laden with food lay on the furs before us and the smells were beyond tantalizing. Bread and cheese were stacked almost a foot high on one of these and on the other lay an array of fish and meat. I recognized pike and salmon and I was certain one of the meats was stag, which I'd had once at the Holy House, but the others I could not identify. Einhard gestured with his hand and grunted something and several Pith women who'd been lounging nearby immediately got up and went to lie down next to Baine and Jebido. I saw Baine grin widely as one of the women whispered something in his ear.

"Sit, sit!" Einhard ordered. He grabbed my arm and dragged me down to a sitting position, then leaned toward me. I could smell the strong odour of drink on his breath. "I've been thinking about you, Ganderman," he said, wobbling slightly. He sat back and took a long drink from the tin mug in his hand, burping loudly before wiping his mouth with the back of his hand. He noticed I sat there empty-handed and he frowned and then banged his mug on the furs. "More beer!" he cried. He looked down at the mug and banged it a few more times; seeming confused when he realized it wasn't making any noise. "More beer!" he shouted again. He gestured to the food. "Eat,

Ganderman. There's plenty for all, courtesy of the kingdom of Ganderland!" I reached for some bread and a hunk of cheese, nodding gratefully to him and I started to eat. It seemed like a long time ago that we'd eaten in the tent and my stomach gurgled happily as I crammed the bread into my mouth. A grey-haired Ganderwoman carrying a metal flagon of beer appeared and she filled Einhard's mug with it. She offered some to the woman who sat beside Einhard but she just shook her head without saying anything and covered her goblet with her palm. The grey-haired woman then offered me a mug and filled it while I held it out. I noticed her hand was shaking as she poured and the moment she was done, she turned and hurried away. I took a gulp of beer and casually glanced at Einhard's companion, surprised to find that she was looking right at me. I quickly averted my eyes and felt my face redden as she laughed. She leaned forward and put her hand on Einhard's arm and said something to him. He made a face and nodded. "Ganderman," he said, turning to me. "My wife tells me that I have the manners of a wild boar."

"And the whiskers to match," his wife said as she nuzzled his beard with her hand. Her deep blue eyes sparkled and she laughed before she took a sip from her goblet. I stared at her and she held my gaze boldly as she drank.

Einhard chuckled and put his hand on her knee. "Just be thankful the Master didn't give me a boar's nose to go with it."

"Praise the Master for that!"

"Ganderman," Einhard said, sweeping his hand toward the woman. "May I present to you my wife, Alesia."

"A pleasure," I managed to mumble. I could feel the heat burning my face and hoped Einhard wouldn't notice.

"Is your name actually Ganderman?" Alesia asked, one fine eyebrow arched coyly. Her eyes were bright and gleamed with intelligence and mischief and I had to force myself to look away.

"Well, no," I said. I downed the rest of my beer and wiped my mouth before replying. "My name is Hadrack."

"Hadrack," Einhard said, looking thoughtful. He glanced at me, looking me up and down as if doubting I spoke true. "Hadrack," he finally repeated, testing the name on his lips. Finally he put a big arm around me and drew me to him in a great bear hug, shaking me as he laughed. It felt like my bones were about to snap from his grip. "I like it!" Einhard cried. He pushed me aside, leapt to his feet and lifted his mug to the ceiling. "To my friend, Hadrack, the Ganderman!"

"To Hadrack!" the few Pith's still awake and sober enough cried in a disinterested chorus as they lifted their mugs.

"Now, Hadrack," Einhard said to me smugly as he half-sat, half-fell back into the furs. "I have a gift for you and your friends." He lifted a hand and motioned to the door where the Piths stood guarding the entrance. One of them nodded and left and I looked for Eriz, but he was nowhere to be seen. The Pith guard reappeared prodding a man and woman ahead of him with his sword point. Behind the three of them more Piths followed, laughing and jeering. Both the man and woman were naked and had their hands tied behind them. The man was tall and heavily muscled and his face looked battered and bruised. Despite this, I sat up in surprise as I recognized him almost immediately. It was the Quarrymaster. As with Fanch, he was older and greyer looking, but it was unquestionably him. The woman was weeping softly and her plump breasts were shining with wetness as the tears fell on them while the Piths walked around her, poking at her and making fun of her heavy thighs and grabbing at the thick patch of black hair between her legs. I assumed she was the Quarrymaster's wife and I tried to keep my face neutral as the Piths teased her. I didn't care what they did to the Quarrymaster; nothing would be too good for that bastard. But as far as I knew the woman was innocent and I wanted nothing to do with what I knew was coming.

"Enough!" Einhard shouted. He was about to bang his mug on the furs again, then thought better of it and banged it loudly on the meat tray. He looked at me as the Piths fell silent, though one or two of the more drunken ones continued to laugh. "Do you know this man?" Einhard asked me.

I nodded my head. "He's the Quarrymaster," I said. "He's the one that sent us down into that hole nine years ago."

Einhard looked over his shoulder at Baine and Jebido and they both nodded as well. "Yes, I thought as much," Einhard continued. He gestured to the naked pair surrounded by the Piths. "My men are going to have some fun with them and I thought you might enjoy watching."

I gestured to the Quarrymaster with my chin. "You can do whatever you like with him," I said. The Quarrymaster glanced my way, then dismissed me with his eyes and stared at the ceiling. He showed no recognition on his face, nor had I expected him to. After all, I was eight the last time he had seen me. The Quarrymaster's face was set in a grim, determined line of defiance, while beside him his wife continued to sob. I motioned to her with my hand. "But the woman has done nothing. Let her go."

"Let her go!?" Einhard cried in mock surprise. The Piths burst out laughing and I noticed even Alesia was chuckling and shaking her head. "Why, in the name of the Master, would I do that?" Einhard asked.

"Because she hasn't harmed anyone and is innocent," I replied. The Piths laughed even harder at that and I felt my face tighten as the white anger started to spread. I opened my mouth to speak, to tell them what I really thought of them, but before I could say anything Jebido appeared by my side and he slapped me roughly on the shoulder.

"You must forgive, Hadrack!" Jebido said loudly. "He's just a boy and knows nothing of the way things work." I started to speak again and he squeezed my shoulder, hard enough to make me wince and clamp my teeth together. "His sister was raped and killed before his very eyes when he was young," Jebido continued, "and the experience has left its mark on him."

"Ah," Einhard said, nodding his head in understanding. He took a sip of beer and smacked his lips loudly. "Well, Hadrack, my friend," he said, looking at me happily. "Then you will be pleased to learn that there will be no rape done here tonight." He grinned widely and looked around at the Piths. "Am I right?" The Piths all shouted in agreement and Einhard laughed, clearly enjoying himself. He jumped down to the floor and stood before the Quarrymaster's wife while the Piths around her moved back and watched. Einhard leaned forward and twirled his fingers in the naked woman's long black hair while he whispered something in her ear. Her eyes widened and she glanced at the Piths in horror and began shaking her head emphatically. Behind the Quarrymaster several Pith women moved to stand beside the naked man. Each of them held a knife in their hands.

"It's not rape if you have a choice," Alesia said with a smile as she slipped over to me. She was suddenly breathtakingly close, her slim white hand now on my bicep, squeezing it gently. I could smell the scent of her and I swallowed as she looked at me in amusement. Her eyes were flashing with excitement and her lips glistened as she prodded them unconsciously with the tip of her tongue.

"I don't understand," I said to her.

Alesia laughed and put her hand on my leg. "My husband is giving her a simple choice," she said with a shrug. "She can either service all of those men down there with her mouth or stand by and watch as my sisters cut off her husband's manhood and feed it to him."

"What?" I gasped. "That's barbaric!"

Alesia just shrugged and pressed herself even closer to me. "Perhaps," she said softly. "But it's all in good fun."

"Fun?" I repeated. I jumped as I felt a hand reach between my legs, pressing and kneading down there. Despite my disgust at what was about to happen to the Quarrymaster's wife, I felt myself responding and I pushed her hand away. Alesia laughed mockingly and moved away from me as she sipped her drink. Below us the Piths were talking heatedly among themselves as Einhard returned and flopped on the robes between us. If he'd seen what had occurred between his wife and me, he gave no indication.

"So?" Alesia said to him.

Einhard nodded. "She'll do it."

"Of course she will," Alesia said knowingly. "Who did you pick?"

Einhard motioned to where the Piths had sorted themselves into a line. "Orixe, number six," he said.

Alesia snorted. "Any woman here can get past six."

Einhard grinned. "That's because you're all whores and have had years of practice." He nodded to the Quarrymaster's wife, who had by now sunk to her knees before the first Pith and reluctantly taken him into her mouth. "I'm guessing she hasn't had much practice judging by that uptight bastard she married."

Alesia laughed. "Probably true, my husband." She frowned as she watched the Quarrymaster's wife. "You're right," she said critically. "The woman has no rhythm at all." She glanced at me where I sat in glum silence. "Don't they teach your women anything in Ganderland?" I felt Jebido's hand tighten on my shoulder and I knew it was a clear message. Make no trouble here or we'll all die.

"So, Hadrack. Care to place a wager?" Einhard asked me.

I felt Jebido squeeze my shoulder again and I looked up at him and nodded, letting him know that I was under control. Jebido seemed to understand, for he nodded back to me before turning to go and sit with Baine and the Pith women. I turned to Einhard. "Why?" I asked, keeping the disgust I felt for all of them from my voice. "It's cruel what you're forcing that poor woman to do. There's no honor in it."

Einhard snorted. "Cruel! I'm giving them a chance, which is more than any Ganderman would have done for us!" I started to protest that we weren't anything like the Piths, but then an image of what the nine had done at Corwick came to me and I slowly shut my mouth. Einhard was right, and there wasn't anything I could say to dispute it. Einhard laughed when he saw the look on my face. "Do you think us stupid, Hadrack? We heard what the old ones told your king to do to us. Kill all the Piths, they said. Leave no man, woman or child of them alive." Einhard took a gulp of beer, his eyes flashing. "Your fat king came to our lands with his army to do the old ones bidding and we sent him scurrying back to them with his tail between his legs." He glared at me. "But not before they had raped and killed our women and murdered any of us that they could find." He gestured to the Quarrymaster's wife. "So don't lecture to me about cruelty and honor! We didn't start this."

"But you raided our lands all the time," I protested. "How can you justify that?"

"Why do I need to?" Einhard asked with a snort. "That's what Piths have always done since the Master made our world. It is our right!" He waggled a finger at me. "But when we came, we always left your Holy Houses strictly alone. Your beliefs are twisted and wrong, yet we tolerated them, which is more than I can say for your fat king."

"But The First Son and Daughter were tricked into thinking you..."

"I don't care!" Einhard snapped. He angrily took a sip of beer and wiped his mouth with his hand; then sighed as he fought to regain control of himself. Finally he looked at me. "Perhaps it's not such a bad thing after all," he said. "Before your king waged war on us, we Piths were hopelessly divided. We constantly fought among ourselves, tribe against tribe and Pith against Pith." He chuckled. "That's all changed now. The Master has lost patience with your kind and He has spoken, and we know now what we must do. For the first time in our history all the Piths stand united under a single king and with a single purpose." He lifted his mug to me in mock salute. "That purpose is to rid the world of your false gods once and for all."

"The Mother and The Father are not false gods!" I protested, horrified that anyone would even suggest such a thing.

"Not to you, perhaps," Einhard said. He pounded his chest. "But we Piths know better. The Master created these lands and all those who live on them. He created the sun and the moon and all the stars above us. This is not debatable. Why anyone would choose to believe different astounds me." He glared at me and his green eyes turned hard. "Mark my words, Ganderman, we will take this war to your fat king and we will destroy your false gods. There is nothing that can stop us from doing this." Shouts arose below us as the Quarrymaster's wife moved on to the next man in line. Silver was changing hands already and Einhard looked away from me and shook his head in wonder. "What kind of fool would bet on her not even getting past one?" he muttered.

"She does seem to be getting better at it," Alesia said to him. She popped a hunk of cheese in her mouth and grinned around it. "Perhaps she's beginning to enjoy it?"

"Perhaps you're right," Einhard said with a chuckle, our conversation seemingly forgotten. "I still say six before she's finished." He looked at his wife with a raised eyebrow. "And you?"

Alesia pointed. "Priam at ten," she said. "He'll be the end of her."

"Priam eh?" Einhard said. "You seem quite sure of yourself."

Alesia laughed. "I've heard rumours of his prowess." Einhard gave her a look and she added, "I talk with my sisters you know."

Einhard grinned at that and rubbed her knee before turning back to me. "So, Hadrack," he said. "What were we talking about?"

"You claimed The First Pair are false gods," I said, not trying to hide my anger. Below us the Quarrymaster's wife had moved on to another man amid cries of glee and disappointment.

"A fact," Einhard said, waving his hand dismissively. "Not a claim. Another time I will show you the path to the Master and you will understand. But for now, we will talk of other things." I just nodded and kept my thoughts to myself. "You spoke of honor earlier," Einhard continued, toying with his mug.

"Yes," I nodded.

"Honor is a silly notion," Einhard said. "It makes you

weak and gives strength to your enemies." He closed his hand into a fist and held it up. "At the end of the day, the only thing the enemy respects is this." He opened his hand and held it out palm up. "If you show them this, they'll cut off your fingers and piss down your throat."

"You can have honor and strength," I said stubbornly. I thought of my father. No one would ever have called him weak, even after his leg was ruined. Yet he had been an honorable man. Honor had made him stronger, not weaker in my opinion. I told as much to Einhard, but I could tell he was barely listening to my words now. The Quarrymaster's wife was one man away from Einhard's wager and he was now completely focused on that. He nodded absently to me and then started talking with Alesia, so I stood up slowly, intending to go sit with Baine and Jebido. I'd had enough of the Piths and their perversions.

Einhard must have seen me move out of the corner of his eye and he grabbed my upper arm with his calloused hand, holding me back. "I'm not done talking with you, Ganderman," he said. He motioned with his head. "Sit." I hesitated and considered pulling my arm away, but then common sense took over and I sat back down, trying hard to suppress my anger. "Did you know that your eyes change color when you're angry?" Einhard said with a grin. I just shook my head and grit my teeth. "Oh yes," Einhard nodded. He drained his mug, then called for more beer before turning back to me. "Grey like a wolf." He chuckled and swayed slightly. "Perhaps that's what I'll call you. Would you like that?" I just glowered at him and he laughed. "Hadrack the wolf. I like it." He made a face. "Well, maybe for now wolf cub would be better. What do you think?"

"Are you going to let us go?" I blurted out just as the grey-haired woman with the beer returned.

She refilled Einhard's mug, then he grabbed mine and had her fill it as well. He handed it back to me and grinned as I drank. "No, I will not let you go. I have other plans for you."

Perhaps the beer was getting to me, or perhaps I'd just had enough of these Piths, I don't know, but I threw caution to the wind and said what I thought. "You're a bastard!"

"True," Einhard agreed without breaking his smile.

"You're going to torture and kill us then?"

Einhard shrugged. "Perhaps. Perhaps not."

I rolled my eyes and, despite myself, I smiled back at him, my anger suddenly dissipating as quickly as it had come. "You really are a bastard, you know."

"Yes," Einhard said. He blinked at me several times and grinned. "I believe we've established that."

"If you're not going to let us go and you're not going to kill us, then what are you going to do with us?" I asked.

"Husband," Alesia said, shaking Einhard's shoulder. "Orixe is next."

"Ah, finally," Einhard nodded. He turned away from me and he and the Piths began to urge the Quarrymaster's wife on as she started to work on Orixe. I glanced at the Quarrymaster and saw that he was staring down at his wife with a mixture of contempt and wonder. Eventually the Piths cheered and Einhard exploded out a curse beside me and then fished into his tunic and drew out several pieces of silver before throwing them down to a grinning Pith.

"The Master thanks you, brother," the Pith said, laughing as he caught the silver pieces nimbly.

"I should have known better than to bet against a woman with a belly like that," Einhard grumbled.

"There, there," Alesia said, laughing at her husband. "Perhaps the next time you'll get it right."

Einhard shrugged at her and turned to me. "Have you sworn an oath to the King of Ganderland?" he abruptly asked me.

I nodded cautiously, surprised by the question and wondering where it was going. "Well, yes, sort of. But that was a long time ago. We were peasants and actually gave the oath of fealty to the Lord of Corwick."

"Not the king?"

"The Lord of Corwick is sworn to the king, which means

so are we."

"Ah, I think I understand," Einhard said. "I have heard of this Lord Corwick," he added. He took a drink of beer and belched. "A good man with a sword, they say."

I shrugged. "I saw him once when my father took the oath and then again one other time." I held my tongue about what had happened at Corwick. I didn't think a man like Einhard would show much sympathy.

Einhard rubbed his temple thoughtfully. "This oath. You say your father took it?"

"Yes," I nodded.

"But not you?"

"I was just a boy," I explained. "As head of our house my father took it for us all. I was there, but all I did was watch with my sister."

"And this oath is important in Ganderland?" Below us the Piths roared and I could see the Quarrymaster's wife was still going strong and had moved on to the next man. Einhard ignored what was happening now and he stayed focused on me. I imagine having lost the bet, his interest in the outcome had faded somewhat.

"Yes, very important," I answered. "In exchange for land to work, we give our liege lord our solemn oath to be faithful to him and to The Mother and The Father and to never cause the lord harm or be deceitful."

"And if you break that vow?"

I shrugged. "Then our lands and lives are forfeit."

Einhard stroked his beard. "When we fought your king, we captured some of his men. Some of them were clearly soldiers, but many others appeared to be just simple men such as you, untrained in war. Does this oath include taking up arms for your king?"

I nodded. "Yes. We're bound to our lord, who in turn is bound to the king. When the king summons the lords to battle, we are expected to join if needed."

"And if you refuse, your oath will have been broken," Einhard said, seeming to understand.

"Yes," I nodded. "The choices for peasants are few."

"But surely the rewards must make it worthwhile?"

"What rewards?" I asked.

"Why, plunder and women of course," Einhard said in surprise. "What else could I mean?"

I shook my head. "Not for peasants. I suppose an occasional ring or such pulled from a body might be hidden but, other than that, peasants are not allowed to profit. Only their liege lord is."

"Your king is a fool!" Einhard stated bluntly. He waved absently at the cheering Piths below. "Does he not know what drives a man? Does he not know what makes a man stand shoulder to shoulder with another man in a shield wall and laugh at death?" Einhard fumbled in his clothing and produced a brown leather sack and untied it. He spilled the contents on the furs before me. "That is what drives a man!" Einhard cried. I looked down at the pile of silver and glittering gems and I swallowed in surprise. Never could I have imagined such wealth even existed. And there it was, lying casually in front of me. Einhard picked up a red ruby and held it in the palm of his hand for me to see. "A man will fight for this, Hadrack. He will charge a shield wall and battle like a crazed beast and not stop because he knows victory is not only for our king and the Master, it is for him as well."

"You share the plunder equally?" I said in wonder.

Einhard grinned and scooped the silver and gems back into his bag. "There is no such thing as equal, my friend. As Sword of the King, I get a quarter of all plunder. Half goes to our king and the rest is divided among the men. It is a fair arrangement." He winked at me. "Compare that to your king, who offers you nothing for your life except what you already have. You have everything to lose and nothing to gain. That is madness. A man who is forced to fight and risk everything for no gain is no match for a man who wants to fight and has much to gain. Wouldn't you agree?" He studied me closely as I thought, my eyes unconsciously following the arc of silver and gems in the bag as Einhard casually tossed it in his hand.

"Yes," I said finally.

Einhard tucked the bag away and nodded in satisfaction. "Good. Now tell me. You spoke of honor earlier. Do you still feel honor bound by the oath your father took?"

I thought about that for only a moment. The Lord of Corwick and his men had murdered my family and all the villagers in Corwick. The oath of fealty was a two-sided pledge, with the liege lord promising on his end to protect his vassals at all times. Lord Corwick had broken his oath as far as I was concerned and so it was an easy answer for me. "Absolutely not."

"Good, good," Einhard said with a lopsided grin. He clapped me heavily on the shoulder. "Then I have decided that I'm not going to kill you after all. The Master has been clear about His wishes, and we, His servants, will be taking the fight even more to these men of Ganderland. Today's battle was just the first step." Einhard looked at me. "As warlord of my tribe and Sword to the king of Piths, I need men to fight this war. Men I can depend on."

"You want us to join you and fight against our king?" I asked in bewilderment as I realized what he was saying. I felt my pulse flutter at the idea and I couldn't help but glance at the bulge in his tunic where I knew the bag of silver and gems lay.

"You and the older one with the big nose and watchful eyes," Einhard nodded. "I have a use for the both of you. The little one I have no interest in."

I frowned and shook my head. "No. He stays with us."

"He's too small," Einhard said dismissively. He swept his arm around the hall. "Any of my sisters could beat him. I don't want him. He'd just get in the way."

"He may be small," I agreed. "But Baine is fast and stronger than he looks, and he's very good with a bow. It would be a mistake to underestimate him." I kept my face neutral as I told the lie. I didn't know it then, but as time would go by my words would become all too true.

"And if I still say no?" Einhard grunted.

"Then I won't join you," I said as I held Einhard's green eyes with mine.

"I could just kill you all and be done with it," Einhard growled, his eyes hardening. "I'd be no worse off than before I met you."

"You could," I agreed. "But if you planned that you would have done it by now."

Einhard sat back and regarded me coldly. For a moment I thought I'd gone too far, but then he threw his head back and laughed. He drained his mug, slurping to get it all, and then looked at me, his face serious now. "You interest me, Hadrack the wolf cub. Give me your oath that you will fight with us and not run away the moment no one is watching and I will let you live."

"All three of us?" I demanded.

Einhard glanced at Baine, who was, I was shocked to see, rutting away quite happily with one of the Pith women. The woman was naked except for leather boots on her feet and she was straddling him, her large breasts bouncing wildly as she rode him. Somehow the naked woman managed to take a great gulp of beer from a mug she held in one hand without missing a stroke or spilling any before with a whoop, she threw the empty mug over her shoulder. I couldn't help but smile to myself at the look of wild-eyed glee on my friend's face as he looked up at her.

"Yes," Einhard grimaced as he looked back at me. "All three of you."

And that is how Baine, Jebido and I came to join the Piths.

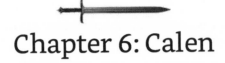

Chapter 6: Calen

Three days of hard riding later, my ass still hadn't gotten used to the unforgiving saddle beneath it or the jerking gait of my horse, and I winced as pain shot up my spine. In front of me the Pith men rode three abreast in a long line while scouts appeared and disappeared like wraiths through the trees in the distance, guarding us from ambush. The women rode behind Baine, Jebido and me and were armed with short swords and light bows and, from what I'd seen already, I knew they knew how to use them both. Behind the women, heavily-laden packhorses carrying plunder and the bodies of the Pith fallen brought up the rear in a solemn column, the corpses flipped over the horses face down and tied wrists to ankles. At the rear of the procession of the dead, several heavy wagons carrying the wounded and drawn by oxen plodded along. The Piths had found the wagons in the compound and had taken them as well as all the horses, though I thought they might be regretting it by now, as the slow-moving oxen had reduced the entire company to a crawl.

Jebido rode easily to my right, his great hawk-like nose jutting out from beneath his new helm, his eyes half-closed as the sun warmed him. Once we'd sworn our oath to Einhard in a completely informal ceremony before a crowd of drunken and mostly sleeping Piths, Einhard had allowed us to take what we wished from the dead Gander soldiers. Jebido now wore a conical metal helm, a mail tunic with a black cloak, and heavy leather trousers. He'd found a pair of hob-nailed boots that fit him perfectly and he carried a short sword on one hip and a long sword on the other. He had a round Pith shield on his left arm and he looked every bit the soldier, I thought with pride. I glanced to my left where Baine rode just as easily as Jebido and I frowned. My friend had taken to riding as if he'd been doing it his entire life, and I can't say that I wasn't just a little bit jealous.

Baine saw my look and he snickered at me. "It still hurts?" he asked in mock surprise. He was dressed in a black-dyed padded leather jacket two sizes too big for him over a white tunic, as none of the armour we'd come across had been small enough for him. He'd also scrounged up some black trousers and black leather boots and I had to admit he looked quite impressive. He reminded me a lot of the small, but lightning-quick black rock snakes we used to see near Corwick. Baine's shield was hung over his saddle and he held a well-used knife in his hand and was flipping it in the air end over end so fast that it was hard to focus on it. His hands weren't large but they were very dexterous, something he told me had helped make him an excellent pickpocket.

"Is it that obvious?" I grumbled.

Baine laughed again. "You look like you could rip a bear in half with your hands right about now."

"As long as I'm on my feet and off this cursed horse, I'd consider it a bargain."

Baine flipped the knife in the air, then stuck his hand out, palm down as the hilt reversed and sat balanced on his hand. He flicked his hand back up and the knife twirled away before he caught it again almost casually. "You'd think with that big soft backside of yours that you'd have enough cushioning."

"Keep talking and maybe I'll rip you in half instead of the bear," I growled at him.

"You'll never catch me," Baine said with a grin. "You're way too slow, what with that giant ass holding you back." I grinned at Baine despite myself and shifted in the saddle, suppressing a groan at the pain in my buttocks. Thankfully, we'd just entered an area of hilly terrain that slowed the horses and wagons even more, making the jolting almost tolerable. I turned and glanced back at the three women riding directly behind me and they all grinned at me. Two of the women were Piths, both with the familiar blonde hair, while the third was plump and had long black hair. Not long ago, the plump woman, whose name was Megy, had been the Quarrymaster's wife, though she'd get mad now if you called her that. As things turned out, Alesia had been right all along and Priam had been Megy's undoing. She'd tried her best, everyone agreed on that, but Priam had just kept going and going until Megy couldn't take it anymore. The poor woman had finally gagged and fallen to her knees, where she'd heaved the entire contents of her stomach onto the floor of the great hall. Megy's failure had prompted the Pith women guarding the Quarrymaster to poke and prod the now terrified man out of the hall at the point of their knives. I never did see the Quarrymaster again, but for hours after you could hear the man's screams echoing across the compound. I had no love for the man, but even now, all these years later, I still shudder when I think about what those last few hours must have been like for him. As for Megy, the Piths had become surprisingly enamoured with her. I suppose they admired her determination and bravery, not to mention her enthusiasm once she got the hang of things. After she'd purged her stomach and stood up, clearly expecting to share the fate of her husband, the Piths had taken a vote and had unanimously decided to let her live. Having nowhere else to go, Megy had decided to come with us and had become a favorite nighttime companion of Eriz, of all people.

"You look very dashing dressed in that armour, Hadrack," Megy called to me with a grin and a wink. "It suits you well and you look happy."

I felt myself sit up straighter in my saddle at her words and I adjusted the shield on my left arm before I smiled back at her. "As do you," I said. And it was true. Megy's hair seemed shiner now and her eyes sparkled with a kind of inner joy. I noticed she'd even lost some weight as well, courtesy of her nightly escapades, I thought with a grin.

"Come see me tonight and we can be happy together."

I tilted my head back and laughed, then shook my head. "Much as I'd like to, Megy, I doubt Eriz would appreciate it if I did." I turned and faced forward and tried to ignore the lewd suggestions coming from the three women about what they would do to me if I came to their beds. I'd already had three such encounters with Ania, a girl no older than myself but with a lifetimes worth more experience than I. Ania was the first Pith female I had seen that night in the compound and I can attest that what the women behind me were saying was, while shameless and most of it physically impossible, not without some accuracy. I smiled to myself as I thought about seeing Ania again that night and absently I let my hand fall to the hilt of my sword. I looked down at it, admiring the gold-plated pommel and crossguard. In the center of the pommel sat a carved, snarling wolf's head, the eyes made with two piercing red rubies. It had originally belonged to the Quarrymaster and I still found it hard to believe that I actually possessed such a treasure. I had outfitted myself as best I could in armour, having had the reverse problem Baine had had. Where he was too small, I was too big. I'd found a sword that I'd rather liked, but when Einhard had seen it, he'd flown into a drunken fit of rage and thrown his mug across the room.

"You can't be seen wearing a toad-sticker like this!" Einhard had cried in disgust, grabbing it from me. "You couldn't cut the foreskin off one of your fat priests with this worthless blade!" He'd tossed it aside in contempt, then called to a Pith nearby and whispered in his ear. The Pith had nodded and left, only to return moments later holding a sword encased in a wooden scabbard surrounded by soft black leather. "You see this?" Einhard said, holding the sword beneath my nose and swaying dangerously. His eyes were red-rimmed and bleary looking as he blinked at me.

"It's a magnificent sword," I finally said, hardly daring to breathe as I stared at it with desire.

"Yes, yes," Einhard muttered, waving away my words. "It is that, but I mean, do you see this?" He pointed at the pommel where a snarling wolf's head sat glaring at me with its ruby eyes. I hadn't noticed it until he pointed it out and I stared at it in surprise. Einhard nodded. "Yes, my overgrown wolf cub." He handed it to me and belched. "It's fate and the Master has spoken to me and wishes you to have it. Besides, I already have a fine sword. So take it."

"I don't know what to say," I said reverently as I took the sword. "There are no words..."

"Then why say them?" Einhard interrupted. He grinned lopsided at me, patted me on the shoulder and then turned away. "More beer!" he cried. And so that's how I came to possess the sword, which I decided obviously to call Wolf's Head. Einhard had told me later, once we'd left the compound and its dead behind, that he'd intended to give me the Quarrymaster's sword all along. He said that it proved what a gracious and caring leader he really was, but personally I think it had more to do with all the beer in his belly, than the kindness in his heart.

"You look quite pleased with yourself," Jebido said beside me, cutting off my thoughts.

I glanced at him and took in a deep breath and smiled. "Well why not?" I said. I motioned to him and nodded at Baine. "Look at us now and compare that to where we were just three short days ago down in that hole. We were slaves, Jebido, not even really alive, and now we're free! Except for riding this blasted horse, life couldn't be much better. I have a full belly, a woman to rut with when I wish, and a sword by my side that would make a king proud. Why shouldn't I look pleased?"

Jebido shrugged. "The Mother and The Father can be fickle," he said. "One moment Their favor shines on you and then," Jebido snapped his fingers in the air, "the next, Their anger. So enjoy it while you can, but don't take it for granted."

I shook my head and laughed. "Are you getting old on us, Jebido?"

"Yes," Jebido said with a grunt.

"Exactly how old are you?" Baine asked with a mischievous look.

"Old enough to peel the hides off both of you with one hand, while scratching my arse with the other," Jebido said. "That's how old I am."

Both Baine and I laughed at that and I took a moment to study Jebido's profile. I realized I hadn't really looked at him closely in a long time and I was shocked to see that his hair beneath the helm he wore was almost completely grey. When had that happened? I wondered. I noticed his face was lined as well, the skin tough and leathery looking. I looked away as I felt a pang of sadness come over me. I realized that my friend might be as old as forty, or even more, which to me at that time seemed ancient. I'd known Jebido for more than half my life and for the first time the idea that one day he wouldn't be there had become very real. I tried not to think about it and instead I glanced back at Jebido. "Are we in the land of the Piths yet, do you think?" I asked.

Jebido shook his head. "I don't think so." He turned and pointed to the northwest, where high-peaked mountains could just be seen far away in the hazy distance. "That's the Father's Spine mountain range over there, which begins at the northern tip of Ganderland and crosses into Southern Ganderland before ending near the coast. I think if we were in the land of the Piths we probably wouldn't be able to see the mountains." He pursed his lips, clearly thinking before adding, "An army on foot usually makes about twenty-five miles per day, on horseback more like thirty-five." He glanced at the decaying bodies swaying behind us on the horses and at the two wagons. "But with all of that slowing us down, I'd be surprised if we're doing even twenty. So if I had to make a guess, I'd say we're still at least three or four days from the border."

We were following an obviously rarely used path that meandered its way through fields of rich green grass dotted with patches of tall pink and purple lavender. A steep hill bristling with jagged stone slabs punching through the grass rose before us with thick trees swaying on each side at the top, separated by the path. To our right the ground inclined toward a wide outcrop of flat, impassive grey granite that looked something like a turtle with its head held in the air. Tough looking yew trees grew almost defiantly in places along the turtle's back in deep pockets of sediment that had been washed into the crevices over the years. More trees grew at the turtle's base and to our left a thick forest of golden aspen and white maple sprawled for miles. From these trees we heard a shout rise up and Einhard lifted his hand, halting the column. Instinctively we began to bunch together, fearing an attack as one of our scouts galloped toward us from the trees and made his way to Einhard.

"What do you suppose that's about?" Baine muttered.

"If I had to guess," Jebido said, looking around with hard eyes. "I'd say The First Pair's favor has just about run out." He nodded to the trees. "As I thought." Mounted men were coming through the thick forest and stopping at its edge to stare at us. I saw more riders on the hill and someone shouted out a warning as more men appeared from the forest behind us and trotted to the road, where they took up a position to block our retreat.

"Mother's tit!" Baine cursed.

Einhard wheeled his horse around and came back to us at a gallop as Alesia rode to meet him. "Get the women up there!" he ordered, pointing to the turtle. "Make every bolt count." Alesia nodded, her face set in a tight mask as she issued orders. Instantly the Pith women turned and raced for the outcrop. I caught a quick glimpse of Megy's black hair and frightened white face and then she was gone in a swirl of pink and purple flowers churned into the air by the racing hooves of the horses.

"You," Einhard said, gesturing to Baine. "You're good with a bow. Go with them."

I saw my friend's eyes widen and he opened his mouth as if to protest, so I leaned over and slapped his horse on the rump, startling it into motion. "Get moving!" I shouted. The horse took off at a dead run with Baine holding onto the reins desperately and looking back at me in confusion. I really should have told him what I'd told Einhard about his archery skill, but it had simply slipped my mind.

"Leave the dead," Einhard commanded. "We'll get them after we're done with these turd-sucking Gandermen." He pointed to two Piths. "Get the wounded out of those cursed wagons and go join the women."

"Yes, brother," both men said in unison.

I glanced to my left at the men in the trees. They'd started their horses into a slow walk, while on top of the hill the riders there had seen the women breaking for the rocks and were now in full gallop, trying to cut them off. I shouted a warning to Einhard and he whirled in his saddle and cursed. "Follow me!" Einhard cried as he drew his sword. There were around eighty or so of us and at least that number of the enemy streaming down the hill, with an equal amount in the trees. How many of them were still at our backs, I didn't know, as there was no time to turn and look. Beside me Jebido drew his sword, his mouth set in a grim line as he kicked his horse into motion, following the charging, screaming Piths as they converged on the enemy coming down the hill. I drew Wolf's Head and followed Jebido, holding onto my horse the best that I could as it raced over the field. In my peripheral vision I could see the riders from the trees were now coming on at a gallop. We'll be slaughtered between the two, I thought, feeling panic start to rise in my chest. "Be calm. Be smart. Be strong," I heard Jebido say in my head. I squashed the rising panic angrily and lifted Wolf's Head above me, then cried defiantly to the sky.

The men on the hill had changed direction now, having given up on the women, heading directly for us bunched into a tight wedge. I could see individual faces clearly and saw that they wore the yellow and black mark of the King of Ganderland. We were racing over the field in a loose bunch, with me and Jebido at the rear. I heard Einhard give a sudden sharp command just as we reached the tip of the enemy wedge. The Piths moved in unison like a great flock of birds at Einhard's words and they swerved to each side, swinging their swords wildly as the Gander horsemen plunged past. Two men at the head of the wedge fell instantly, mortally wounded, and several horses behind them tripped over their fallen bodies and flipped forward, tossing their riders from their saddles. It was a marvellous feat of horsemanship by the Piths, clearly something that could only be done by the most expert of horsemen. Unfortunately, I was not an expert horseman and I reacted much too slow. I saw Jebido wrench his horse's reins to the side and I felt relief flood over me as he just managed to get clear, then I lost sight of him as the rush of riders were upon me. Horses swept past me on both sides and instinctively I lifted my shield to protect my head as first one, then a second sword clanged against it. I winced as I felt pain vibrate up my arm all the way to my shoulder. A rider with a black beard and snarling face was bearing down on me with his sword in the air and poised to strike and I ducked desperately under the man's wild swing. I automatically lashed out with Wolf's Head and felt my blade slash through his mail and cut deep into his midriff. I had but a moment to see his eyes widen in surprise and then he was past me and gone. Something collided heavily with my horse and I was wrenched sideways and would have fallen if not for the press of men and horses milling around me in confusion. I looked over my shoulder and saw that the Piths had swung back around and had completely surrounded the Gandermen. They had them hemmed in now, pushing the leaders back as the panicked horses behind continued to try to get through. I felt something bang heavily against my helmet and then everything went black. Feeling slightly dizzy and unable to see anything, I started to swing my sword wildly around me at the pressing bodies, expecting a sword thrust to take me at any moment. I could smell the sweat of the horses and the fear of the men and I cried out as something pierced my upper thigh. With my left hand I pushed my helmet back where it had fallen over my eyes and I just managed to bring up my sword in time to deflect a blade that had been aimed at my throat. The soldier whose sword I'd blocked cursed me and he swung his rectangular shield at my face. I leaned back as far as I could and the shield whizzed over me, just grazing the tip of my helmet. I let the shield pass and then stabbed forward, cursing back at him as I heard the man scream like a hog as Wolf's Head took him in the chest.

For a moment I was free of attackers and I looked down

at my aching thigh, shocked to see a Pith arrow jutting out of it. I realized that the women were shooting down at the encircled Gandermen from the rocks above and that they didn't know that I was trapped among them. I heard a shout and saw Eriz and several Piths battling on the other side of a wall of Gandermen and I urged my horse in their direction with my feet. Around me Gandermen were falling as the arrows were starting to hit their marks and my shield was almost wrenched off my arm as an arrow punched a third of the way through it. I noticed that the wicked barbed point had just narrowly missed my upper arm and I said a quick prayer of thanks to Mother Above for watching over me. Another arrow glanced off my chest armour with a loud twang and I knew that if I didn't get out of there soon, one of those arrows was bound to find my flesh whether The Mother was watching or not.

I sensed rather than saw movement to my left and tried to raise my shield just as a big man with a red-splattered beard swung an axe at me. The axe head barely grazed my shoulder armour, then deflected off my shield and collided with my horse's head. The poor beast didn't know what had hit it and it dropped instantly. I tried to fling myself to the side as the horse fell, but I only half succeeded, and I landed heavily with the lower part of my injured leg trapped under the dead animal. I screamed in agony as the big man with the beard leapt from his horse and stood over me with his great axe held in both his hands. He grinned down at me with brown broken teeth and raised the axe. I lifted my left arm to ward off the blow that I knew was coming before realizing with dismay that I'd somehow lost my shield. The bearded man opened his mouth to say something to me, what it might have been I'll never know because a Pith arrow took him directly in the mouth and it flung him backwards almost contemptuously. I think I must have fainted from the pain for a moment after that because the next thing I knew I felt a hand on my shoulder and I looked up into the concerned face of Jebido.

"Are you all right, Hadrack?" he asked me anxiously.

I wiped at my eyes, surprised to see blood on my hand, then looked up at him and grinned weakly. "Never been better, my big-nosed friend." Jebido laughed and slapped my shoulder as together he and another Pith pulled me out from beneath the horse. I grit my teeth to keep myself from screaming as fire burned along my leg from ankle to hipbone. Jebido saw the arrow sticking out of me and frowned and, in one quick motion, yanked it from my flesh. I screamed again and passed out a second time. When I came to, I found myself lying at the base of the turtle, where Ania was working at cleaning and bandaging my wound.

Ania smiled at me and motioned to my leg. "It's not as bad as it looks. You should be fine in a week or so."

I nodded and glanced over her shoulder to where the Piths were just finishing off the last pocket of resistance. Dead Ganderman lay everywhere, many of them having been struck down by multiple arrows. "So we won," I said, wincing as Ania tightened the bandage on my leg.

Ania snorted. "Of course we won." She motioned with her head contemptuously behind us. "Those Gander dogs can't stand up to Piths."

"True," I agreed. "You women and your arrows made the difference."

"Yes," Ania said matter-of-factly. "Your friend did well," she added, unable to keep the smile from her lips. "Though, if the truth were told, I'd wager he'd never picked up a bow before today."

I glanced to where Baine stood beside Jebido on a small knoll of grass as they watched the Piths finishing off the Gandermen below them. Baine had a bow slung over his shoulders and he must have sensed my eyes on him, for he turned and looked back at me. He grinned when he saw me awake and said something to Jebido, who also turned. I nodded to them both and they smiled back at me before turning away.

"There," Ania said. "All done."

I glanced down at the wound, which Ania had wrapped

with rags torn from a tunic. "My trousers?" I asked her.

"Here," she said, holding them up as she rose to her feet. "Stand up and I'll help you put them on." I did as she said and winced as I put weight on my bad leg. It hurt something fierce, but I found it was tolerable. I lifted my injured leg and Ania bent and gingerly fit my foot through, then did the same for the other side. She pulled the trousers up, stopping to fondle my man-hood before pulling the trousers all the way up. "Will I see you tonight?" she asked coyly.

I rolled my eyes at her and grinned. "You Piths are insatiable!" I said with a snort.

"Yes," Ania agreed with a wide grin. She held Wolf's Head out to me and I took it, belting it around my waist. "I have to go now," she said. "There are others wounded." I nodded in understanding and gave her behind a slap as she moved away, then limped over to stand with Jebido and Baine.

"Have a good sleep?" Baine asked me with a twinkle in his eyes.

"Ania tells me you held your own up there," I said, ignoring his jibe and motioning to the outcrop.

Baine shrugged. "I missed more than I hit, but I'll get it."

"I hope you weren't aiming for me," I said, pointing to my leg.

"If I had, you'd be fine right now," Baine said. Both Jebido and I chuckled and Baine's face turned serious. "I saw you fall and thought you were done."

"So did I," I agreed.

"As long as there's breath in your body and strength in your sword arm you're never done," Jebido said. Below I saw that the fighting was now over and most of the Gandermen were dead. Some soldiers, I noted, had thrown down their weapons and were begging for mercy. I had no illusions of how that would turn out. As expected, the Piths were in no mood for mercy this day, and they quickly sorted the prisoners into a line and were ordering them to their knees.

"They're going to play bloodline now?" Baine asked in

wonder.

I opened my mouth to reply and then hesitated as something about the first man standing in the line caught my eye. His head was lowered and I couldn't see his face, but something about him seemed familiar as he slowly kneeled. "Mother Above!" I suddenly exploded as I started forward. "He's short!"

"What?" Baine called out in confusion to my back.

"Hadrack, wait!" I heard Jebido shout.

All the prisoners were now on their knees with their heads bent and I saw Eriz with his sword raised over the first man. "Stop!" I cried at the top of my lungs.

Eriz hesitated in mid-swing, staring at me in surprise as I limped up to him. "What is it, brother?" he asked with a look of bewilderment on his face.

I ignored Eriz and looked down at the kneeling man. My shadow had fallen across his body and I studied his sweat-encrusted, thinning blond hair before finally, slowly, the man looked up. It was Calen. There was no question in my mind. He was a youth no longer, now a grizzled soldier of twenty-six or twenty-seven, but it was unquestionably him. He looked up at me with eyes that had come to grips with his death, seeing me, but not really seeing me as I towered over him. "Do you know who I am?" I asked him in a whisper. My voice sounded odd to me, raspy and hoarse and I could feel my hands start to shake with anger. I let my right hand fall to the hilt of Wolf's Head to steady it and I waited for him to speak.

"Brother?" Eriz said again. "What is this?"

"Just wait!" I screamed at him, barely able to control my rage. I saw Einhard standing behind Eriz. He was looking at me with a mixture of puzzlement and surprise on his face. Baine and Jebido ran up to join Einhard and I saw Jebido move as if to come to me, but Einhard lifted his hand and stopped him, for which I was thankful. I wanted no interference in what I was about to do. I turned back to look down at Calen. "I asked you if you remember me?" I said to him.

Calen wet his dry lips and looked around at the watching

Piths, then focused on me. "Never seen you before," he said.

"Well I've seen you before!" I growled at him.

"Good for you," Calen said with a shrug.

I brought my good knee up and crashed it into Calen's face, feeling his nose shatter with a satisfying crunch. He screamed and fell backward onto his rear, holding his ruined nose in both his hands as he stared up at me in shock and fear. I grabbed him by his hair and pulled him back up to his knees, where he stayed swaying back and forth as he held his nose. "Corwick!" I hissed at him. I had a good grip on his hair and I shook his head roughly and then dragged it back as far as I could, exposing his throat. Calen screamed and he let go of his nose with his hands as he spread his arms helplessly. "Nine years ago!" I shouted. "Do you remember Corwick nine years ago, you bastard?"

"Corwick?" Calen sobbed. "What about it?"

"You chased me into the bog," I said, grinning coldly as I saw the light of recognition in his eyes.

"You're the boy!" Calen whispered in shock.

"Yes," I nodded. "I didn't die in the quicksand that day." I pulled his head back even farther, ignoring his whimper of pain. "You took my family away from me!" I hissed in his ear.

"No! No!" Calen protested. He tried to move his head but I held him firmly by the hair. "I didn't have anything to do with it! I swear!"

"You were there. I saw you."

"Yes!" Calen gasped. "I was there, but I didn't kill your family! That was someone else!"

"You helped kill the others, though," I growled.

"I had no choice!" Calen protested.

I let go of his hair and stepped back as Calen slumped forward with his chest heaving. I looked around at the silent Pith's watching. Even the women had come to watch and I saw Ania and Megy in the crowd. For a moment I caught Alesia's eye where she stood watching me with an excited look on her face, then I let my gaze drift to Jebido and Baine, then on to Einhard, before finally I refocused on Calen. "We all have choices," I said. "You killed innocent people."

"Lord Corwick ordered us to!"

"Did he order you to rape and murder those women too?" I snapped. I saw Calen's eyes widen in surprise and then he quickly looked away from me to hide the guilt that I knew lay in his eyes. I glanced down at the stag emblem of the king that I'd come to hate that lay across Calen's chest. I pointed at the crest. "Why do you wear the king's banner and not Lord Corwick's?" I asked.

Calen hesitated for a moment, looking puzzled by the change in topic. "I was transferred to Klanden Garrison four years ago," he finally said. "All the garrison troops there wear the king's mark."

I glanced at Jebido and he nodded that it was true and I nodded back to him, feeling a calmness coming over me. I turned back to Calen. "Where are the others?"

"What others?"

"There were nine of you that day," I said. "Where are the rest?"

"I...I don't know for sure," Calen stammered. "Some are still with Lord Corwick, I think."

"And the others?"

"Probably garrisoned along the border, if they live at all," Calen answered. "I don't know."

I sighed, knowing I'd gotten everything I would from Calen. I turned to Eriz. "Throw him your sword."

"What?" Eriz said, gaping at me in astonishment.

"Your sword," I repeated. Eriz turned to Einhard, who stood studying me until finally the Pith leader shrugged and motioned to Eriz. The big Pith muttered something to himself and then threw his sword in the grass in front of Calen. "I made a vow to my sister and my father and to all those people who lived in Corwick," I told Calen. "I swore to them that I would find their murderers and kill every one of them." I pointed down at him. "You were just a kid then. No older than I am now, and I know you're not the worst of the nine that was there that day. For this reason I'm giving you a chance to die like a man. Pick up the sword."

I moved back, drew Wolf's Head and waited. Calen looked up at me and I'm sure he could read the hatred in my eyes and he knew that if he didn't pick up the sword I'd fall on him anyway. Around us the open field was deathly quiet, not even a bird chirped as Calen slowly reached out and grasped the sword in his right hand. He stood shakily and wiped some of the blood from his face, and then he nodded to me that he was ready. Calen was no longer a boy but a seasoned soldier, and, as it turned out, a very good swordsman made even better by desperation. I was young, wounded and inexperienced, but on that day, none of it mattered. As Calen lifted his sword I let the white rage that had been building up inside me have free reign and I attacked. Whatever Calen tried, be it defence or offence, I smashed past, pounding away at his guard with sheer single-minded rage. I nicked his leg, then his cheek, then his arm, ignoring a slash from his sword that got through and shaved some skin off my temple. I used Wolf's Head like an avenging hammer and barely noticed when Calen's sword spun from his hands and he fell. My sword continued to rise and fall, as over and over again I struck downward, pulverizing Calen into a wet, sticky mess of splintered bones, meat and blood. Finally, when it was done, I dropped my sword to the ground and fell to my knees. I grabbed the Pair Stone that still hung around my neck after all these years and I said a prayer of thanks to The First Pair for delivering Calen to me.

After a time, I felt a gentle hand rest on my shoulder and I looked up at Jebido. "Come, let's get you cleaned up," he said softly.

I nodded and, with his help, I got to my feet. Baine rushed to my other side and with them supporting me, I limped away. "That leaves eight of the bastards," I said to my two friends.

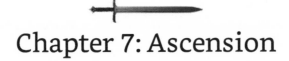

Chapter 7: Ascension

For the rest of that day and the next we travelled steadily southward, while in the distance we could see Gander scouts riding in pairs and studying our progress. It was obvious to all of us that despite the overwhelming defeat they'd suffered at our hands, we'd not seen the last of the Gandermen. Einhard tried sending warriors on fast horses after the scouts at first, but he had finally given it up as pointless as the watchers only came within eyesight of us and then disappeared at the first signs of pursuit. On the afternoon of the second day after the battle, we came to a shallow stream no more than eight feet across at its widest point and Einhard called a halt to rest and to refill our canteens. I gratefully dismounted, rubbing my backside gingerly as Jebido, Baine and I led our horses to the stream to drink. Einhard approached us and let his horse drink beside ours as he studied the Gander scouts. "What are they waiting for?" Einhard finally asked Jebido, motioning to where the men watched us silently from a safe distance up on top of a hill. "Why don't the Ganders just attack and get it over with?"

Jebido frowned. "After what happened to them the last time, I'm betting they're waiting to have enough men to overwhelm us completely this time. They're probably keeping an eye on us while moving troops around us like a net."

"So then we're just minnows waiting to be swept up and swallowed by Gander dogs at their pleasure?" Einhard said sarcastically. "How long do you think we have?"

Jebido shrugged. "Impossible to say. It'll depend on how many troops they have at their disposal and where they want to attack us."

"And if we try to slip away from this net?" Einhard asked.

Jebido motioned to the men on the hill with his chin. "They'll always be watching, so that won't be an easy task with a group as large as we are."

"Probably not worth the effort anyway," Einhard said. "My gut tells me they already know where we're heading." He bent down on his haunches and used his fingertip to draw a long line in the soil near the stream edge. "This is the border between Southern Ganderland and the land of the Piths," he said. He then stabbed at the ground. "This is approximately where we are right now." He then made five marks all along the length of the borderline. "The Gandermen have been busy in recent years building garrisons along the border." He glanced up at us and grinned. "I guess they weren't too happy with us raiding them whenever we wanted to and they figured this would deter us. The good news is only two of the western-most garrisons are complete so far." He pointed to the eastern corner of the borderline. "This is where we crossed into Southern Ganderland. I'm hoping to get us back the same way. The White Rock river runs along the border, here, and there's only one passable ford for more than a hundred miles. Once we get across that ford the only way through the mountains to our lands is a narrow pass." Einhard made a face. "It's possible the Gander's know about it and, if they do, trying to fight our way through there will be costly." He gestured to the ground. "There's an unfinished garrison several miles from the pass guarding one of their new bridges, with several other bridges further west." He glanced up at us. "If the pass is blocked, we'll have no choice but to try and get across one of those bridges."

"How far along are they on the garrison?" Jebido asked.

Einhard shrugged. "Last I heard, not even halfway." He grinned at us. "And that's how it will stay for the time being thanks to our raid at the quarry."

"Won't they just send more soldiers and slaves to Father's Arse and start up again?" Baine asked.

Einhard chuckled and shook his head. "Not without the stonemasons they won't."

"They weren't slaves," I said, seeing a flaw in his logic. "They'll just go back to work when it's safe and start cutting blocks again. You'll have gained nothing."

"Now that would be a trick I'd like to see," Einhard said with a laugh. "We Piths are not fools, my young friend." He used his fist to make a large depression in the ground some distance away from the border line and then drew a wiggly line that snaked close to the eastern-most garrison. "We learned that all the stone used for building these garrisons came from only one place."

"Father's Arse," Baine said.

"Yes," Einhard agreed, motioning to the large depression. "We didn't show up there by accident. The Ganders transport the shaped stone by wagon from the quarry to the river, here." Einhard touched a spot on the wiggly line. "From there it's floated downriver on barges and then loaded back onto wagons and distributed to the garrisons." He glanced at us. "We needed to stop construction until we're ready to attack them."

"And the only way to do that was to stop the flow of building stones," Jebido said with a nod.

"Exactly," Einhard acknowledged. He grinned. "But it's not like we could just destroy the quarry. It's too big."

"So you killed all the stonemasons," I said, finally understanding. "That's why you attacked. Not to take the fort, but to get to the stonemasons."

"Yes," Einhard said. "The builders need stone cut exactly to specifications. Something only a skilled stonemason can do properly. Since almost every stonemason in Ganderland worth anything at all was working in that quarry, their deaths should mean construction will grind to a halt. At least for a while."

"How long do you need?" Jebido asked.

Einhard shrugged. "That depends entirely on the Master's will. We must wait until He gives us His blessing." He grinned. "So, in the meantime, we prepare and we plan as best that we can." He gestured to the ground. "Keeping these garrisons weak is part of that plan." Einhard straightened up. "It's time to move."

"One moment, if I may?" Jebido said with a slight frown.

He gestured to where two Piths sat their horses about a hundred yards away and downwind from us, watching over the fifteen dead men and one woman draped over the backs of horses. "How exactly do you expect us to get through the Ganders while being slowed down by those?" The two Piths guarding the dead kept swatting at the air angrily as a host of buzzing flies swarmed around the decaying corpses. I heard one of the Piths spit out a curse as he slapped at his face.

"We'll find a way," Einhard said with a shrug.

"It makes a lot more sense to bury them here," Jebido said stubbornly. "Continuing on with them makes no sense and could be the end of us."

"I will not leave our brothers and sister behind!" Einhard snapped irritably.

"Then we will probably all die," Jebido said flatly.

Einhard glared at Jebido and his eyes flashed before finally he grunted and handed me the reins of his horse. "Wait here!" he commanded before stalking away. He approached Alesia and said something to her and her eyes widened, then she shook her head emphatically. Einhard said something else and she started to protest, but was silenced by a curt word before the Pith leader strode back to us. "Tonight I will attempt to send the spirits of the fallen on the path to meet the Master." He put his hands on his hips and nodded at Jebido. "I intended to bring them to the Ascension Grounds where it would be done properly, but, as our friend here pointed out, with them slowing us down our chances at success are low." He glanced at the corpses. "Doing the ceremony here, under these conditions, is not something I wish to do and, if there were any other way, I would take it. I just hope that it will work." Einhard took the reins of his horse from me and he swung into the saddle, shouting to his men to do likewise. Baine, Jebido and I shared a look and they both seemed just as confused by the entire matter as I was. We mounted up and followed the Piths as Einhard led us down the shallow bank and across the narrow stream. We travelled for the rest of that day, never stopping for a break before finally Einhard gave the word to make camp. Every evening since Baine, Jebido and I had joined the Piths we'd built a rough, rectangular palisade made of heaped earth and sharpened stakes pointing outward to protect us for the night. This evening was no different, though I noticed as we worked that the palisade was much larger this time and that some of the Piths were setting posts into the ground positioned closely together in the center of the enclosure. I saw Ania working with Megy and several of the other Pith women and I walked over to her.

"What's that all about?" I asked, motioning to the posts.

Ania smiled pityingly at me. "Sometimes I forget you haven't found your way to the Master yet and still cling to your insane beliefs." She glanced over her shoulder. "The only way for our fallen brothers and sister to find the path to the Master is to release their spirits to the skies."

I saw several Piths piling dead scrub brush at the base of some of the poles and I realized what she meant. "You burn them?" I asked in surprise.

Ania's pretty face turned angry. "We don't burn them, Hadrack!" she snapped, shaking her head. She looked upward. "We release their essence from their earthly bonds so that they can ascend. Only once the body is no more can a spirit be truly free to find its way back to the Master." She sighed and looked sadly at the posts being erected. "It's always preferable to bring our dead back with us and release them in the Ascension Grounds, which is the birth place of the Master. It's a sacred place and the only one where the spirits are guaranteed to find the true path." She looked down at her hands and toyed with her fingers. "I know the Sword of the King is right and I trust his judgment, but I'm afraid it might go badly for our brothers and sister to do the ceremony now."

I glanced at the poles and frowned. "What happens if something goes wrong and they don't get...uh...released properly?" I caught myself as I almost said burned.

Ania looked at me sadly. "Then they are doomed to try

to find their way to the Master on their own." We were camped on open land about a mile from a large forest of oak and elm trees and Ania swept one hand toward the trees. "For a spirit not given the proper light of ascension, trying to find the path would be like trying to find one particular leaf in all those trees." She shook her head. "Not impossible, but it would take years to accomplish, if at all." She shuddered. "I can't think of anything worse than spending eternity wandering the earth looking for a path and not even knowing when you found one if it's the right one."

I watched several Piths tamping the ground around a pole they'd just placed in the ground and I motioned to it. "So if all they need is to have their spirits released this way, then why don't you think it will work?"

Ania blew air through her mouth angrily and then gestured to the waiting dead, who were now lying in a neat row along one wall of the palisade. "Because one of our fallen brothers was the Pathfinder!" She glanced at me and raised a hand to stop my question. "The Pathfinder is like a guide," she explained patiently. "As the essence rises in the ascension ritual, the Pathfinder's words help to illuminate the true path to the Master for them." She frowned and glanced again at the corpses. "His name was Urdin and he was not supposed to join the fighting. He knew this better than any, yet he let his lust for battle overcome common sense and now he's dead. Because of Urdin's selfishness, he has jeopardized all of their chances of finding the right path to the Master."

"These other paths," I said. "Where do they go?"

Ania wrapped her arms around herself and pursed her lips. "Dark, terrible places," she whispered. She looked up at me and I could see the fear in her eyes. "Once an essence takes the wrong path there is no turning back and it will be forever doomed to spend eternity there." She turned away and watched as the Piths, having finished with their work, began to carefully pick up the dead from where they lay and bring them to poles. "It's almost time," Ania said.

I watched as the Piths gently tied the dead bodies to the posts and was surprised to see that more than one of the tough warriors had tears on their cheeks. More Piths arrived and they began scraping circles on the ground at points all around near where the bodies stood lashed to the poles. I counted twelve of the circles all made roughly the same size. "What are those for?" I asked.

"Rutting rings," Ania said with just a ghost of a smile on her lips.

"You're joking?" I said in surprise as I studied the rings.

Ania shook her head and smiled. "I promise you, I'm not. As the spirits ascend, we celebrate their lives by coupling beneath the eyes of the Master. Each man and woman will take a turn in the rings as we give thanks to Him for giving our fallen brothers and sister life, and for accepting them back in death."

"But there are four times as many men as women!" I protested.

Ania just laughed. "I guess we'll be busy then," she said with a wink. She motioned over my shoulder. "It's starting."

Einhard and Alesia appeared and they walked solemnly across the compound and stopped near the dead as the Piths assembled in a large group behind them. Several Pith women with torches walked along the perimeter of the palisade and lit bonfires that had been prepared earlier. I noted that a few Piths remained watching the open lands outside the palisade walls as Ania leaned closer to me. "The Sword of the King will speak the words normally spoken by the Pathfinder. As far as I know, this has never been done before. Hopefully the Master will not be too angered by it and will decide to show our brothers and sister the path."

Einhard spread his arms wide and lifted his face to the sky and Alesia moved back into the shadows as the Pith leader began to chant loudly in a language I'd never heard before. "What's he saying?" I whispered to Ania.

"He's speaking the ancient language of the Master," she whispered back. "Right now he's thanking the Master for giving us time with our brothers and sister." She cocked her head, listened for a moment and then nodded to herself. "Now he's imploring the Master to hear his words and show the spirits the true path to His side as the ascension begins." Einhard made a gesture with one hand and the Pith women with the torches ran forward and lit the dry brush on fire beneath the corpses. Flames shot up and instantly lit the enclosure and I turned in surprise as Ania began to strip her clothing off. When she was completely naked, she put her hands on her hips and smiled at me as the shadows from the flames danced across her white skin. Ania was no taller than my shoulders and slim, with small, pert breasts capped by large pink nipples that stood erect and proud. I stared at her flared waist with the soft blonde down nestled between her thighs and I felt instant desire come over me. I started to move toward her but she just laughed and held up her hand. "You have to wait your turn, Hadrack," she said. Ania walked past me and ran her hands down the armour covering my chest, pausing to lean into me so that her mouth was close to my ear. "Promise that you'll wait for me and not go with anyone else into the rings," she whispered huskily.

I swallowed noisily and nodded my head. "I promise," I whispered back. Ania kissed my cheek and then walked slowly toward the large group of Pith men. Her skin gleamed in the light of the flames and I thought she looked like a goddess as the Piths silently parted to let her through. I lost sight of her in the press of men for no more than a few heartbeats and then she reappeared holding Eriz's hand. She led him to one of the rutting rings and I felt a moment of jealousy come over me as the big Pith stripped and followed her into the ring. More naked Pith women were selecting men now and stepping into the rings, while the fires raged and Einhard continued to chant to the sky. I glanced again at Ania and grit my teeth as I saw Eriz on top of her and I forced myself to look away. I had no claim to Ania, I knew, and I was determined not to let my anger get the better of me and maybe cause me to do something stupid.

Jebido walked up to me shaking his head. "These Piths

sure do things different," he said as he stopped beside me. He chuckled. "I'm too old for this kind of thing."

I laughed, glad to have someone to talk to and distract me from Ania. "You didn't seem too old last night with that girl as I recall."

Jebido just grinned sheepishly at me. "I didn't want to hurt the young things feelings. You understand, don't you?"

"Of course I do," I said with a laugh. "You're good that way." I glanced around the compound. "Have you seen Baine around?" Jebido snorted and pointed and I followed his finger to one of the rutting circles on the left side of the raging fire near the back. A Pith woman with large breasts was on her hands and knees facing us while Baine knelt behind her with his hands on her ample hips. The woman's breasts were jiggling with each of Baine's enthusiastic thrusts. He saw us looking and he grinned happily and waved before turning his attention back to business.

"I think that boy must have been sired by a Pith," Jebido grunted.

"That would explain a lot," I agreed with a laugh.

"Uh oh," Jebido whispered in warning, gesturing with his chin as Megy ran up to us. She was naked and grinning widely with excitement as she held her hand out to me. "Come with me, Hadrack!" she cried. Her eyes were bright and gleaming in the firelight. "I've been looking forward to this all day!"

"I can't!" I protested as she grabbed hold of my hand and tried to drag me toward the fires.

"Oh, don't be shy," Megy said with a laugh. "I promise I won't hurt you."

"I really can't, Megy!" I said as I pulled back from her. "Maybe some other time." I saw the hurt expression on her face and I looked to Jebido for help, but he just shrugged at me with a blank face. I turned back to Megy and leaned closer to her. "It's not you, Megy," I said. "I promised Ania I'd wait for her or else I'd go with you."

"Ah," Megy said in understanding. She patted my arm and

grinned. "Can't say that I blame you, Hadrack. Maybe another time then." She turned to Jebido and held out her hand to him. "What about you?"

Jebido looked at Megy and a wide grin broke out across his face. "Well why not!" he exclaimed with a laugh. He quickly stripped and he and Megy made their way to an open rutting ring while I tried not to laugh at the sight of my friend's skinny white ass hurrying along behind her. I looked for Ania, hoping that she and Eriz were finished, but I was disappointed to see that she was now with the ox-like Pith named Tato. I cursed under my breath in frustration and turned away from the fire and then stopped in surprise and stared at the naked woman standing behind me.

"Are you enjoying your first Ascension Ceremony, Hadrack?" Alesia asked me with an amused look on her face. Alesia was tall for a woman, reaching almost to my nose and she held my gaze and studied me openly. Her breasts were large and heavy and her deep blue eyes sparkled in the firelight as she held out her open hand to me. "Come into the rings with me, Hadrack," she whispered. Without even realizing it, I reached out to her and put my hand in hers. She smiled and slowly drew me toward her, rubbing my hand along her naked belly, then between her breasts before drawing it to her mouth where she lightly ran her tongue across my knuckles. She turned and guided me toward an empty ring and I moved in a daze, unable to resist her. At some point I must have removed my clothes, or Alesia had done it for me, I truly don't remember, and we lay down together in the ring and coupled as flame and smoke rose skyward around us. I don't know how long we rutted, but at one point I became aware of a voice chanting and I realized that it was Einhard, standing not far away from us with his arms still spread as he continued to call to the Master. Alesia was on top of me, grinding her hips into me and groaning softly as I glanced up at Einhard's face. The ancient words were still coming from his mouth, but he was no longer looking up at the sky as before, but was instead staring down at the two of us. Our eyes met and I felt a stab of fear deep in my gut as I saw the coldness reflected back to me in those bright green eyes. Then Alesia started to move on me more urgently and I turned back to her, all thoughts of Einhard or anything else forgotten.

Hours later, long after the fires had burned themselves out and most of the Piths were asleep except for the sentries, Jebido and Baine found me where I sat in the darkness with my back against the cool mound of dirt that made up the northern palisade wall. Jebido sat down with a light groan to my right, while Baine glided smoothly and silently down to my left. I just stared at my hands that lay propped up on my bent knees and waited, knowing what was coming. Finally, after many minutes of silence, I glanced at Jebido. "Well?" I said to him.

"Well what?" Jebido grunted back.

"Aren't you going to tell me what a complete fool I was?" I asked.

Jebido flicked something off his elbow and looked at me with one eyebrow raised. "If you already know that, then why do you need me to tell you?"

I sighed and looked away from him, leaning my head back against the dirt. "What in the name of The Mother was I thinking?" I said to the sky.

"That's just it," Baine said with a chuckle. "It wasn't you. It was your cock doing the thinking for you."

"Yes," I agreed bitterly. "And because of it we all might be dead by the morning."

Jebido shrugged. "Maybe. We'll just have to wait and see."

I remembered the cold look in Einhard's eyes and I shook my head. "No. You weren't there. You didn't see the way he looked at me." I glanced at my friends. "I'm the one who did this, not you. Hopefully Einhard will take that into consideration and spare your lives."

Baine snorted. "You're his favorite." He motioned to himself and then to Jebido with his thumb. "He just tolerates us. If he decides to kill you he'll kill us too."

I felt the anger growing in me and I slammed my fist

against the ground. "How did it come to this!?" I hissed. "I was waiting for Ania. I wanted to be with her."

Baine put his hand on my shoulder. "Don't worry about it, Hadrack," he said. "The Mother and The Father will watch over us." He grinned, his eyes suddenly twinkling. "Besides, there isn't a man alive that could have resisted a woman like that." He made a face, clearly thinking. "Except maybe a eunuch I suppose. I'm not really sure how that works, but then again, even a man without balls probably couldn't say no to Alesia either."

"That's very helpful," I said to Baine sarcastically. I felt Jebido lightly touch my shoulder and he motioned with his chin to me in warning. Ania was making her way across the compound to where we were sitting and as she reached us, Jebido hurriedly stood up.

"Well, I think it's time we got some sleep," Jebido said, motioning to Baine to rise as well.

"But, I want to..." Baine started to protest.

"Now!" Jebido growled. Baine stood up reluctantly and together he and Jebido walked away as Ania sat down cross-legged in front of me.

"You didn't wait for me," Ania said point blank.

I spread my arms helplessly and looked at her, trying to come up with an excuse. Finally, I just decided to tell her the truth. "I don't know what happened," I confessed. "One minute I was waiting for you and the next I was following Alesia into the ring." I let my arms fall to my sides and I shrugged. "I was a fool and now Einhard is probably going to kill us."

Ania looked at me in surprise. "Kill you? Why would he do that?"

"After what I did with his wife right in front of him," I said. "What else can he do?"

Ania shook her head and laughed, clearly amused. "Oh, Hadrack," she said. "You have much to learn about us Piths." She leaned forward and put her hand on my arm as I stared at her, completely confused. "The Sword of the King is not angry with you."

"He's not?" I said in bewilderment.

"Not at all," she said. "He knows it wasn't your fault and he holds nothing against you for what happened." Ania made a face. "Alesia should not have done what she did. She took advantage of the Ascension Ceremony to rut with you, knowing that there was nothing that Einhard could do about it."

I rubbed my hand over my eyes, feeling overwhelming exhaustion come over me and I blinked at her, trying to understand. "So I did nothing wrong?" I finally asked, hardly daring to believe that it could be true.

"Well," Ania said with a soft smile. "It wasn't the smartest choice you could have made, but no, because it was done during the Ascension Ceremony, you have done nothing wrong." She looked at me with warning in her eyes. "Had you rutted with her outside the ceremony, however, then Einhard would be justified in killing the both of you."

"None of this makes any sense," I said in exasperation.

"It's simple," she said. "When a Pith man and woman marry they can choose to be exclusive with their spouse or open."

"By open you mean rutting with whoever they wish?"

"Yes," Ania nodded. "But it must be agreed upon by both or else it isn't valid and would then be considered a crime." She laughed. "Despite what you must think of us, we take adultery very seriously and it can sometimes be punishable by death."

"So then most Pith couples must be open," I said, thinking about all the rutting I'd seen in just the few days I'd been with the Piths.

Ania shrugged. "Some are. Some, like the Sword and Alesia are not. It depends on the couples' preferences. Most, like me, choose to be selectively open."

"Like you?" I gaped at her. "You're married?"

"I am," Ania confirmed. "Eriz is my husband." I just stared at her in shock and Ania laughed. "Does this surprise you, Hadrack?"

"Well, yes," I admitted. I shook my head, trying to make sense of it all. I looked at her. "But we've been together every night since I joined up with you and I thought…" I hesitated, not really sure what I had been thinking about Ania. I changed the subject. "What about Eriz? He's all right with it?"

"As I said, we are selectively open, so yes, he is all right with it."

"What does that mean, exactly?" I asked. "Selectively open?"

Ania grinned. "It means, Hadrack, that Eriz and I do not just rut with anyone at our whim. Very few Piths actually do that. At least the married ones, anyway. Instead, we each select one or two people who we are attracted to and we make a formal pact that we'll only rut with them when the desire comes upon us. We call these people our other-mates." Ania looked at me coyly. "Up until I met you, Eriz and I only had one other-mate each."

"Tato," I said, realizing instantly who her other-mate was.

"That's right," Ania said. "Eriz's other-mate is married to Tato, but she stayed behind as she is heavy with child."

"Is it Eriz's or Tato's?" I asked, instantly regretting it and expecting an angry reply from Ania.

She just smiled and shrugged. "Who can say for sure?"

I shook my head at the strangeness of it all before a sudden thought stuck me. "So Eriz agreed to me becoming an other-mate to you?"

"Yes," Ania nodded.

"Then that probably means you had to agree to one for him. Is that right?"

"Well, sort of," Ania said with a laugh. "In fact, it was Eriz who came to me first. I agreed and decided since he was bringing a Gander woman into his bed; it seemed only fair that I bring a Gander man."

"Megy," I said, understanding.

"Indeed," Ania said. "My husband finds her quite fascinating." She looked at me and her eyes sparkled with mischief. "I had originally decided on the older one with the big nose, but then I changed my mind and chose you instead."

"Why me?" I asked, grinning back at her. The thought of her and Jebido rutting was too ridiculous to even contemplate.

Ania stretched and stood up and she looked down at me with a knowing smile. "Older men don't have the stamina they had when they were young. Half the time in bed is spent just trying to wake up their one-eyed snake." She laughed. "Happily, I have come to learn that your snake is always awake and rarely seems to want to sleep." She grinned widely and held her hand out to me. "Your snake isn't tired right now, is it, Hadrack?"

A moment ago I'd felt confused and exhausted, afraid I'd ruined everything, and now I felt elation wash over me. We would live to see another day and all was right with the world.

I stood up and Ania giggled with delight at the sight of my snake trying to push its way through my trousers. She took my hand and led me across the compound and to her bed. I didn't resist. Why would I?

Chapter 8: The Gatehouse

Hours later, I was awakened by a boot roughly prodding me. Ania and I were lying near the eastern palisade wall on top of a thick layer of boxwood shrubs that she'd gathered and then covered in furs. I was lying on my back, with Ania on her side and snuggled into my chest. The furs were pulled all the way up to our chins and I noticed absently that her hair smelled faintly of a mixture of sweat and shrubbery. She muttered softly in her sleep as she pressed herself deeper beneath the warmth. I groaned groggily at the intrusion and cracked one eye open.

"The Sword of the King wishes to speak with you," Eriz said gruffly when he saw that I was awake.

I blinked up at him. "Now?" I whispered as Ania moved beside me. The sky was still dark with hundreds of bright stars winking down at me and a small crescent moon hung low in the sky, illuminating the campground weakly. "What does he want?" I asked hoarsely.

Eriz snorted. "It's not my place to tell you what the Sword wants. Nor is it yours to question it. All that you need to know is that he wishes to see you."

"Fine," I grumbled as I cautiously pried myself away from Ania's warm body and slipped out of the furs. Whatever this was about, it was obvious that Eriz was in no mood to explain it to me.

Eriz frowned at my nakedness as I stood shivering in front of him. "Get dressed," he ordered. "Wear your armour and bring your weapons."

Beneath me, Ania sighed and turned onto her back on the bed and then opened her eyes. She blinked several times, looking up at Eriz first, then shifting her eyes to me. "What's happening?" she asked sleepily.

"It's nothing," Eriz said dismissively. He bent to one knee

and kissed her on the cheek gently. "The Sword just wishes to speak with Hadrack." He carefully pulled up the furs that had fallen off her shoulders and adjusted them around her like a mother tucking in a child. "Go back to sleep. There's nothing to worry about."

Ania's eyes narrowed. "What does he need to speak to Hadrack about at this time of night?" she asked suspiciously.

Eriz frowned. "That will be revealed in the morning. For now, all you need worry about is getting some sleep."

Ania pursed her lips and sat up, her face tight with growing anger. Around her the furs fell unnoticed from her upper body. She crossed her arms over her small breasts and looked at Eriz defiantly. "Tell me what this is about!" she demanded.

While they were talking I'd hurriedly gotten dressed and had just finished belting Wolf's Head around my waist. Eriz saw that I was ready and he motioned for me to follow him. "Eriz?" Ania called to our backs. "I'm talking to you!" Eriz ignored her and I glanced back at her and shrugged helplessly, grinning despite myself at the look of outrage on her face. Better she be mad at him than me, I thought to myself as I followed Eriz. He led me around sleeping Piths and the still smouldering remains of the dead to where a single square tent of black canvas stood silhouetted in the weak moonlight. I saw that Jebido was standing near the closed tent flap, clearly waiting for us, and he nodded in greeting as we approached.

"What's going on?" I asked him.

Jebido just shrugged. "I've no idea."

I noticed that like me he was fully armoured and wore both his long and short sword. "Where's Baine?" I asked.

Jebido grinned. "His bedding was empty when Eriz woke me. If I had to guess, knowing that boy, I'd say he's sharing a bed with someone else tonight."

"Go on," Eriz interrupted roughly, motioning us in as he swept aside the tent flap.

Jebido and I both had to lower our heads to pass through the opening. "Ah, there you are," Einhard said, smiling widely as we entered. He was standing in the middle of the tent holding a battered tin mug in one hand, while his other hand was braced on his hip. I glanced around at the sparse furnishings. Two small wooden stools, a black bearskin rug covering the dirt floor and a raised bed at the back made from poles covered by straw stuffed into canvas. Two squat candles made from sheep fat sputtered on one of the stools, weakly lighting the interior and filling the tent with smoke and a heavy musky scent. Alesia sat reclining on the bed with her legs covered in a blanket of fur and she smiled at Jebido and me politely when we looked her way. She was dressed in a simple, sleeveless white tunic and as Einhard walked toward us with his arms outstretched, Alesia slowly moved the furs aside as she held my gaze, revealing her bare legs with just a shadowy hint of blonde hair nestled between them. She grinned at the look on my face and I caught a spark of mischief flare in her eyes before she glanced down, pretending to be surprised and quickly replaced the fur over her lower body. I silently grit my teeth and touched my Pair Stone, praying to both The Mother and The Father that she wouldn't cause any more problems. Einhard stood before Jebido and embraced him warmly, then moved to me and gave me a mighty squeeze that took my breath away.

"Did you enjoy the ceremony?" Einhard asked. Jebido and I shared a glance and both of us nodded at the same time.

Behind us Eriz entered the tent and stood off to one side with his arms crossed over his chest.

"Good. Good," Einhard said as he stepped back and took a drink from the tin. "It certainly wasn't traditional," he added with a short laugh. "But I believe it was successful and the Master showed our brothers and sister the true path."

"Of course He showed them the true path," Alesia said. "How could He refuse? You were magnificent. Not even the best trained Pathfinder could have done as well."

"You think so?" Einhard said, turning to look at her.

"Absolutely," Alesia said.

"Well," Einhard said modestly. "We all played our part."

He smiled without humour. "Some more so than others," he added dryly. He turned to face us and I saw Alesia's expression stiffen at his words. "Forgive me for waking you," Einhard continued, "but before the ceremony began I sent out several of our men to try and capture some of those bastards watching us." Einhard's eyes turned hard and I knew he was still upset that several of our own scouts had been missing for days now. "They're good," he conceded, "but I needed information before we move against the Ganders and I hoped that the Ascension Ceremony would distract them." Einhard grinned at us. "It worked and we managed to kill one and capture another." Einhard paused to sip from his tin. "That man gave us the information I needed, though truth be told, most of it is far from good." He gestured to us with his hand. "You recall the other day I told you about the ford where we crossed the river?" Both Jebido and I nodded. "Well, as I suspected, the Ganders have discovered it and are lying in wait in the pass expecting us to return that way."

"How many men?" Jebido asked.

Einhard shrugged. "More than enough, by the sounds of it." He shook his head. "Only a simpleton would lead his men into that trap." He grinned at us ruefully. "I like a fight as much as any man, but I'm no simpleton, so the pass is out."

"What other options are there?" Jebido asked.

"Few," Einhard said. "The White Rock river runs parallel to our position about five days ride to the west of us, then curves around across our path, heading east to the pass."

"Effectively boxing us in," Jebido muttered as he rubbed his chin. "You mentioned bridges before."

"Yes," Einhard nodded. "There are two of them to the northwest and a much bigger one near the pass." He grimaced. "That bridge is heavily guarded with a gatehouse on each bank, not to mention the unfinished garrison close by."

"And the other two?" Jebido asked.

"Nothing quite as elaborate," Einhard said with a sigh. "Unfortunately, they are both many miles away and in the wrong direction."

"We should go for one of the smaller western ones," I said. It made sense to me. The Ganders were expecting us to head for the pass and might not be expecting us to turn and the bridges wouldn't be as heavily defended. I said as much to Einhard, who listened patiently before shaking his head.

"They're ready for that too," he said. "They have men spread out in a wide arc along the river and they're watching the bridges just in case. The moment we turn west they'll know and will be ready for us. We're going to need to move fast and catch them by surprise if we want to get away."

"So that leaves us with the bigger bridge," Jebido said.

"Yes," Einhard nodded. "It's our only chance."

"If it's anything like what you say it is," Jebido said, "then getting through those gatehouses won't be easy."

"Nothing ever is," Einhard grunted.

"Couldn't we just swim the river at some point?" I asked. I wasn't all that enthused with the idea myself, since all the swimming I'd ever done had consisted of splashing around in the lagoon down in Father's Arse but, just the same, I thought it needed to be said.

Einhard snorted. "Not a chance! The White Rock is wide and deep with treacherous currents that would pull us all under. We'd never make it." He shook his head. "The only option is the southern bridge. The good news in all this is the prisoner tells me they don't expect us to attack there, so surprise will be on our side." He grinned at us. "I believe the man's words were, only a fool would do that."

"Surprise is all well and good," Jebido said, "but getting through those two gatehouses will take a lot of time and a lot of lives."

"Perhaps," Einhard chuckled. "Perhaps not. The gatehouses are indeed well guarded, and I understand that there are at least several hundred men being held as reserves in the garrison. If my plan works, then by the time we get there most of those men should be gone." He gestured to Eriz, who bent down and picked up two surcoats with the King of Ganderland's stag crest on them, which I'd failed to notice lying in a heap on the floor. Eriz handed Jebido and me a surcoat and then stepped back. "I want you two to go to the bridge ahead of us and pose as Gandermen," Einhard said. I looked down at the surcoat in my hand, trying to understand how doing that would help our cause as Einhard continued, "Our Gander friend told me that there are more scouts out there and that they always work in sets of two." He glanced at Jebido. "Does he speak true?"

"Yes," Jebido said. "They usually do it that way."

"Very well," Einhard said, nodding to himself. "You and Hadrack will take the Gander horses we captured and make your way south, heading for the bridge." He glanced at Eriz. "We'll create a diversion for you so you can slip out without those other scouts seeing you. With the darkness you should be able to get away undetected."

"And then what?" Jebido asked.

"The bridge is roughly a day's ride from here and I want you two to be well on your way before the sun comes up. I don't want those scouts seeing you and wondering what you're up to. I have other plans for them." Einhard nodded to Eriz beside us. "Eriz and Tato will leave with you and will hide in the forest and wait. First thing in the morning the rest of us will break for the bridge at full speed. That should alarm those Gander scouts and I'm sure they'll race back to their masters to report what's happening. They'll be moving fast to stay ahead of us and most likely won't be as cautious as they normally would be, so it should be easy for Eriz and Tato to eliminate them. We can't have them showing up and contradicting what I want you two to say. When you get close to the bridge, wait for Eriz to contact you that all is well and that the rest of us are getting close. That's when you two ride in and tell the Ganders that, as expected, we've attacked at the eastern pass. My understanding is that this news will draw some, if not all of the garrison force away. The rest of us will hold far enough back so that the Ganders won't see our dust. If they fall for it, Eriz will let us know and we'll attack."

"That might work," Jebido said as he rubbed his chin thoughtfully. "But there's no chance they're going to leave that bridge undefended."

"I know that," Einhard said. "If you and Hadrack can take the first gatehouse, then we can rush the second one and overwhelm it before they know what's happening. The key is getting rid of as many men from the garrison as we can so they can't reinforce that second gatehouse. Once we're across the river, they won't have a chance of catching us."

"What about Baine?" I asked, realizing there had been no mention of him. "Why isn't he going with us?"

Einhard shrugged. "For this to work they have to believe you two are Gander scouts and we now know they only work in pairs. Baine will have to stay with us." He gestured to the tent flap. "There's only a few hours or so of darkness before dawn breaks, so you'd better get going."

"One moment," Jebido said, lifting a hand to stop us. He looked at Einhard. "This scout you captured. Is he still alive?"

"Yes," Einhard said with a frown. "Why?"

"I need to speak with him," Jebido said.

Einhard shook his head. "There's no time."

"We'll have to make time," Jebido insisted. He lifted a hand to stop Einhard as the Pith leader began to protest. "When I was in the army we always had a watchword. Nobody comes into camp without it. I don't know what the protocol is at that gatehouse, but if we show up without that word they might suspect something is wrong."

Einhard grunted and made a face. "Very well," he said. He turned to Eriz. "Take them to the prisoner and get what you need from him, but in the name of the Master be quick about it!"

"Of course, brother," Eriz said. He turned to us and motioned us out.

I nodded to Einhard and, as I turned to follow Jebido out, I stole a quick glance at Alesia, even though I'd promised myself that I wouldn't. Alesia saw my look and she wiggled her fingers playfully at me in farewell and grinned. I quickly shifted my eyes away and ducked my head low as I followed Eriz and Jebido through the entrance. Everything was in darkness outside, as the weak crescent moon had slipped behind a thick bank of heavy clouds. At Eriz's signal, a huge bonfire suddenly roared to life at the northern corner of the compound and Pith warriors began milling around it drinking and laughing as one of the women stood up and began to dance naked in the firelight.

"We must be quick," Eriz said, leading us to the western wall of the palisade where I saw a man lying on the ground with his back propped up against the heaped bank of soil. His head was pulled back at an angle and a thick rope encircled his neck, the rope then tied to the wooden palisade wall above him. Blood covered his chest and one eye was swollen completely shut. Both his arms were spread to each side with rope tied around each wrist and lashed to the wall. I saw that he was awake and his one good eye followed us fearfully as we approached.

Eriz motioned to Jebido, who squatted down in front of the Gander soldier. "It's not looking so good for you right now, friend," Jebido said.

The Gander soldier blinked his good eye and studied Jebido. Then his mouth curled in a sneer. "You're one of us, you traitorous bastard!"

Jebido grunted. "I was, but that was a long time ago." He drew his short sword and stared at the soldier. "Tell me the watchword."

The Gander soldier's eye widened in surprise. "Why would you need to know that?"

Jebido lowered his sword until the tip was resting on the man's right kneecap. "My reasons are my own. What is the watchword?"

The soldier shook his head. "You're going to kill me anyway, so why should I tell you?"

Jebido shrugged. "Because there's quick dying," he said, "or there's long dying." Jebido moved his wrist and the soldier screamed as blood began seeping through his trousers at his knee. "Tell me the watchword and I promise you'll die quick." He pushed again with the sword and the man cried out a second time. "Don't tell me and I'll make sure you take a long time to die." He lifted his sword into the air and looked at the bloody blade critically. "The choice is yours. I've got all night and if I get tired, I can always turn you over to the women." Jebido gestured to where several Pith women stood watching and encouraging the naked dancer in front of the bonfire. "They really are savages, you know. You wouldn't believe the things that they do to their enemies." He leaned forward and whispered in the soldier's ear and I saw the man's eye widen in shock and his face turn even paler than it had been. He glanced at the women and swallowed, then looked back at Jebido. "You promise you'll end it if I tell you? No more pain?"

"You have my word," Jebido said.

The soldier nodded. "The watchword is Tyro."

"The king's son?" Jebido said.

"Yes," the soldier whispered. He closed his eye and looked away. "He's in command."

"Ah," Jebido said. He glanced at me. "He was just a boy nine years ago." I nodded to him in understanding and Jebido stood up and looked down at the soldier. "Thank you," he said. He leaned forward and without hesitating, drew his sword blade swiftly across the soldier's exposed neck, cutting through rope and cartilage. The man shuddered as blood spurted and then he sagged forward, hanging limply by his bound wrists. Jebido turned to us and nodded. "We can go now."

Eriz lead us to where Tato and Ania stood waiting, holding the reins of five horses at the open southern gate. "What are you doing here?" Eriz demanded, glaring at his wife.

"Going with you, of course," Ania said, looking at him defiantly. She wore light leather armour and had a bow strung over her shoulder. A short sword was strapped around her waist.

"No!" Eriz snapped. "You will stay here."

"There's no time for this, brother," Tato cut in. He looked

up at the sky. "Dawn is coming soon and you know your wife. If she wants to come with us, there's not much you or anyone else can do to stop her."

Ania grinned at Eriz and the big Pith finally snorted and looked away. "So be it," he said as he turned to Jebido. He pointed to the sky. "Do you see those four stars bunched together there?" he asked. When Jebido nodded Eriz continued, "Keep them always before you and you'll come to the river and the bridge."

"Understood," Jebido nodded.

"Good," Eriz said. "We'll walk the horses out from here. Don't get into the saddle until you're far enough from the compound that you won't be seen." He glanced at each of us in turn. "Good luck, brothers."

"And you," Jebido replied.

Eriz motioned us forward and the five of us led our horses on foot through the gate, which was a simple barrier six-feet wide made from crisscrossed sharpened stakes that had been removed by two Piths and was quickly replaced by them once we passed through. Eriz, Tato and Ania immediately turned and led their horses to the west, heading for the trees, and they rapidly disappeared into the darkness, leaving Jebido and me alone.

"So, what do you think?" I asked softly as we walked. Above us the weak crescent moon suddenly appeared from behind the clouds, casting a faint glow that we could barely see by. To the west I could see the black mass of the forest just distinguishable from the sky above it. To the south in front of us lay more fields wrapped in darkness, with half-seen lumps of rocky hilltops looking like giant heads wearing odd misshapen helmets breaking the openness. Something stirred in the long grasses in front of us and both Jebido and I reached for our swords, then we relaxed as the mischievous face of a fox appeared in the moonlight before it was abruptly gone.

"It might work," Jebido finally said as he glanced up at the sky. "If we're lucky."

"You don't sound too enthusiastic," I said.

Jebido laughed softly. "One thing I've learned over the years, Hadrack, is plans rarely go the way you want them to." He motioned with his thumb. "Mount up. We've come far enough now."

I nodded my head and awkwardly pulled myself into the saddle, hissing slightly as my leg protested. For a long while we rode in silence. Gradually the terrain beneath our horses' hooves changed from lush grasslands to large areas of open bedrock, with only the odd weed clinging stubbornly to it. The rock-strewn hills we'd seen in the distance earlier became more common now and we had to navigate around them more and more as we progressed. I noticed a faint glow beginning in the east as the sky lightened and, as each minute went by, the sky became a little bit brighter, pushing the stars back. To our left a high barrier ridge rose in shadowy jagged sections. It looked to me as though a giant knife had slammed down and cut wedges from it at random. "Dawn's almost here," I finally said to Jebido.

"Uh huh," Jebido grunted. He gestured to the sprawling forest about a mile away to our right. "Let's get over there. We'll be harder to see in the shadows of the trees when the sun rises. Hopefully the forest runs right up to the river and it will give us cover."

I followed Jebido around the base of a hill and we headed for the trees. I could hear birds calling out from the branches all along the treeline as the sun gradually rose, lighting the patches of conflicting grass and rock with its warmth. "How will we know when we're getting close to the river?" I asked Jebido as I caught up to him.

"You'll hear it before you see it," Jebido said as he motioned to his horse with his chin. "The horses will let us know first, when they catch the scent. Then you'll hear the water."

I nodded my understanding and shifted my bulk in the saddle, wincing as another twinge shot through my bad leg. I watched as a hawk circled high in the air above us, gliding easily as it rode a thermal column upward. Finally I glanced back at Jebido as a thought struck me. "Do you think this is the way King

Jorquin came when he invaded the Piths?" I asked.

"I doubt it," Jebido said. He pointed over the trees. "They probably crossed somewhere to the west." He turned in the saddle and gestured with a thumb northeast. "Over that way somewhere is Corwick Castle, and much further north from there you'll find Gandertown. I talked to Eriz about it and he told me King Jorquin marched on them with three thousand men." Jebido chuckled. "Not that it did them much good. The way Eriz told it, the Piths ran circles around them and they ran home like whipped dogs." He leaned sideways and spat on the ground. "Eriz said that while they fought the Ganders at home, they sent raiders into Southern Ganderland and sacked and pillaged towns and villages all along the border in retaliation." Jebido made a face. "That's the price for underestimating the Piths, I suppose."

"Do you think the Piths can win this war, then?" I asked.

"Maybe," Jebido said. He grimaced. "Either way, I can tell you it's going to get ugly. Eriz told me the raiders targeted the Holy Houses and burnt them all and killed any of the priests and priestesses they could find. Their way of sending a message to The First Son and Daughter I expect."

I frowned at the thought of the Piths firing Holy Houses and killing priests and priestesses. Their ways were so different from ours. Yet in only a few short days I'd come to think of many of them as my friends, which was something, other than Baine and Jebido, I'd had very few of in my life. The destruction of the Holy Houses and murdering of priests and priestesses though, that was something I couldn't forget about, no matter how much I liked the Piths. I told as much to Jebido and he listened patiently while I explained my thoughts.

When I was done, Jebido nodded to himself and then he glanced at me. "I understand that you cannot forgive them for what they've done. Neither can I. And yet, despite their crimes, would it be fair to say that you're content being with them, Hadrack?" he asked.

I looked at him in surprise. I actually hadn't really

thought about it much, but I realized that I was. I grinned at him. "Well, I'd prefer it if we didn't have hundreds of Gandermen breathing down our necks trying to kill us, but yes, I'd say over-all that I am."

Jebido waved an arm around him. "Do you think The First Pair guided you here, then, with these Piths?" he asked. "Giving you happiness and contentment now where they never did so before?"

I frowned, puzzled by the question. "I suppose so," I said weakly. "Why do you ask?"

Jebido sighed and looked away from me, his hooded eyes watching the hawk soar lazily above us. "I just find it curious, is all." He looked back at me. "The Piths believe in the Master and claim He created the heavens and the earth. We believe it was The First Pair." He paused to chuckle dryly. "One of us has to be wrong."

"Well, it's them," I said quickly, starting to feel annoyed at Jebido. "Of course they're wrong."

"Why?" Jebido countered.

"Why what?"

Jebido snorted. "Don't be stupid with me, Hadrack," he said. "You know what I mean. Why are the Piths wrong and we're right?"

"Because," I hesitated, trying to think as Jebido grinned infuriatingly at me.

"Because?" Jebido prompted.

"Because we have to be!" I snapped at him.

Jebido tilted his head back and laughed as I glowered at him. "Well," he finally said once he'd composed himself, "you got me with that one."

"Why all the questions?" I snapped at him. "Don't tell me you're starting to believe in the Master now?"

"Of course not," Jebido said. He rested his fist over his heart. "I know The Mother and The Father created this world." He glanced at me out of the corners of his eyes and I saw one side of his mouth rise in a faint smirk. "Not because it has to be true," he said, banging his fist to his chest several times, "but because I know in here that it's true."

"Then why did you make it sound like you didn't?" I protested.

"I'm just trying to understand Their plan," Jebido said. He lifted his hands, palms up. "As you said, the Piths burned our Holy Houses and killed the priests and priestesses. They believe it to be justified, but to us it's an unforgivable act. They should be our enemies, not our friends, and yet, I can't help but feel we've been guided here for some purpose. I just can't figure out what it might be."

"Maybe The First Pair want us to try to convert the Piths," I said jokingly as I tried to lighten the mood.

Jebido shook his head seriously, clearly having missed the joke. "I'm no priest and neither are you. That can't be it." He glanced at me. "You do realize if we actually get out of this, that we're going to have a big problem?"

"Such as?" I asked.

"Such as the Ganders have sworn to destroy the Piths and the Master along with them and the Piths have sworn to do the same to the Gandermen and anything to do with The First Pair. A war is coming, and from the sounds of things, neither side is willing to let the other survive." He waggled his thumb between us. "That leaves you, me and Baine in a very awkward situation."

"I hadn't really given that much thought," I admitted.

"Perhaps it's time you did," Jebido said.

The sun was now high in the sky and, even beneath the intermittent shade of the trees, I could feel the heat building as sweat rolled from beneath my helmet and ran down the back of my neck. We rode about five feet from the edge of the forest, navigating as best we could around long dead branches and here and there the occasional rotted stump. Jebido's horse suddenly whinnied softly and its ears swivelled forward. My horse's ears twitched as well. "They smell water," Jebido said. "We're probably at least several miles from the river. As soon as we hear the water we'll stop and wait." I nodded my understanding and in another ten minutes or so, the first faint sounds of running water reached us. Jebido motioned us further into the shadows of the trees and we halted under a massive elm. I glanced behind me, looking for the Piths, but so far there was no sign of anyone.

I fingered the black and yellow surcoat that lay over my armour. "Do you really think they'll believe we're scouts?" I asked Jebido.

Jebido slapped at a bug that landed on the back of his neck. He glanced at his hand and made a face, then wiped his hand on his trousers. "I don't see why not," he said. "We've got the watchword and they have no reason not to believe us."

I adjusted Wolf's Head on my hip and eased my sore leg out of the stirrup and let it dangle, sighing at the relief. "Maybe we should dismount for a while?" I suggested. "Give the horses a rest."

Jebido shook his head. "No. We might have to move fast. Best to stay mounted. It could make all the difference."

"It would make a bigger difference for my ass if we got down," I grumbled unhappily. I hesitated as I looked behind us again, thinking this time that I'd seen movement near one of the larger hills in the distance. I stared at the spot and then nodded to myself. I had seen something. "Looks like we have company," I said as three riders on horseback became visible, picking their way around the hill.

"Is it them?" Jebido asked as he shielded his eyes with his hand and squinted.

"Looks like it," I said as I studied the approaching riders. I saw a flash of golden hair in the sunlight and recognized the slim form of Ania. Beside her rode the thick body of Tato and in front of them the great bulk of Eriz. "It's them," I said with a grin. Jebido nodded and he kicked his heels against his horse's sides, guiding it out from beneath the shadows of the trees and into the sunlight. I followed suit and we rode for about twenty paces until we were sure that the others could see us and then we stopped, waiting for them.

"Greetings, brothers," Eriz said as the three Piths rode up

to us.

"You two look like you're nice and relaxed," Ania said with a smile. She wiped the sweat off her brow and adjusted the bow slung across her shoulder. A quiver full of white-feathered arrows sat strapped to her back within easy reach of her right hand.

"Have any trouble?" Jebido asked.

Eriz snorted. "Those fools rode right into our laps. Their heads were off their necks before they even knew what was happening." He removed his helmet and ran his fingers through his sweat-slick hair. "Any trouble on your end?"

"Nothing," Jebido said. "We haven't seen anyone all morning." He gestured over his shoulder with a thumb. "I'm guessing the river is about a mile or so from here judging by the sounds of it."

Eriz put his helmet back on, looked to the south and nodded. "Probably about right. The Sword of the King and the others are two miles back." Eriz pointed to the southeast. "You two cut across that way until you see the river and then follow it west until you reach the bridge. I want the Ganders to think you're coming from the pass."

"That makes good sense," Jebido said with a curt nod.

"Tato and Ania will return to the Sword and let him know all is well," Eriz said. He turned to Tato. "Guide them to this point and wait until you hear from me."

"Of course, brother," Tato said.

Eriz turned back to Jebido and me. "In the meantime, I'll get as close to the bridge as I can and wait until the Gandermen leave. Make sure they understand they have to move quickly. The longer we sit out here waiting for them to leave, the better the chances are that someone will discover us."

"And if they don't fall for it?" I asked. I had visions of other scouts riding up just as we we're telling the Ganders the lie and revealing us as imposters.

"Then they'll kill you and Tato will win his wager," Eriz simply said. I glanced at Tato and he just shrugged back at me.

"Either way," Eriz continued, "we will be attacking that bridge within the hour."

"Then we'd better be on our way," Jebido said as he yanked on the reins and turned his horse.

"May the Master watch over you both," Ania said. I smiled and nodded to her as I followed Jebido and she called out to my retreating back, "Oh, and just so you know, Hadrack, I bet on you to fool them, so I'd appreciate it if you don't go and get yourself killed."

I glanced back at her over my shoulder and laughed. "I'll do my very best," I said. I turned in the saddle and followed Jebido as we headed out at a trot, moving southeast. The sun was beating down on us mercilessly now, as the noon-day heat baked everything beneath it. I caught up to Jebido and we rode silently for a while. I could see rivulets of sweat trickling down his temples to his cheeks, then following his jawline before dropping to stain his surcoat. I wiped at my own brow and grabbed my canteen, offering some to Jebido, but he just shook his head. I took a long drink of the tepid water, then replaced the stopper and returned it to my saddlebags. Ahead of us our view was cut off by a small forest of towering white pines and when we reached it, we guided our horses through the trees cautiously. Sounds of rushing water reached us clearly now, echoing through the trees and the pace of the horses picked up as they headed eagerly for the river. Jebido moved right, around a crumbling old oak tree and I guided my horse around it to the left. I cursed under my breath as a large spider web spun in a wide net over several branches enveloped me like a cloak and I fought to pull the sticky threads from my face. Jebido glanced over his shoulder and he chuckled as I glowered at him, daring him to say anything. He stopped his horse and waited patiently as I extricated myself from the web.

"I can see the banks of the river through the trees," Jebido said, having to practically yell over the noise of the rushing water as he looked to the south.

I wiped the remnants of the web on my trouser leg and

nodded as I guided my horse close to him. The forest line ended twenty yards from where we sat and beyond that, a wide-open section of green grass sloped toward a rock-covered bank that led to a wide river seething with white-foaming rapids. On the far side of the river an equally rocky bank rose up steeply and then met a mixed wall of white birch forest and stone cliffs.

Jebido looked at me and he took in a deep breath. "Are you ready for this?"

"Ready," I nodded as I gripped my reins tighter.

"As soon as we break from the trees, let your horse go and try to keep up," Jebido said. He studied me for a moment, then added, "Whatever happens, let me do the talking." He turned away and then looked back at me. "And keep that temper in check. Got it?"

"Got it," I said, feeling my pulse quicken.

Jebido nodded and he guided his horse through the trees with me close behind him. We stepped out into the sunlight and Jebido immediately shouted and kicked his heels against his horse's flanks, startling it into a gallop. I did the same, barely noticing the pain in my leg as my horse seemed to explode beneath me, racing after Jebido's quickly retreating form. From in front of me I could hear Jebido calling out, "Ha!" over and over again as he held his horse's reins with his left hand and slapped its rump with his right. Every few seconds or so he'd look back over his shoulder, staring past me before turning away and urging his horse onward. I knew it was an act, but, even so, I found myself emulating him, almost expecting to see a horde of bloodthirsty warriors directly behind us in hot pursuit. We reached a stand of short scrub brush and our horses burst through it without slowing, both Jebido and I ignoring the clawing branches as they sought to hold us back. Once through, we urged our horses onward down a steep slope toward the bridge that I could see rising in the distance. It was made of stone and, though it spanned the river at its narrowest point, it was still massive and seemed to go on forever. I counted twenty-two arches built on thick stone piers. Each arch was roughly twenty-feet across and probably twice that in height. At both ends of the bridge rose a towering square stone gatehouse two stories high with rounded turrets at each of the corners. Long yellow banners with the black stag insignia draped down from the turrets of both gatehouses and they fluttered lazily in the breeze coming off the river. I could see four or five archers watching us warily from the battlements of the closest gatehouse. Half a mile from the far bank of the river rose the dark mass of the unfinished garrison Einhard had told us about.

I turned my attention back to the gatehouse, where four horsemen sat talking in front of two arched doors that lay open. A heavy grilled portcullis made of wood and lined with metal hung suspended above the doors along two grooves cut in the stone. I followed Jebido as he headed directly for the mounted men, shouting and waving his arms. The Ganders swung toward us as Jebido pointed behind him urgently. "The pass!" he shouted. "The Piths are attacking the pass!" One of the mounted men guided his horse a few steps forward. He wore a fur-lined cloak over his armour and surcoat and the cloak was clasped around his shoulders by a large Blazing Sun pendant. His eyes were brown and suspicious beneath his helm and his mouth, barley seen through his thick grey beard, was turned down with disapproval. Be careful, Jebido, I thought to myself as we came to a shuddering halt in a cloud of dust ten paces from the mounted men. "The Piths!" Jebido repeated, panting as he pointed to the east. "They're attacking the pass!"

The man with the grey beard frowned. "Have you forgotten protocol, soldier?" he asked.

"But the Piths," Jebido said weakly. He glanced at the unfriendly faces watching us. "They're overrunning the pass as we speak!"

Several of the mounted men snickered and even the man with the grey beard almost smiled. "While I doubt that very much," he said as he straightened in his saddle, "first things first. My name is Rand Lassan and I am the gate commander here. What is the watchword?"

Jebido slapped his hand against the top of his helmet. "Of course," he said. "My apologies, Sir." He shrugged his shoulders and grinned, looking very much like a simpleton I thought, as I admired his performance. "The watchword is Tyro."

"Very well," Lassan said. He flicked his eyes from Jebido, to me, then back to Jebido. "What's this about then?"

"As I said, Sir," Jebido replied. "The Piths have attacked the pass." He hooked a thumb at me. "Hadrack and I barely got away. They were everywhere."

Lassan frowned beneath his helmet. "We expected that," he said with a shrug. He turned and glanced at the man nearest him, a brown-haired youth with a thin beard and scarred face. "Dolon, take seventy-five men and go support our men at the pass as we discussed." The scar-faced youth turned to go and Lassan added, "Make sure every one of those Pith bastards is dead, understood?"

Dolon grinned. "Understood."

"Do you think that will be enough men, Sir?" Jebido asked timidly.

"Eh?" Lassan muttered, turning his hard eyes on Jebido. "Why wouldn't it be?" he said dismissively. "There's only eighty or so of these Piths and some of them are women. They can't break through the pass and we'll box them in and wipe them out."

"But there's more than that!" I blurted out. Jebido gave me a look of warning, but I ignored him.

"What do you mean there's more?" Lassan growled.

"They appeared out of nowhere," I said breathlessly. "Hundreds and hundreds of them and they joined up with the others and rode for the pass. We tried to get around them to warn our men at the pass, but the Piths kept chasing after us until we had to flee, so we decided to come here. Isn't that right, Jebido?" I said, glancing at my friend.

Jebido scratched his hooked nose and nodded. "As sure as Mother Above is watching over us, it is," he said enthusiastically. "There's got to be almost a thousand of the screaming heathens out there!"

Lassan pursed his lips and his eyes narrowed as he thought. Finally he seemed to come to a decision and he turned to Dolon. "Roll out the entire garrison!" he snapped. "And send someone to Prince Tyro's camp and let him know what's happening."

"Do we ask him for help?" Dolon asked with a blank look.

Lassan made a face. "Just let Prince Tyro know what's happening and carefully suggest to his Highness that it would be wise to send men to reinforce the pass from the south. Make sure that he understands the urgency of the situation." He smashed his fist into his palm. "I don't know where all these new Piths came from, but I swear by The Mother and The Father that not one of those murdering bastards will get away!" Lassan turned to us as Dolon headed through the gatehouse doors at a gallop, his horse's hooves clacking loudly against the cobblestones as he disappeared from view. "You two will come with us when we ride out."

I opened my mouth to say something, what I can't imagine, but Jebido cut me off with a hard look and then he smiled at Lassan. "We wouldn't have it any other way," he said. Lassan barely nodded at us and then he swung down from the saddle, barking orders to his men. Jebido also dismounted and I did the same, hardly able to contain myself as I looked at Jebido desperately.

"What are we going to do?" I whispered fiercely as I glanced over my shoulder at Lassan. "We can't go with them!"

Jebido shrugged and I automatically followed him as he walked closer to the river before stopping to stare out over the fast-flowing water. Finally, he handed me the reins of his horse and undid his trousers, pissing all over a small, thorny-looking weed with a spiked purple flower at its head that grew stubbornly among the rocks. "What choice do we have?" he asked as he finished and retied his trousers. "If we try to run now they'll know something is wrong." He removed his helmet to wipe the sweat from his forehead and glanced at the sky. "Don't worry,

Hadrack, I'll think of something."

We both turned and watched as the gatehouse doors on the far bank swung open and riders emerged into the sunlight, riding three abreast. Each man held a glittering lance with a yellow banner at the haft and each was dressed in mail and wore the king's banner on his chest. They pounded across the bridge and behind them men holding long pikes trotted on foot in disciplined rows. Lassan mounted up and as the first riders passed through the gatehouse he kicked his horse into motion ahead of them. He pointed at us as he passed. "You two fall in behind."

Jebido nodded to him and swung into the saddle, waiting as I clumsily pulled myself up onto my horse. We sat there as grim-faced riders passed us by, row after row of them moving at a fast trot, then fell into step behind the last of the mounted men. Behind us the foot soldiers were already falling behind as one of the riders in front of us turned in his saddle to grin at us in a friendly fashion. I realized he couldn't be any older than I was.

"Are we really going to finally get a chance to fight the Piths?" the youth asked us eagerly.

"Sure looks that way," Jebido muttered dryly.

"Mother's tit!" the young Ganderman said happily. "It's about time!"

"Careful what you wish for," Jebido said to him, but the youth had already turned away and he didn't seem to have heard.

We'd already lost sight of the bridge and were following a well-worn trail along the river, riding near the pine forest along the crest of the ground before it started to slope down toward the water. The foot soldiers behind us were nowhere to be seen by now and Jebido gave me a warning look before he called out to the young soldier in front of us, "Hey!" he shouted over the roar of the river. Jebido pulled up on the reins of his horse and it faltered, slowing down and I did the same as the Ganderman circled back to us.

"What's wrong?" the youth asked as Jebido dismounted.

Jebido reached down and lifted his horse's right foreleg,

bending it back to stare at its hoof. He snorted in disgust and let the leg go as he straightened up. "Looks like I've thrown a shoe."

"Ah," the Ganderman said, not looking that concerned. He glanced over his shoulder at the disappearing column of mounted men and it was obvious that he wished that he hadn't stopped.

"Don't worry about it," Jebido said, waving his hand at him. "Go join the others. It doesn't look too bad and this big lad with me is the son of a smith. He'll have this fixed in no time and we'll be right behind you."

"That's wonderful," the youth said, glancing at me and looking hugely relieved. "You better hurry up, though. I can't promise I'll leave you any Piths to kill if you take too long." Jebido laughed and waved in acknowledgement and the young Ganderman spun his horse around and galloped away.

"Not bad," I said as Jebido hauled himself back up into the saddle.

"Smart and handsome is what my mother always used to say about me," Jebido said with a smile.

I grinned back at him. "Well, she was half right."

Jebido laughed at that and then motioned us into the trees as we could hear the marching feet of the foot soldiers rapidly approaching. We waited impatiently as they trudged past us and then finally, once they were gone, we returned to the open. "Now what?" I asked.

"Now we head back to the bridge and take command of that gatehouse."

"How many men do you think are in there?" I asked.

Jebido shrugged as we turned and headed back the way we'd come. "I've no idea, but chances are most of them will be archers, which will make it easier." We rode back as quickly we could and Jebido motioned forward with his chin as we pushed our way through the stand of shrubs and the bridge came into view. "We'll find out soon enough either way," he said. "As soon as we get close enough, ride your horse inside and kill anyone who tries to stop you."

I nodded that I understood and stood up in the stirrups, pleased to note that my leg only protested a little bit as I glanced to the north. I could see a faint cloud of dust rising and I knew Eriz had returned to Einhard and told him that the ruse had worked.

"They're coming," I said to Jebido as I sat back down in the saddle. Jebido nodded, but said nothing as we guided our horses down the steep slope that led to the bridge and then we both halted our horses in dismay. The gatehouse doors were closed!

Chapter 9: The Bridge

"Shit!" I hissed under my breath as we drew closer to the gatehouse. I saw a single archer watching us from the ramparts as we trotted forward. "What do we do now?"

"We get them to open the gate," Jebido said calmly out of the side of his mouth.

"Einhard will be here any minute," I whispered back.

"I'm well aware of that, Hadrack," Jebido grunted. We stopped our horses about twenty feet from the gate and looked up at the archer peering down at us. "Open up!" Jebido barked at the man.

The archer shook his head. "Can't do it."

Jebido blew air out of his nose angrily. "What do you mean you can't do it?" he demanded. "We need to get inside." I glanced nervously over my shoulder, expecting to see the Piths charging toward us. Thankfully there was no sign of them yet, but the dust cloud was getting nearer and I cleared my throat, trying to warn Jebido and hoping that the archer would stay focused on us and not notice the dust.

"The Commander said to keep the gate locked and not let anyone in," the archer said with a shrug.

"He didn't mean us you simpleton!" Jebido shouted up at him. "He meant the Piths you fool! Do we look like piss-drinking Piths to you?"

The archer studied us thoughtfully and I rolled my eyes and grit my teeth. "No, you don't," the man finally said. "Just the same, I can't let you in."

Jebido flung his hands up in exasperation. "Fine, then you can explain to Captain Lassan when he gets back why he didn't have his favorite sword." Jebido glanced at me and shrugged as I looked at him in surprise. The story was weak. He knew it and I knew it, but the Piths would be here any time now and we needed that gate open, so it would have to do.

"His sword?" the archer muttered, looking confused. The head and upper body of another archer appeared, then a third man leaned over to look down at us.

"What did he say?" one of the new men asked.

"He said Lassan forgot his sword and sent them back to fetch it," the first archer replied.

"He was wearing his sword when he left," the third man volunteered. "I saw it."

"Are you sure?" the first archer asked. "I don't remember seeing him wearing it."

Jebido and I shared a look, as, for the moment it seemed we'd been forgotten as the three men argued over whether or not Lassan had actually taken his sword with him. "Not that sword!" Jebido finally shouted, cutting them off. "His other one."

"Eh?" the first archer called down. "He has another one?"

"Sweet Mother's tit!" Jebido swore up at them as he dismounted. "The one with the black and gold hilt he keeps in the garrison you blithering imbeciles! Surely you know which one I mean? The sword he keeps for special occasions. That's the one he wants. Now open the doors and be quick about it! If we don't return with it before we fight the Piths it'll be someone's head!" Jebido glowered up at them as he stood with his hands on his hips. "And I swear by The Mother and The Father that it won't be our heads rolling in the dirt, it'll be yours!"

"All right! All right!" the first archer called down. "There's no need for that now. I'll tell them to let you in!"

"Finally!" Jebido grunted. I dismounted and stood next to Jebido and he glanced at me. "Be ready," he said. "Just follow my lead and don't do anything until I do." I nodded as we heard a thud and a screech and then the great wooden doors swung slowly inward.

From where we stood, the entrance was cast in deep shadow and we hurried forward, leading our horses through the high archway. I glanced up at the massive portcullis with its sharpened spikes hanging above us as we passed under it and I involuntarily shuddered at the thought of being pinned beneath those wicked points. A soldier stood to either side of the doors holding them open for us and I sighed in relief at the coolness inside the building after the scorching heat of the sun. The men-at-arms immediately closed the doors behind us and we blinked in the gloom and paused, waiting for our eyes to adjust. Torches burned weakly along the walls and it took a few moments before I was able to make out the faces of the Gandermen. I was pleased to see that there were just the two of them. Above our heads rose a high-vaulted ceiling made from cut stone and supported by a network of oak beams. I noticed large circular holes had been cut here and there through the stone and wood, giving the men above a good view of the gatehouse floor below them. Though I'd never seen them before, I knew that these were called murder holes, as Jebido had told me about them once. He'd explained that a common tactic used to snare an attacking party was to leave the castle or gatehouse doors open, inviting them in. Once the invaders entered, the portcullis at each end would then be dropped, trapping them inside, while from above the defenders would shoot arrows or throw rocks or whatever else they could find down onto the helpless men through the murder holes.

"This way," one of the soldiers grunted disinterestedly, cutting off my thoughts as he motioned to a set of doors at the far end of the gatehouse identical to the ones we'd just passed through. The man was short and thin, with a pock-marked face and long yellow teeth that gave him a vaguely rat-like appearance.

"One moment," Jebido said, raising a hand to halt the soldier. Jebido gave me a warning glance and I tensed, knowing what was about to happen. I casually let go of my horse's reins and turned my head, marking the other man's position in my mind. The Ganderman was tall and lanky and stood three paces back from me by the doors. He'd just finished sliding the huge oak bar into place and he nodded to me and grinned black stumps. I noticed that the bar was supported by a metal plate about six-inches wide and almost an inch thick, and that it slid closed through a set of four iron brackets. I casually rested my right hand on the hilt of Wolf's Head as I nodded back to the man in a friendly fashion.

"As you probably heard, we're looking for a sword," Jebido told the rat-faced soldier. "Sort of like this one." Jebido drew his sword and showed it to him.

The Ganderman glanced briefly at the blade Jebido held casually in his hand and then shrugged. "Why should I care?" he asked with a bored look.

"You make a very good point," Jebido conceded. "Just like this sword here," he continued, "has a very good point." Jebido stabbed outward, punching through the man-at-arm's mail and reaching almost halfway up the blade as its tip burst out his back. The rat-faced man's eyes bulged and he gasped in surprise and instantly collapsed. I heard the second Ganderman cry out in shock and I slapped my horse's rump, startling it out of my way as I drew Wolf's Head from its scabbard and turned on him. The soldier fumbled to draw his sword, cursing as the hilt caught in his surcoat just as I slashed deeply into his neck, silencing him. A cry arose from the floor above us and I thought at first we'd been discovered as an archer came sprinting down the stone staircase that rose in a spiral to the right of the doors.

"Piths!" the archer cried out as he jumped the last two steps to land heavily on the cobblestones. "They're attacking!" the man shouted, pointing to the closed doors with one hand, while holding a large bow in the other. I realized it was the first archer we'd spoken to earlier and his face sagged almost comically when he saw us standing over the two dead bodies of the men-at-arms. "But?" the archer said in confusion.

Jebido took two great strides toward him and he ran him through, barely giving the dead man a second glance as he slumped to the floor. On the other side of the doors we could hear the Piths as they shouted their war cries and advanced on the gatehouse. "Get the doors open!" Jebido grunted to me. He glanced up at the second floor. "I'll take care of the rest of them." I nodded and Jebido sprinted up the staircase as I ran for the doors. A round iron ring the size of my hand was set into the bar and I pulled on it, drawing the heavy beam backward out of the brackets. I swung the doors open and had just a moment to register what was happening, before I flung myself backward and to the side just as a horde of angry-faced Piths using a thick tree as a battering ram came racing toward me. Eriz and Einhard were at the front of the ram and both of them looked shocked as they plunged past me through the suddenly open doors and into the gatehouse. The Piths momentum took them more than half-way across the width of the building before they were finally able to gain control and stop.

Einhard shouted for them to lower the ram and he turned to face me. "That was something of a surprise," he said with a laugh. He came toward me and hugged me to his chest. "A little warning next time would be nice."

"I'll try to remember that," I said with a grunt as he crushed me in his arms.

"You're unhurt?" he asked as he put his hands on my shoulders and studied me.

"Not a scratch," I reassured him.

"We thought you'd failed," Einhard said, his face turning serious.

"No," I said with a smile. "Just delayed a bit." Behind me Jebido appeared on the stairs and he grinned at us as he descended. I saw a long slash dripping blood along his cheek, but, other than that, he seemed unharmed. More Piths were coming through the open doors on horseback and Einhard and I hurriedly stepped to the side to let them pass. The Piths had abandoned the wagons, I noted, and the wounded were riding as best they could, some of them tied to their saddles to keep them from falling. I saw Baine enter with Alesia, Ania, Megy and the rest of the Pith women.

"Is that everyone?" Einhard demanded.

"Yes, brother," Eriz said as he stood in the open doorway

and peered outside.

"Close and bolt the doors," Einhard commanded. Eriz nodded and he and Tato slammed the doors shut before Eriz levered the oak bar into place and locked us in.

"I'll drop the portcullis," Jebido said, turning to run back up the stairs to the second floor. Within moments we could hear a rattling coming from outside and then a loud crash that vibrated the floor beneath our feet. Jebido returned back down the stairs and nodded to Einhard. "Just in case anyone tries to get in behind us, that'll make things difficult for them," he said.

Einhard turned to Alesia as she and the other Pith women dismounted. "Take your sisters up top and keep a look out until we move."

"Of course," Alesia said. She was dressed in leather armour with a cloak lined with wolf's fur thrown casually over one shoulder. A quiver of arrows lay slung over her back and she carried a long bow in her left hand. She gave me a quick glance as she passed me and I was struck again by the rawness of her beauty as she ordered the other women up the stairs. Ania stood with Tato, and I saw her put her hand out and grin as Tato placed several silver fingers into her palm. Ania laughed and winked at me before she tucked the fingers into her tunic and then followed the other Pith women up the stairs. Baine waved to us and flung a leg over his saddle and nimbly dismounted, pausing to hand the reins of his horse to one of several Piths that were trying to corral the animals into one corner of the gatehouse, before he headed our way.

"You two had us all worried there," Baine said. He hooked a thumb behind him. "Everyone but Tato, I guess."

"He should have known better than to make a losing bet like that," Jebido said.

"A good thing he lost," Einhard said. He gestured to the battering ram, which was as thick at the base as my waist and perhaps as much as thirty-feet long. "I'm not sure our ram would have survived trying to break through this gate and the one on the other side of the river as well." I noticed the Piths had notched the end of the ram like an axe head and they had trimmed the branches all along it, cutting them off two feet from the stump to give them handholds. It was crude, but to my eye looked like it might be effective. Einhard cupped his hands around his mouth and he called up to the battlements above us, "Anything, Alesia?"

Alesia's pale face appeared at one of the murder holes. "Nothing to the north, but I can see some troops moving around behind the gatehouse on the other side."

"How many?"

"No more than twenty I'd guess."

"Are the gates closed?"

"Yes," Alesia said. "They know we're here."

"Can't say I'm surprised," Einhard muttered. "Are there archers on the battlements?" he asked Alesia.

"Ten or so is all I can see," Alesia confirmed.

"Excellent!" Einhard said with a satisfied grin. Eriz and Tato joined us and Einhard removed his winged helmet to scratch at his scalp, then he thrust it back on his head determinedly. "Eriz, when we attack the other gatehouse with the ram, you and the others will follow behind us on horseback. The moment we break through the doors, you charge in and kill the defenders."

"And our sisters?" Eriz asked.

"They'll follow behind us on horseback as well," Einhard said. "We'll need their arrows to keep those Gander archers at bay so we can get to the doors."

"There's a small armoury up top," Jebido said, gesturing with his thumb above us. "Some swords and shields and plenty of arrows the women can use."

"Good," Einhard nodded as he gestured to the southern doors. "Open them up. I want to see those Gander bastards." Two Piths ran to the far doors and unbarred them as we followed Einhard to stand in the opening and peer down the length of the bridge at the other gatehouse. Heat shimmered across the rough cobblestones of the bridge and from where I stood, I could see archers watching us from the upper battlements. The heavy yellow stag banners were now hanging limply along the ramparts in the still air as Einhard took several steps out into the blazing sunlight. His golden helmet and armour instantly gleamed like a brilliant beacon and when the Ganders saw him they started to yell, waving their bows above their heads and encouraging us to come out. Even from where we stood, we could clearly hear the insults drifting across the bridge.

Einhard turned to us and smiled wryly. "Bastards are eager to die, I see," he said with a chuckle as he glanced at Tato. "Hadrack will take Eriz's place on the ram."

Tato just nodded as Jebido, Baine and I moved to stand beside Einhard in the sunlight. Curious, I crossed to the side of the bridge and supported my body with my hands against the rough stone as I stared down at the surging water fifty feet below me. A wooden dock rose on the southern shoreline, jutting thirty feet out into the river and was supported by heavy wood pilings stained dark from the water. A narrow road of rounded stone wound its way up the embankment and then curved behind the far gatehouse before leading to a massive garrison that stood dominating a hill half a mile to the south. I studied the fortress, noticing that the entire northern and eastern walls were incomplete and rose no higher than a man's eyes. The Gander's had reinforced the unfinished walls with a wooden palisade, which seemed quite flimsy to me compared to the heavy stone; stone I realized with a grimace that I had probably dug from the earth with my own two hands. A wide ditch bare of any trees or shrubs and almost full with murky brown water surrounded the garrison. The road ended in a high ramp at the edge of the ditch that sat facing the open gates of the garrison. A heavy timber drawbridge supported by thick chains lay open in invitation where it spanned the ditch and rested on the ramp.

"You'll be in range of their arrows before you even get halfway across," I heard Jebido mutter as he studied the far gatehouse critically. I turned back and joined them as Jebido suddenly frowned and shielded his eyes. "Mother's tit!" he cursed.

"They've dropped the portcullis."

Einhard shaded his eyes and stared at the gatehouse, and then nodded. "So they have. Is that going to be a problem?"

Jebido grimaced and glanced back at the battering ram. "Breaking through those doors with that is one thing, but the portcullis is designed to withstand a battering ram."

"Are you saying it can't be done?"

Jebido shook his head. "No, it can be done. It'll just take a lot longer is all."

Einhard just shrugged. "It can't be helped."

"Einhard!" Alesia shouted down to us. Einhard frowned at the note of urgency in her voice and he stepped back into the gatehouse. He looked up at her face thrust through the murder hole. "Riders coming from the east!" she said.

"The Master is surely testing us today," Einhard muttered to himself. "Are there many?" he asked his wife.

"Plenty of the bastards," Alesia confirmed, "and still more coming behind on foot."

"Archers too?"

"Could be."

Einhard nodded his understanding. "Keep them back from the doors."

"It will be done," Alesia said grimly before disappearing from sight.

Einhard turned to Jebido. "It looks like our ruse was only halfway successful. You said there were shields in the armoury, if I recall?"

"Yes," Jebido said.

"The big Gander shields like we saw at the quarry?"

"The same," Jebido agreed with a dry smile. I realized why he was smiling, as the bigger, heavier Gander shields would instantly offer us better protection on the ram than the small, round Pith shields we all had strapped to our backs.

"Good," Einhard said. He gestured to Tato. "Go upstairs with your brothers and get the shields." Tato nodded and Einhard cupped his hands around his mouth. "Alesia?" Within moments Alesia reappeared. "What are they doing?" he asked her.

"The same thing we did," Alesia said with a snort. "Making a battering ram."

Einhard nodded, not looking surprised at all. "Leave three of your sisters up top to give them something to worry about. Bring the rest down." He glanced at me as Alesia's face disappeared. "At least they'll have the same problem here as we do with the other one."

I nodded to him as Tato and the other warriors reappeared with the big Gander shields on their arms. Tato silently handed one to me and one to Einhard. I glanced out the doorway at the far gatehouse that seemed to be swaying in the distance, though I knew it was just an illusion from the heat. For just a moment one of the banners flapped weakly as a momentary gust of playful wind toyed with it before disappearing, leaving the banner to hang limply. I was thinking about us running across the bridge carrying the ram and trying to break through the portcullis and gatehouse doors while arrows rained down from above, when suddenly an idea began to form in my mind. I glanced at the long battering ram, then back to the gatehouse. Would it work? I wondered. I felt excitement rise in me as I again looked down at the ram. It just might, I realized.

"I have an idea," I said, causing Einhard to pause in mid-step as he moved to the front of the ram. He turned and stared at me, waiting calmly with a look of interest on his face. Thinking back on it now, these many years later, one of the things that always struck me as surprising about the Piths was the deep respect they had for every member of their tribe. Each man or woman was listened to seriously, regardless of their stature or the situation, and rarely if ever ridiculed for their opinion. I didn't know that at the time, of course, and I felt a moment of anxiety, hesitating to put into words my idea as the Piths just stared at me in expectant silence.

"Well?" Einhard finally said with a smile. "Am I to guess or will you make it easy and just tell me?"

"My father once told me to use my brain first and only

use my fists when all else had failed," I said, trying to gather my thoughts.

"Sound advice," Einhard nodded. "Your father was a wise man."

Behind us the women came hurrying down the stairs, most, if not all of them, with two or more quivers of arrows slung over their shoulders. I noticed Ania wasn't with them and I felt a momentary jolt of fear for her, as I knew she'd offered to stay behind and guard our backs. I saw Megy move to stand off to the side near the wall with a look of uncertainty on her face and I gave her a quick smile of encouragement.

Einhard glanced at the approaching women and then turned back to me. "I don't see how that sound advice can help us today, though, my friend."

I pointed down to the battering ram. "What if instead of using this like a fist, we use it like wings?" Einhard frowned, while around him the other Piths were muttering among themselves, clearly confused.

"What are you jabbering about?" Baine whispered beside me out of the side of his mouth.

I ignored him and turned to Jebido. "Will we be able break through the portcullis with this on the first rush?" I asked him.

"Not a chance," Jebido said with a quick shake of his head. "It's made of solid oak and reinforced with iron. Because it's set into the walls of the gatehouse, you can't just burst it open like you would the doors. We need to bash it apart, and that will probably take four or five tries. That's if we're lucky."

"I thought as much," I said, feeling confident now in my idea as I turned back to Einhard. "And how many men will we lose trying?"

"That can't be helped," Einhard said as he glanced around the room. "We all know the risks. If we don't get through, then we all die anyway."

The Piths were nodding in agreement with Einhard, but I pressed on regardless. "What I'm suggesting is we rush the gates just like we planned." I gestured to the female Piths who were listening intently. "The women will support us, also as planned, but when we get to the gate, instead of ramming into it, we flip the ram up on its end." I showed them what I meant, using my arm as the ram and holding it out and then flipping it up at an angle. I turned and pointed to the far gatehouse. "You see that banner hanging to the right of the gate?" Everyone turned and looked. "We head for that and lean the ram against the wall right below it and use the cut branches as steps. If we can reach the banner, we can pull ourselves up it and over the ramparts while the Ganders are hiding from our arrows. They won't know what's going on until it's too late."

"Will the banner hold?" Jebido asked doubtfully.

"There's only one way to find out," I said.

The room fell silent as everyone digested the idea and finally Einhard's face broke into a wide grin. "Not even the Master himself would have thought of that!" he exclaimed. He came forward and wrapped me in his arms in a giant bear hug as the Piths cheered. Einhard let me go after almost squeezing the life out of me and he put his hands on his hips. "We will do as Hadrack suggests!" he said confidently. He glanced at Eriz. "As soon as the ram is in place, you and your men will go up and clear the top floor." He turned to Jebido. "How is the portcullis raised?"

"There's a small room off the armoury on the top floor that houses the winch. You'll need at least two men to turn it."

"Good," Einhard nodded, turning back to Eriz. "Get that portcullis up and the gates open as soon as possible so we can get the horses inside." Eriz merely nodded his understanding. "Alesia," Einhard continued, turning to his wife. "Follow them up and guard the ramparts. As soon as we have possession of the gatehouse, send someone back here to get the others. Once we have everyone inside we'll drop the portcullis again to slow those Gander bastards down." He looked around at our faces. "Any questions?" When no one spoke, he grinned and nodded his head. "Then let's do this!" he cried as he moved to the front of the ram on the left side, while I moved to take the right.

"Be careful, Hadrack," I heard Jebido call out as he, Baine and the other Piths mounted up.

I nodded my head, but said nothing as Einhard gave a sharp command and we bent and lifted the ram. With twelve men to lift it, the tree seemed to weigh nothing at all and we surged forward, out into the sunlight. I squinted at the brightness and lowered my head as we started across the bridge at a fast trot, while in the distance, the men on the far ramparts started to jeer at us. My Gander shield was on my left arm and I found if I angled my arm with my elbow jutting up at the sky I could grab the branch fairly securely from above with my left hand while I wrapped my right hand underneath it. This way the rectangular shield was covering most of my body and face and I was just able to peer around the corner to see. Behind us the women and Baine rode their horses in a jagged line across the bridge, while behind them the rest of the able-bodied Piths and wounded followed with the remaining horses in tow. We were almost halfway across the bridge now and several impatient archers loosed arrows at us, which fell well short. The arrows cracked against the cobblestones and ricocheted crazily in all directions and I made a mental note of where they'd landed, knowing that once we reached that spot we'd be in their range.

For the first few moments of the attack I knew we'd have to take the brunt of those arrows, as Einhard had told Alesia to let the Ganders shoot at us until we were closer. Once we were in position, the plan was the women would rush forward and rake the ramparts with arrows to force the Ganders to take cover. We knew they wouldn't stay under cover for long, and that's when we would flip the tree up against the wall.

We were three quarters of the way across the bridge now and I glanced over at Einhard. He saw my look and he grinned at me as his green eyes flashed with excitement beneath his winged helm. He's actually enjoying this, I realized, grinning back at him as I realized that I was too.

An arrow thudded into the head of the ram and another smacked into Einhard's shield and then careened crazily away.

We were in range now and Einhard shouted for more speed, urging us forward as we began to run faster, aiming the ram straight at the massive portcullis blocking the doors. I could see the men clearly on the ramparts now as they leaned over to shoot down on us. I heard a grunt behind me and stole a quick glance over my shoulder to see that Tato had fallen with an arrow through his throat. Our pace faltered slightly, but then the rest of us compensated for Tato's loss and we kept going.

Einhard was grinning like a madman, spittle flying from his mouth as he took great gasps of air into his lungs and finally he shouted, "Now!"

From behind we heard the battle cries of the women rise as they spurred their horses forward and then the sounds of their arrows smacking against the stone battlements. I watched as the Ganders above us ducked beneath the onslaught and we whooped with delight as an arrow caught one of the archer's in the shoulder, spinning him around before he dropped from sight. We were closing in on the gatehouse now and both Einhard and I shared a knowing look. He nodded and gestured with his chin and we shifted away from the doors, aiming now for the wall to the right of the portcullis. Any moment now, I knew, watching as we bore down on the thick stone wall. I bit my lip, thinking Einhard had waited too long, and then he cried out the command to stop. We plunged the head of the ram down and into the ground, while behind us the Piths in the middle broke off and headed to the back of the ram, where together, the rest of the warriors heaved upward. The ram slowly rose to a vertical position as we struggled to keep it in line with the wall, then, at a signal from Einhard, we let it fall toward the gatehouse. The back end of the ram crashed into the wall, causing a great puff of dust and dirt to rise from the stone and we had to move quickly as the cut base of the tree started to slide along the cobblestones. Several of the Piths ran to support the center of the ram and they heaved it back just in time, and then, with all of us grunting and groaning, we lifted it up as high as we could. The ram now lay angled at a steep pitch against the wall, but I realized with dismay that the branches were aligned up and down rather than side to side.

"Turn it!" Einhard urged us as the women continued to pour arrows up at the ramparts. One of the braver Gander archers had chanced taking a look and I saw him peering down at me from directly above my head. His eyes widened in shock as he realized what we were doing, and a shout of warning rose from him before an arrow struck the stone near his face and he gave a frightened squawk and disappeared.

"They know!" I called out to Einhard.

The Piths had just righted the tree so the branches were facing out and without thinking, I cast aside my Gander shield and began clambering up as fast as I could. I heard Einhard call to me but I ignored him. I made it to the top of the ram and I looked up, cursing as I stretched as far as I could but found my fingers still two-feet short from the end the banner. I felt a body pressing close against my legs and I looked down at Einhard, who'd followed me up.

"Get on my shoulders!" he shouted up at me.

I nodded my head and stepped onto his left shoulder, then pushed up with my foot. I heard Einhard grunt below me and I reached upward with my left hand, this time just able to get hold of the banner. I held on as tight as I could and then swung my right hand in an arc and grabbed the banner with it as well. I said a silent prayer to The Mother and The Father that the banner would hold me and then I started to drag myself upward. Hand over hand I pulled my way up, while below me I could hear the Piths cheering me on. A head appeared above me and I realized it was the same archer as before. He was leaning over the parapet no more than five feet above me and I saw him grin as he placed an arrow in his bow and aimed down. There was nowhere for me to hide. I considered just letting go, deciding a fall to the ground was better than an arrow through the head, but then the Ganderman stiffened as an arrow buried itself in his right eye and he collapsed forward, lying draped over the parapet. The bow he'd held fell from his lifeless hands and I had to look away quickly as it cracked across my helmet before plunging to the ground. I glanced down over my right shoulder and grinned my thanks to Alesia where she sat watching me from atop her horse. She grinned back and saluted me with her bow before drawing another arrow and notching it and taking aim at the parapet above me.

I felt a glorious surge of energy rush through my body and I turned back and climbed the rest of the way up, pausing once I'd reached the top to wrap my left hand over the rounded stone of the parapet to support my weight before I let go of the banner with the other. I swung my right arm up and grabbed the parapet, then hauled myself over it in an awkward dive. An arrow whizzed past my head and then cracked against the stone behind me as I landed heavily and I instinctively rolled and then came to my feet while drawing Wolf's Head. Behind me I could hear grunts of effort as someone labored to pull himself up the banner and I knew more Piths were on the way. Gander archers sat huddled all along the parapet walls, pressed into the stone as they waited for a break in the barrage of arrows, while in front of me another archer was crouched down in a covered archway near the top of the stone stairwell that led below into the gatehouse. This man must have been the one who'd just shot at me, I realized, as I noticed he had an arrow embedded in his shoulder. The archer seemed unaware of the shaft jutting out of him, however, as he drew another arrow and swiftly notched it to his bow. I bellowed and rushed at him, slashing out with Wolf's Head and crushing his bow and slicing his left arm off at the elbow. The archer stared down in shock at the stump spurting dark red blood, while behind him I could see a wall of men-at-arms racing up the stairs. I kicked the archer in the chest as hard as I could, sending him careening backward down the stairs and nodded in satisfaction as his tumbling body collided with the soldiers, sending them into disarray.

A narrow passageway led off to my left and another to my right, but I ignored them both and turned back into the open. I bounded to the nearest archer along the wall, who was aiming at Eriz as the big Pith hauled himself over the parapet. A quick slash with my sword and the Ganderman fell with a scream. I continued on, hacking and smashing my way through the archers as Eriz ran to join me. Together, we finished off the last of them and we turned as angry shouts rose up from the stairwell. The men-at-arms had sorted themselves out by now and were pouring up the staircase and out through the archway into the open, screaming in rage. I counted at least ten or more of them holding heavy swords and shields and I could hear even more pounding up the stairs behind them. By now Einhard had jumped over the parapet and he and I shared a quick look. The Pith leader smiled happily at me before he unstrapped his round shield from his back and then dashed toward the Ganders with his sword raised high over his head.

"Kill the bastards!" Einhard cried as he crashed his shield into a Ganderman's face, punching in the man's nose guard.

We ran to support him, the three of us lined up hacking at the Ganders as more Piths came over the wall and joined us. Slowly we pushed the Gandermen back though the archway and to the top of the stairwell. The fighting was desperate and fierce now, men spitting and cursing at each other as the Ganders desperately fought to make room for the soldiers coming up the stairs behind them. The smell of unwashed bodies, piss and shit hung over us all like a cloud as Ganders and Piths screamed and died all around me. I barely noticed as Jebido appeared by my side, and together we forced a huge Gander with a long brown beard and surprisingly tiny eyes backward into the seething mass of men coming up the stairs.

"Finish them!" Einhard cried as he dodged a swung sword and then lashed out with a foot, kicking his attacker along the side of his leg. I heard a snap and the man screamed in agony as he dropped to one knee. His helmet fell off and one of the Piths fighting alongside Einhard swung down with his sword, loping the man's ear off before Einhard finished him with a quick thrust.

"Hadrack!" Jebido cried out in warning.

I'd taken my eyes off the Gander with the long beard for just a moment, thinking he was done for, but somehow he'd regained his balance and he came at me, growling like a man possessed. I managed to bring my shield up to block his sword and the blade slid off the raised iron boss with a screech. Seeing an opening, I lunged forward with Wolf's Head, but the big Gander just laughed and swatted my blade away with his sword, and then he rushed at me with his heavy shield held low in front of him. I had only a moment to brace myself for the impact before he crashed into me, jarring me to the bone. I was flung backward through the archway and I landed heavily with the wind knocked from me as my shield spun away, rolling along the stone floor to come to a halt against the parapet wall. I lifted my sword over my head to block the big Gander's downward thrust that I knew was coming and I kicked out at the man's leg like I'd seen Einhard do. My foot caught him between the legs, higher than I'd intended, but the result was the same and he gasped, doubling up above me. Instantly I sprung to my knees and, with both hands wrapped around the hilt of Wolf's Head, I stabbed upward. The point caught the big Gander at the base of the throat and I pushed hard, severing cartilage and bone before my blade burst out the other side. The man sagged above me and I almost gagged on the smell of his fetid breath as I struggled to hold him up before finally I managed to shove him aside.

"You like to live dangerously," Jebido muttered as he offered me his hand.

I grinned up at him and accepted his help as I got to my feet, then turned to watch as lithe Pith women carrying their bows over their shoulders poured over the rampart wall. Within moments there were at least five of them, led by Alesia, and then Baine's grinning face appeared along the parapet and he rolled nimbly over the stone and landed cat-like on the floor of the gatehouse.

"Out of the way!" Alesia commanded as she and the rest of the archers brushed past us to spread out in a semi-circle around the archway. "Einhard!" Alesia shouted as the archers drew their bows.

Einhard glanced over his shoulder as he fought and he grinned when he saw her. He gave a quick shouted command and the Piths instantly fell back and ducked into the passageways, leaving the surviving Gandermen open to the Pith arrows.

"Now!" Alesia cried. Six bowstrings hummed in unison and several of the Gandermen screamed and fell, writhing in agony as the metal-barbed arrowheads pierced their armour and flesh. "Again!" Alesia called. I stood and watched in awe as the Pith women moved with practised ease, notching and letting fly arrow after arrow, decimating the Ganders relentlessly. Baine stood in the middle of the line, and though he wasn't as fast as the Piths, he still managed to shoot one arrow for every two the Piths did. How accurate he might have been, I can't say, though I figured even I could have hit such easy targets as the boxed-in Ganders on the stairs. Within moments it was done, and, save for one Gander who had turned and fled back down the stairs, the rest lay dead or dying draped all along the length of the stone steps.

"Move!" Alesia ordered, motioning the archers to spread out along the southern ramparts. She looked down over the edge. "The spineless bastards are running like rabbits," she spat as she aimed and shot downward.

"They always run!" Einhard said with a grin. He waved his sword toward the stairs. "Follow me! Kill any who stand in our way!"

"Where's that winch?" Eriz grunted at Jebido as the rest of the Piths rushed down the stairs.

"This way," Jebido said, heading along the left passageway.

Eriz and I followed him past an open doorway, where I caught a quick glimpse of swords, shields and spears, before he turned into a second doorway leading into a room lit by bright sunlight coming through a slot cut through the stone along the northern wall. A block of granite several feet wide and long lay on the floor, and mounted to this was a metal winch with an iron handle twice as long as my arm. A rope thicker than my wrist was attached to the winch and rose above us, where it looped over a pulley and then disappeared into the wall through a rectangular hole in the stone. Eriz grabbed the handle and I joined him, and together we slowly turned the winch, both of us grunting with exertion.

"It's moving," Jebido said as he leaned out the window slot to look down at the gate below us.

The portcullis rose slowly, protesting loudly, but eventually we had it most of the way up and Jebido nodded to us that it was enough. Eriz set the lock in the teeth of the winch and we headed back down the hallway. We made our way over the bodies on the stairs and down to the first floor, with Baine and the Pith women following us. The north-facing doors were open by now and the rest of the Piths were riding into the gatehouse with the extra horses. I noticed they'd stopped to get Tato's body and I thrust his death from my mind. I stared across the bridge at the other gatehouse and studied the far bank, where I could see Ganders massed just out of bow range as they waited for the ram they'd fashioned to do its work. I could hear shouts and occasionally the odd crash as the ram impacted mightily against the portcullis. I knew Ania and the other Piths had made the Ganders pay for each attempt, but I also knew that it was only a matter of time before they broke through. I could see Gander archers ringed around the gatehouse and shooting up at the ramparts and I prayed to The Mother and The Father that Ania was all right. As if in answer to my prayers, three riders burst out of the gates and rushed toward us across the bridge. One of them was listing in the saddle, clearly wounded, and for a moment I was convinced it was Ania, but then relief flooded over me as I realized she was in the lead. I stepped aside as the three women burst through the open gates and came to a shuddering stop.

"Welcome back!" I called to Ania.

She gave me a weary smile and then turned to look down at Einhard. "They're almost through," she managed to gasp.

"It doesn't matter now," Einhard said with a grin. He gestured to Eriz. "Destroy the ram and then close the portcullis and bolt the doors. It's time we left this cesspool of a place called Ganderland!"

Everyone cheered his words and I went to join Baine and Jebido, who were holding my horse for me. I mounted up as the sounds of battle axes rang out as the Piths chopped up the ram. Once they were finished and had returned, the portcullis behind us crashed down with a resounding bang. Then the light and the view to the north was cut off as two Piths closed and barred the doors.

When we were all mounted and ready, Einhard drew his sword and pointed out the open southern doors. "Home!" he cried. "And let no man stand in our way!"

"Home!" the Piths echoed as we trotted out into the sunlight.

Most of us were smiling and chatting happily when we rode out through those doors. We had slipped through the Gander net and accomplished the impossible and, now with open land and horses beneath us, we knew that we couldn't be caught. Unfortunately, our happiness would prove to be short lived. Einhard warily held up his hand, halting us as we spread out in a loose semi-circle behind our leader. We sat there in silence, smiles wiped from our faces as we stared at the mass of mounted men facing us and stretched out across the road and the fields to either side. There had to be hundreds of them, I realized. Behind us I heard a crash, and then a great cheer rose up and I knew the Ganders across the bridge had broken through the gates.

"Shit!" Baine said softly.

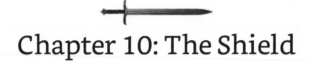

Chapter 10: The Shield

It's been more than fifty years since the assault on the bridge, but I can still remember the feeling of elation I had felt at our success, only to have it squashed in the blink of an eye and replaced with mind-numbing despair. We were truly and completely trapped this time. We all knew it, and by the triumphant looks on the Ganders faces, they knew it as well. As it turned out, Einhard and the Piths had been seen after all, and the watchers had waited just long enough to ensure the Piths were truly attacking the bridge before chasing after Lassan and telling him of our trickery. Lassan had turned about immediately and returned to the bridge, first instructing a rider to ride as fast as possible to the pass and tell them what had happened and that they should take the southern route around the cliffs to cut us off. Rarely, in all the years I would know Einhard, would I see him look as utterly disappointed and defeated as he did that day. He sat hunched over slightly on his horse, his sword still bared in his hand as he stared with hooded eyes beneath his winged helm at the mass of men surrounding us. His right hand holding the sword twitched several times as if eager to cut through Gander necks and I wouldn't have been the least bit surprised to see him charge the men in front of us.

What was going through Einhard's mind at that moment, I can't say. Remorse? Rage? Regret? Probably all of those things, I thought, as I knew that was exactly what I was feeling and probably everyone else as well. It seemed to me as though that particular moment was frozen in time and no one moved, as all eyes, Piths and Ganders alike, focused on Einhard the Unforgiving, Sword of the King, and waited, unsure what he was going to do. Would our leader have us charge the Ganders and die beneath their blades, or would he have us flee back into the gatehouse and try to make a doomed stand? I didn't know, nor, I'm sure, did anyone else. I stole a glance at Jebido, who like me sat his horse in stunned silence. The color of Jebido's face matched the grey of his hair and his lips were pursed tightly together in anger. He saw my look and his face relaxed somewhat and then he shrugged slightly as if to say, what can you do?

Four riders at the center of the massed Ganders moved forward, breaking the moment, with two of them falling back respectfully behind the other two men. One of the men was young, perhaps no more than twenty-years old, and was built wide like a bull. His polished armour shone in the sunlight and his hair was long and black like mine and was swept back from his high forehead. A fine purple cloak was thrown over his shoulders and was clasped with an oversized Pair Stone.

"Prince Tyro, the king's heir!" Jebido hissed in a whisper as he leaned toward Einhard.

If Einhard heard him, he gave no sign of it. He just sat stone-faced as the Ganders approached. I turned my eyes to the rider beside the prince, realizing with dismay that this man was much older and dressed in the black flowing robes of a priest. Jebido and I shared a worried look and I knew he was thinking the same thing I was. Killing Gandermen was one thing, but killing a priest was a sin that there would be no coming back from.

"Einhard, Sword of the King!" Prince Tyro boomed as he halted his horse ten paces from us. He was holding a lion-headed golden helm under his arm and his face was flushed red, whether from excitement or from the heat I could not tell. His beard was carefully trimmed, almost daintily I thought, as he grinned brilliant, perfect white teeth at Einhard. "You are the man known as Einhard the Unforgiving, are you not?" he asked with a smirk.

I disliked him the moment he'd opened his mouth and I dearly hoped that Einhard would run his sword through the man's pompous face.

"I am he," Einhard acknowledged, barely nodding his head.

Prince Tyro took in a deep, self-satisfied breath and then let it out noisily. "You and your little band of heathens have certainly been an annoyance lately," he said. "Much like a fly buzzing around your head, annoying, but easily swatted when the mood strikes."

"I think you'll find there are no flies waiting to be swatted here," Einhard growled at him.

Prince Tyro laughed. "Perhaps a little more dangerous than a fly," he conceded as his horse stamped its feet and shook its head. The prince snapped hard on the reins, yanking its head up and he glared down at the animal with cruel eyes before turning back to Einhard. "But in the end, your fate will be the same."

"It's easy for a weak man to talk strong words when he has swords at his back to do his fighting for him," Einhard said contemptuously.

The prince's face turned even redder and he spit on the ground in rage. "You'll regret saying that, you shit-eating heathen bastard!"

Einhard grinned. I saw his green eyes light up and I felt a rush of relief. Whatever happened here today, whether we lived or died, at least the Einhard I'd come to know was back. "I'm thinking about shoving my blade up your pompous ass," Einhard said, "but judging by the looks of you, I'd wager that would be something you'd probably enjoy."

Prince Tyro dropped his hand to his sword, his body visibly shaking with rage. "I'm going to hang you from a tree and peel the skin off you myself you worthless turd!"

Einhard threw his head back and laughed heartily, then tossed a leg over his saddle and dropped easily to the ground. "Why don't you prove to all these soldiers of yours what a big man you are and come and kill me then," he said. He waved his sword at the watching Ganders. "Your prince talks big words in front of you," he said, raising his voice so all could hear. "But I have fought you for days now and know that you are real men. Men to be respected in a fight." Einhard grinned at them. "I don't like you," he said. "I admit that openly and will gladly kill any of you that I can. But even though most of you are uglier than a dog's puckered arsehole, I still respect you as fighters."

Many of the Piths laughed at that and I even heard some of the Ganders chuckling as Einhard pointed his sword at the prince.

"This one, though," Einhard said, "this one I do not respect." He moved several paces forward as Prince Tyro fought to control his horse. "Words are easy," Einhard said, glaring up at the prince. "I think that's all you have. I think under all your finery, you're just a spineless coward and will run like a scared rabbit the first time you face a real man." Einhard plunged his sword into the ground and then stepped back. "A real man wouldn't accept what I just said to you. A real man would have to kill someone who said what I did or die trying." Einhard put his hands on his hips and he tilted his head sideways. "But a coward would get his men to kill me for him." He grinned up at Prince Tyro. "So which man are you?"

Prince Tyro opened his mouth to speak, then hesitated as the priest guided his horse closer and whispered something into the prince's ear. The priest was thin, with greasy brown hair flecked with silver and thick red lips under a wide nose. A large Rock of Life pendant hung around his neck, suspended by a golden chain. I don't know what the priest said to Prince Tyro, but the fire of anger went out of the prince's eyes and he began to nod as he listened, before finally he lifted a hand to the priest. "As much as it would give me great pleasure to rip your heart from your chest and piss on it," Prince Tyro said after a moment, speaking loud enough for all to hear. He motioned to the priest. "Son Oriell has forbidden it."

Einhard snorted. "So you choose to hide behind the skirts of one of your lying priests, then?" he said. He spit at the feet of Prince Tyro's horse. "You are a coward!"

"His Highness does not waste his time with the likes of you," Son Oriell said in a surprisingly high voice.

Einhard laughed loudly as he turned his attention to the priest. "You look familiar," he said. "Do you have a twin?"

"I do not," Son Oriell said with an impatient frown.

"Really?" Einhard said doubtfully. "Because you look exactly like what dropped out of my ass this morning!"

"How dare you insult a Son of The Father!" the priest hissed. Behind him, it was now the turn of the Ganders to grumble in outrage.

"Enough of this foolishness!" Prince Tyro snapped. "The time for talking has ended." He glared at Einhard. "Have your men," he paused to sneer, "and your women, lay down their arms."

"And why would we do that?" Einhard asked. "So you can kill us like sheep?" He pounded his chest with a fist. "Unlike you, we Piths do not run from a fight."

"You are outnumbered four to one," Son Oriell said slowly and carefully as though he were talking to a child. "You have no chance here. Throw down your weapons and I will confer with Father Above. Perhaps, if some of you choose to renounce your heathen god and accept His embrace, The Father will be merciful."

"Merciful?" Einhard spat. He swept his arms behind him. "We are Piths you simple-minded buffoon. None here would worship your false gods. We would rather die."

"Then die you shall," Son Oriell said with a sigh. He let his eyes roam across us and his skinny face was set in an expression of distaste. We were sweat-encrusted and filthy, with most of us covered in blood, and I imagine we must have looked half-crazed to his eyes. He glanced at me and then looked away, then frowned as his puzzled gaze came back to me. "That man!" Son Oriell said loudly, pointing a shaking finger at me. "That man is no Pith!" The priest pointed to Baine and Jebido as well. "Nor are they! These men are Gandermen!" He turned to Einhard. "What is the meaning of this?" he demanded. "You have taken hostages?"

"Of course not," Einhard said with a smile. "Do they look like hostages to you? These men chose to join us."

"Impossible!" Son Oriell said, looking horrified. He turned and glared at me. "You there! What's your name?"

"I am called Hadrack," I said reluctantly.

"Does this creature speak true?" the priest asked, gesturing to Einhard. "Did you and your companions join these heathens wilfully?"

"Yes, Son," I said, unable to hold his eyes. I knew that The Son's and Daughter's of The First Pair were the link between this world and the next. To lie to one of them was a deadly sin and I swallowed, worried by the look of anger and betrayal flashing in Son Oriell's eyes.

"Father Below!" the priest whispered as he clasped the Rock of Life tightly against his chest. He stared at me in disbelief. "Do you mean to tell me that you have forsaken The Mother and The Father in favor of a heathen god?" he demanded, his face white with fury.

I knew I couldn't lie and I opened my mouth to deny it, to tell him that I had not, nor would I ever forsake The First Pair, but then the priest's horse skittered sideways and I got a good look at the face of the man sitting his horse behind him. He was heavily built, with a scarred face and he sat stooped over in the saddle. I saw he wore a great axe strapped across his back and I felt a bottomless rage explode across my mind. I remember Jebido had told me years ago down in Father's Arse that the man's name was Searl Merk, but I never thought of him by that name. For me he would always be Crooked Nose, the man who'd killed my father.

All reason and logic fled from my mind and I screamed in fury, ignoring the startled look of fear on Son Oriell's face as I drew Wolf's Head and kicked my heels against the sides of my horse. Cries broke out all around me as the Piths and Gandermen converged on each other, but I only had eyes for one man and I urged my horse directly at him at full speed. Crooked Nose saw me coming and he tried to turn his horse, but I was on him too fast and the animals collided heavily as I swung Wolf's Head wildly at the other man's head. Crooked Nose ducked and he lost his balance and tumbled from the saddle to land heavily on the ground. I saw his helmet go careening away and I flung myself off my horse as Crooked Nose got to his feet and drew the axe from his back.

"I don't know what your problem with me is," Crooked Nose said as he hefted the axe with both hands. "But I'm going to cut your head open with this and spit on your brains."

"You bastard!" I hissed in fury, lashing out at him with Wolf's Head.

Crooked Nose looked surprised by my speed and he dodged backward to safety, then swung my father's axe at my head in one fluid motion. I barely managed to avoid it, ducking low in desperation as it whooshed over me, realizing even as I did so that it was a mistake as I saw his knee coming for my face. I couldn't avoid it and light exploded behind my eyes as his knee crushed my nose. I fell back, just able to keep on my feet and spitting blood, trying to see through the tears filling my eyes. Crooked Nose was coming on fast and I backed away from him. My shield was still strapped to my back and I couldn't take the time to reach for it. I cursed myself for being stupid and rushing into this even as I sidestepped a murderous overhead swipe from Crooked Nose. My father's axe buried itself halfway into the ground in the spot I'd just been standing on and, as Crooked Nose fought to pry it free, I lashed out at him with my left fist, catching him on the cheekbone and splitting it wide open. I swung Wolf's Head around in a vicious overhand cut, but Crooked Nose had the axe up by now and he blocked my sword with the handle. I saw a chunk of the carved wood go flying off and I ducked and whirled, trying to take the feet out from my opponent. Crooked Nose grunted and leapt over my blade, then swung down with his axe. I felt the edge graze my helmet and I cried out as the blade cut through my forehead, down my eye, and along my cheek. I gasped and fell back, swinging Wolf's Head desperately as I tried to see. My right eye was full of blood and I didn't even know if it was still there or not. Crooked Nose was grinning at me now as he stalked toward me with the axe held low. I shook my head, trying to focus. This wasn't the end, I told myself. I would not die here. This man had killed my father and I would have my revenge! I bellowed like a wounded animal and I charged with Wolf's Head held out in front of me like a spear. Crooked Nose had thought me finished and his eyes widened in shock and surprise as I ran the blade of my sword through his side. I spit wetness from my mouth and smiled bloody teeth at him. "For my father and my sister, you bastard!" I rasped as we fell to our knees together. Crooked Nose swung my father's axe at me one-handed and I partially blocked it with my left arm just in time. I grunted as I felt the blade slice into my side and then I grabbed the carved handle and yanked it from his grasp. I tossed the axe aside contemptuously and stared into his eyes, our faces only inches apart. "Remember Corwick, you turd-sucking son of a whore?" I rasped at him. "I was the boy in the bog!" I saw Crooked Nose's eyes flinch, the sudden light of understanding filling them before they hardened and he drew his head back and smashed his forehead into my ravaged face. I screamed and thrust Wolf's Head deeper into him and he stared at me, trying to say something before he finally collapsed backward. I fell forward on top of him, gasping for air as I watched the light fade from his eyes before darkness took me and I knew nothing more.

The hour grows late now, and my hand holding the quill shakes with fatigue as I write these words of events that happened so long ago. I pause to rub the scar on my forehead and I allow my fingers to trace its length downward, across my cheek and through my beard to my chin. I remember my last thought that day as the blackness was settling in. All I could think of was that I'd failed. That I was dead and would not live to fulfill my vow to my family. The sense of failure hung heavy over me in those last moments of clarity before my death and, I confess, no one was more surprised than I was when finally I was able to open one eye and blink up at a rough stone ceiling.

"What?" I managed to croak. I was lying on a four-posted bed in a small room with an open-slot window that let in sunlight that warmed a rectangular section of the stone floor to my right. I could only see out of my left eye and instinctively I raised a hand to my face, stopping as I encountered heavy bandages. I groaned as I shifted in bed, feeling a sharp pull in my side and I peered under the soft fur that lay over me. I was naked from the waist up, I saw, and my entire left side was bandaged as well. I noticed that a small trace of blood had seeped through the cloth bandage. I looked up as the door creaked open and I frowned in puzzlement as a girl of no more than thirteen stood in the doorway with a bowl of water in her hands and a sheet of rough cloth hanging over one arm.

"Oh!" the girl squeaked in surprise. "You're awake." She was plain looking, but in a pleasant way, and the few strands of hair that had managed to escape her wimple were dark brown in color. Her eyes were blue and enormous and filled with good-natured kindness. I liked her immediately.

"Where am I?" I asked.

The girl moved to a small rectangular cupboard about chest high and she placed the bowl and cloth on it before turning to me. "You're in Gasterny Garrison, my lord," she said.

"Gasterny Garrison?" I said in puzzlement. "Do you mean the garrison near the bridge?"

"Yes," the girl nodded happily. "My name is Betania, lord."

"You've been caring for me?" I asked, still trying to understand how I lived at all. Clearly the Gandermen had won the battle at the bridge and for some reason they'd saved me and decided to bring me back to health. Why, I couldn't imagine. I wondered what had become of Baine, Jebido and the others, but was afraid to voice my concerns to Betania, reluctant to know the answer.

"Yes, lord," Betania said. She picked up the bowl and cloth and set them on the floor near the bed, then sat down next to me. "May I?" she asked, gesturing to my face. I absently nodded as I thought about what my next steps should be. "Keep your right eye closed until I tell you, all right?"

"Yes," I said, unconsciously holding my breath. Would the eye work or would I be blinded the rest of my life? I wondered.

Betania carefully removed the bandages from my face and I studied her with my one good eye, looking for some hint in her expression at how bad it might be. "This is healing nicely," she said after a moment as she gently probed at the wounds with soft fingers. "Does that hurt?" I shook my head and she moved on. "How about here?"

"No, not at all," I said truthfully, surprised that it didn't. "How long have I been like this?" I asked.

"Almost three weeks," Betania said.

"What?" I gasped in surprise.

"You came down with fever and raved like a lunatic for days," Betania muttered. "We were convinced you were dying." I felt her fingers on my eyelid, pushing and probing gently. "Any pain when I do this?"

I started to shake my head and she admonished me to stay still. "Sorry," I said.

Betania nodded, looking satisfied as she sat back on the bed. "All right, my lord, try opening your eye."

I slowly did as she said, expecting only blackness and I felt a rush of relief pour over me as my eyelid opened. I could see. Praise The Mother and The Father, I could see! There was some blurriness in the eye, but I could make out everything just fine and I told her that.

"The blurriness should pass," Betania said, "and you've healed well enough now that we can leave the bandage off your face. Now let's have a look at your side." She moved the fur away and undid the bandages, nodding to herself distractedly as she washed and cleaned the wound. I looked down at the gash in my side from my father's axe and I knew that I'd been lucky. If it had gone in any deeper, I wouldn't be alive today. I thought about Crooked Nose, feeling a moment of intense satisfaction. He'd wounded me grievously, but he was dead and I wasn't. My vow to revenge my family remained intact.

"There," Betania said as she bandaged my side with fresh cloth. "All done, my lord." She stood up and smiled at me, turning her head to look at me critically. "You don't look nearly as bad as you might think," she said. She giggled and grinned at me. "Quite dashing, actually, with that crooked nose and scar."

My nose, I thought, putting my hand to it and exploring it with my fingers. I felt a bump where the bone had snapped beneath Crooked Nose's knee and I smiled ruefully at the irony of it.

"I'll be back later to check on you, my lord," Betania said as she opened the door.

"Why do you keep calling me lord?" I asked as she left.

"Because that's what his lordship said we must call you," she answered over her shoulder before disappearing.

I frowned at that, picturing the red face of Prince Tyro, angered that I could be beholden to such a man. I glanced around, seeing a small wardrobe in the corner, and I flung the fur off me and got shakily to my feet. I crossed to the wardrobe and rummaged through it until I found a tunic that would fit me and I gingerly pulled it over my head. I stepped to the door and opened it, expecting armed guards waiting there, and surprised when there wasn't. I had no idea what I planned to do; I just knew I needed to do something.

A hallway led off to my left and a wide set of stone stairs rose up to my right. I chose the steps and carefully climbed them, keeping my hand pressed to my side and hoping the exertion wouldn't start the bleeding again. I came to a landing that led to another set of stairs and I climbed those as well, breathing in the fresh air as I stepped out onto the battlements. I crossed to the ramparts and leaned out, staring across to the bridge in the distance where we'd fought and lost so many weeks ago. I saw some riders trotting over the bridge and thought I saw a winking of blonde hair, knowing that it was likely just a trick of the eyes. I knew the Piths were all dead, knew it in my gut, and nothing I could do or say would change that.

"I do hope you're not considering jumping after all we did to save your life," a voice said behind me.

I whirled around, wincing at the stabbing pain in my side

and I stared in disbelief at Einhard as he came toward me. The Pith leader was grinning wildly and he spread his arms as he approached. I just gaped at him stupidly, expecting one of his crushing hugs, but Einhard just put his hands around me gently and hugged me.

"But how?" I stammered as Einhard stood back. "How did you survive? Have they taken you prisoner too?"

Einhard threw his head back and laughed deep and long before finally moving to stand beside me and lean against the rampart. "I'm not a prisoner," he said with a chuckle. He wiped some dust off the stone and grinned at me. "In fact, I'm now the master of this garrison." I must have looked like a simpleton to Einhard as I just stood there staring at him with my jaw hanging open. "Actually," Einhard continued, "the people here call me his lordship." He winked at me and grinned. "Can you believe that, Hadrack? Gandermen calling a Pith his lordship."

"I don't understand," I managed to say.

Einhard patted me on the shoulder and he turned to look out over the ramparts to the bridge. "You've missed a lot, my friend," he said. He grinned sideways at me. "Do you remember we lost several scouts on the way here?"

"Of course I do," I said.

"Well, it turns out one of them survived." He glanced at me and grimaced. "Barely survived, actually. But he made it back to our lands and when the king heard of our plight, he sent the Shield of the King with five hundred warriors to find us." Einhard grinned and his green eyes twinkled. "The Gandermen were so focused on us after your outburst, that they never even saw the Shield arrive and we smashed them completely."

I shook my head in wonder, then frowned. "What about Baine and Jebido?" I asked, unable to keep my voice from quivering.

"Alive and well," Einhard said. "They'll be anxious to see you I'm sure, though they might change their minds when they see how ugly you've become."

I grinned back at Einhard, feeling the scars on my face

tighten as I did so. "What about Ania, Eriz and the others?"

"Most are well," Einhard confirmed. "As you know, we lost Tato," he continued, "along with some others. The Gander-woman, Megy, was killed as well."

I nodded sadly, turning to stare out at the bridge as Einhard clasped my arm and squeezed. "I'm glad you're well, Hadrack." He gestured to the land beneath us. "Stay here. Enjoy the fresh air and warmth of the sun on you. I have some duties to look after, but I'll seek you out later. I'll tell Jebido and Baine you're up here. I'm sure they'll want to speak with you." I nodded my head and stared down at the river and the bridge as Einhard turned away. "Oh, and I have something for you," he said as he stooped down and reached around the wall of the stairs. He grinned mightily as he held up my father's axe, then crossed over and handed it to me. I took it, unable to say anything as Einhard smiled. "Jebido found it after the battle," he said with a smile. "It was lying near the body of the man you fought and Jebido knew you would want it."

I nodded my thanks to Einhard and, as the Pith leader strode away, I held my father's axe in both my hands, caressing the carved handle. I felt a single tear slide from my damaged eye and slither down my scarred face and I turned back to the ramparts and stared outward as I gripped the axe to my chest. I was seventeen years old and still alive, and now I had my father's axe. I thought of the surviving men of those nine that day in Corwick and knew that in the not too distant future, I'd meet them all again.

AUTHOR'S NOTE

First, I'd like to thank you, dear reader, for taking a chance on an unknown author. I know there is a lot of content out there, and I am truly humbled you chose to spend time with Hadrack, Jebido and Baine. Writing The Nine was one of the most enjoyable things I have done in a very long time. Hopefully you enjoyed reading it as well. Please consider leaving a review on Amazon or Goodreads.com, as the only way for a writer to continue to improve is to know what people think of their work

I wrote several fantasy novels, as well as a young adult novel almost ten years ago and, sadly, had to abandon writing for a time. While the idea of a 'starving artist' may seem romantic in some ways, the grim reality is it does not pay the bills when you have a family to support. Thankfully, I am now at a stage in my life where I can turn my attention back to writing, which has always been my passion. The second book in The Wolf of Corwick Castle series, titled The Wolf At Large, has now been released and is available through Amazon.

Terry Cloutier

OTHER BOOKS BY THE AUTHOR

Made in the USA
Columbia, SC
19 April 2020